MATTHEW P. GILBERT

SINS OF THE FATHERS BOOK 1

DEAD GOD'S DUE

©2019 MATTHEW P. GILBERT

Print and eBook formatting, and cover design by Steve Beaulieu. Artwork provided by Dusan Markovic.

Published by Aethon Books LLC. 2019

ACKNOWLEDGMENTS

Many helped along the way. Some, I have forgotten, and for that I apologize. Some have forgotten me, and for most of those, I make no apology.

- My wife, Jessica, for listening, suggesting, correcting, musing, and sharing the dream with me.
- Paul Steed for prodding me years ago to actually write. The news of his passing hit me quite hard, and made me all the more resolved to finally get this done.
- Jeff King for convincing me it was good enough to publish.
- The many friends who offered criticism, proofreading, and suggestions, as well as encouragement that the tale was worth telling.
- Tom Thompson for sparking my imagination and amusement regarding a certain character.

PROLOGUE
ONE MILLENNIUM PAST

THE MONSTER simply would not *die*. More than an hour after he had been hoisted outside the praetorium, the fiend still kicked furiously at the air, leering down at the men who had come to celebrate his well-deserved end. Somehow, he had turned even his execution into another chance to sow discord. At least the noose kept his poisonous tongue from inciting yet more trouble, but the whole affair was not merely futile, it was disruptive of good order. If the Monster would not die, leaving him hanging bordered on the obscene, yet what could be done?

Imperator Publius Xanthius Bellicus had any number of problems due to both his position and the situation at hand, more than one of them the sort that could cause a man to lose his grip on sanity, but this was by far the most pressing. A failed execution was a clear statement that a leader lacked resolve, and that was not a message he could permit, whatever the circumstances. He wiped sweat from his brow, cursing the heat. Weeks past the end of summer, the evening ought to have been cooler. *They* were, *until today. It's as if we are cursed.*

Husam al Din, Xanthius's second, strode around the corner of the command tent and made a beeline for Xanthius. At six and a half feet tall and thick as a bull, Husam was intimidating enough. In motion, with grim resolve plastered across his face, he was positively terrifying to the lower ranks, a force of nature that would exact penance from the insubordinate and indolent.

Xanthius almost smiled at Husam's approach but caught himself before it could show on his face. *I suppose I am his target, now.*

Husam stopped a pace from his commander, snapped to attention and hammered a fist against his breastplate in salute.

Xanthius raised an eyebrow at the sight of his friend and trusted officer. It seemed only yesterday that Husam's skin was a chocolate brown, but now it was almost black, his eyes seeming to glow in his darkened face. Had there been a day when he was between shades, Xanthius wondered? It must have been so, and yet he had not noticed it until now. The time had simply slipped away, unaccounted for, like so much else. "At ease. Report."

Husam looked at his feet and ran a hand over his great bald head, shaking it slowly back and forth, a gesture that Xanthius had come to recognize as indicative of the man's disapproval. Husam growled to himself briefly, then spoke. "The sorcerer wishes audience." He spat upon the ground in disdain.

Xanthius inclined his head toward the Monster, still dancing at the end of the rope. "About him, I presume."

Husam nodded, still scowling. "Presumably."

Noting the subtle undertone in Husam's voice, Xanthius raised an eyebrow. "You disapprove? You're the one who brought him to me."

Husam's mouth twisted in a sour expression. "So it was, and Ilaweh knows, I have fought many men and befriended them later. But these men are treacherous."

Xanthius clapped him on the shoulder and gave him a fatherly smile. "Strange times, strange bedfellows. I'll see him inside."

Husam snapped a salute and turned to carry out his task. Xanthius took one last look at the Monster, still leering down, then removed his galea, tucked it under his arm and turned toward the command tent. As he reached for the tent flap, he paused, his attention wandering toward his second biggest problem: The Wall. He looked up at the barrier, knowing it would not be enough to stop his army should he choose to enter the city, but the cost would be high. *I will need to make a decision on that soon, as well.*

Xanthius's camp was well out of arrow range, but close enough to observe the defenders. He watched them briefly as they ambled back and forth between merlons, full of nervous energy that had to be walked off, most not even bothering with helmets or mail in the heat. *Fools. I could rush you with archers and kill half of you before you even understood what was happening.* But they knew no better. They had never trained to resist a siege. They were farmers, guards, bureaucrats, even a few criminals, likely, but not a soldier amongst them. The soldiers were encamped outside the wall with their Imperator, awaiting his command to breach.

Huddled behind the wall, terrified, the civilian populace prayed for salvation, as if there were anyone who could accomplish such a thing. The wretched politicians and lawyers who had brought them to this state had no doubt reserved the better accommodations for themselves, but there would be little enough for any of them soon enough.

A sea of steel and flame spread before Xanthius, campfires lining the ground to the limits of his vision, light glinting orange and deadly from sword, shield, and breastplate. They had been more, almost ten times as many when Alexander fell, but extricating themselves from Prima had been months of butchery. There was no telling how many of the enemy they had killed, how many would go unburied, food for the crows in a blasted land once known as the cradle of civilization.

Without Alexander and the Eye, there was no hope of coordinating his men, much less the logistics. Starvation and disease would come soon, and then the infighting. Without the supplies within the city, another nine in ten of his men would be dead within the month, and the rest reduced to cannibalism. Xanthius cursed under his breath. The fools behind the wall refused to see reason. *They leave me no choice.*

Xanthius forced his thoughts back to more pressing matters and ducked into the command tent. Despite how he had downplayed things to Husam, the sorcerer would be a prickly issue. Xanthius laid his helmet on one of the several tables and turned to the washbasin and mirror, privileges of rank. He dipped a cloth in the tepid water and cleaned sweat and dirt from his face. *These sorcerers are heavily influenced by such inconsequentialities. Best to present the right image.*

From outside, Husam called out, "Imperator, your visitor."

"Come," Xanthius answered, and turned toward the entrance to meet his former enemy. *Though 'former' is, perhaps, too strong a word.*

The tent flap parted, and the sorcerer entered. Husam followed him in and stepped to the side, wary, one hand on his sword. "Amrath of Laurea," he announced with a sneer.

Amrath was not a small man. In fact, he was fairly muscular and stood a good six feet tall, but next to Husam, he seemed almost a child. He wore a simple green tunic cinched with a rope belt, but no armor or weapons, nor even jewelry. His blonde hair was bound tight against his head in a bun. There was absolutely nothing about him that was extraordinary, and yet for all that, Xanthius could feel the man's presence like one might feel the sun on his face at high noon. Amrath's deep green eyes stared at Xanthius with unnerving energy, a touch too bright to seem fully sane. *At times, it's as if they're looking right through you.*

Imperator Xanthius knew that he, too, was imposing. And he was also the victor, pyrrhic though his victory might be. He said nothing and waited, refusing to concede anything to his vanquished enemy.

Amrath raised an eyebrow and flashed a grin like the sun peeking from behind a cloud, still probing with his eyes. Xanthius ground his teeth, refusing to smile back. This was sorcery, some sort of charm, but it would not work. *Not here. Not now.*

Xanthius's visitor let the smile on his lips twist into a wry grin and sighed. "Amrath of nowhere and nothing," the sorcerer said with a shrug. "You can call this place what you will, but it will never be Laurea. We have all robbed the world of her heritage forever."

Xanthius could feel his jaw clenching as he suppressed the urge to shout. "I think you overstate things."

Amrath waved a hand in the direction of the wall. "You think this misbegotten backwater can ever replace what was lost?" He spat on the ground. "A cheap simulacrum, nothing more, and you are but a fool with a barbarian horde."

Husam bristled at this. "You call us barbarians?" he asked, his voice soft and menacing as he tightened his grip on his sword.

The sorcerer spun and regarded Husam with contempt. "What else could you be? Can you even appreciate what you've done?"

Husam looked down at the sorcerer, his hand loosening on his sword as his gaze grew distant. His lips trembled, and a muscle beneath his left eye jerked spasmodically, pain, rage, and shame vying for dominance of his face. "We have killed the world," he said softly. "We are as damned as your Council of Twelve. Would a barbarian appreciate that?"

Amrath gaped a moment before answering. "No," he said softly, shaking his head, his cheeks bright red and burning. He cleared his throat and spoke again, his voice stronger now, more confident. "He would not. Forgive me. The war has been difficult. It was easier to kill you if we thought of you as beasts."

Husam nodded in agreement. "At least you don't bear the shame of the Monster being one of your own."

Xanthius folded his arms and scowled at this, shaking his head in slow denial. "Your people recognized him for what he was. It is our shame that we did not until it was too late."

Amrath nodded in silence. He looked back and forth at them and finally voiced the unspeakable. "The rope would seem to be less effective than we had hoped."

Husam shook his head in frustration. "I told you before how it must be done."

Xanthius covered his face with a hand for a moment. "It is barbaric, to burn a man alive! Wouldn't your Ilaweh object to such a thing?"

Husam was unmoved, his face stoic. "Ilaweh expects good men to destroy evil. Fire is a sure way. The other Fallen succumbed to the flame where steel failed. And he is not truly alive, at any rate."

The sorcerer's face grew pinched as if he had eaten a lemon. *So even the Meites have their limits. Good to know.* "You tried everything?" he asked. "Even beheading?"

Husam heaved a great sigh and lifted his arms to the heavens as if to ask for strength to repeat a lesson he had already explained many times. "Fallen in two pieces, or eight, or ten, they are still *Fallen*. What is already dead, you cannot kill. You must destroy it utterly."

Xanthius suppressed an urge to chew at his lip, knowing it would present a poor image. "Semantics."

Husam's face grew even darker. His nostrils flared as he spoke in a low, flat tone. "*There is no other way.*"

Xanthius was not the sort of leader to argue in the face of the inevitable. Husam spoke truth, and they all knew it. "Cut him down and bring him to me," he ordered. "I will not do this without looking him in the eye."

Amrath scoffed. "That will be difficult."

"This is hardly a time for cheap humor," Xanthius said with a scowl.

"On the contrary," Amrath replied, somber once again. "It is a time when humor is desperately needed."

Xanthius nodded to Husam. "Go." He waited until Husam was well away, then turned an accusing eye toward the sorcerer. "Where is the Eye?"

"Safe. That's all you need to know."

"How dare you speak to me as if I am a child! What have you done with it? If it should fall into the wrong hands…"

Amrath picked at his sleeve, seemingly distracted. "All men are tempted by power, Xanthius, even you."

"The arrogance of such a phrase coming from the lips of a Meite is beyond words."

"Aye, there is some irony there, to be certain," Amrath said with a nod, looking Xanthius in the eye again. "But we understand power, too, in ways few outside our sect ever will. No one could have imagined what it did to Alexander, not even the Monster." He paused a moment, studying Xanthius's face, searching for something; though if he found it, he gave no sign. "The Eye is safe, Xanthius, in ways that only Meites could think of to make it."

"And I am supposed to simply trust you?"

"I can't see how you have any choice. But consider, if we intended to use it, would I be here now?" Amrath's eyes seemed sincere. *But they all lie well.* "We Meites understand how to balance power, surely you must know that. None of us would want it in anyone's hands, not even our own. It does not even belong in this world."

Xanthius allowed a nod at this. *They* are *quite jealous of one another.* "Probably true. But how could anyone ever trust you after—"

Amrath's face grew dark with anger. "I am well aware of the treachery we practiced on Alexander!" He paused a moment, fuming, holding a finger in the air as if to reserve his right to speak. After a moment, he continued, "If you think it doesn't haunt me *every day*, then you know nothing of my beliefs."

"He was offering you the chance to surrender!"

"To surrender and leave him with the Eye!" Amrath's gaze was like a green flame, his confidence in his own cause like a physical force, undeniable. "You don't fully understand the significance, and I won't do you the evil of explaining it. A warrior needs his sleep, eh? But even a simple warrior like you can appreciate the madness of his command to slay the entire continent!"

Xanthius looked away, not wanting his eyes to reveal all of his thoughts. "I did not obey that command," he said softly.

"He *gave* it, Xanthius! To everyone! The damage was done the minute they all knew. Surely you have to see what that thing did to him!"

There was no arguing that point. "Tell me you destroyed it."

Amrath sighed and ran his fingers through his hair, looking suddenly older. "I don't think it *can* be destroyed. Yorn was able to pry its eyes out and cut the thing in half along a seam, but beyond that, it was impervious to everything we tried."

"Can it be reassembled?"

"With terrifying ease."

Xanthius pounded his fist into his hand in frustration. "We are cursed by the gods themselves!"

"Aye," Amrath said. "More so than you realize."

Xanthius raised an eyebrow at this, waiting for more.

Amrath looked for a moment as if he thought Xanthius was toying with him, then shook his head vigorously. *As if he were denying a bad memory.* "Those mad fools in Torium were trying to kill a god, to steal his power. They almost succeeded, *would* have if we hadn't attacked them. They may still, in the long run."

"Gods visit Torium regularly, eh?" Xanthius sneered.

"Once was enough."

Xanthius tried to take this in stride and give no further insult, but Amrath's frown suggested this effort had not been entirely successful. "Sorcery is difficult enough for me to accept, and I have seen it with my own eyes," Xanthius admitted. "I respect your and the Ilawehans' beliefs, but I do not share them."

Amrath was obviously offended, but that seemed a fairly normal state for Meites. *They squabble like children.* The sorcerer scowled at him a moment, his lips pressed hard together. "Then you are a fool," he declared.

"This would hardly be the first time I was pronounced such."

Amrath opened his mouth to deliver what Xanthius expected to be a significantly more artful insult when the sounds of a struggle outside interrupted their conversation. A dark hand pulled open the tent flap, and a man came hurtling through the opening and collapsed in a heap, face down on the floor, long dreadlocks splayed about his head. The noose had been cut from the pole, but it was still tight about his neck, and his hands were bound behind him as well. Husam strode in and delivered a savage kick to the downed man's ribs.

Instead of screaming, the prisoner turned his gaping, empty eye sockets toward his captor and let out a deep, sinister laugh. "That which does not kill me." His voice was deep and gravely, made even more so by the noose.

Husam grabbed the end of the rope and jerked the prisoner to his feet. They were almost the same height, though Husam was thick and hale, a stark contrast to his gaunt, ashen captive.

"The day is not yet done, Monster," Husam growled as he

shoved the man forward. "Amin al Asad," he announced, then, with less enthusiasm, added, "of the Ilawehans."

The prisoner turned his head toward Husam, his features twisted in fury, "Kafir! Traitor! How dare you name me such!"

Husam returned the glare, then nodded quick assent, and announced, "Amin al Asad, of Elgar."

Al Asad held Husam's gaze briefly before returning the nod, then turned back to face Xanthius. "The name of a dead man," he muttered. "I am Carsogenicus now."

Amrath feigned wonder and admiration, spreading his arms wide to the prisoner and plastering on a false grin. "Amin al Asad, Carsogenicus, Odio Sinistera: the list keeps growing. Have you thought of any new names while you were swinging?"

Husam kicked Carsogenicus again, this time in the back of his leg. "You will not escape justice by changing your name, dog. Ilaweh will know you, whatever you call yourself."

Al Asad staggered but kept his footing. He turned and spat in Husam's face. The huge warrior reached for his sword, but Xanthius raised a hand to stop him. If ever a man deserved to be tortured or murdered, here stood the one, but such things were barbarism. At some other time, one might risk descending into a touch of brutality but not here, not now. Civilization was but a candle flickering in the wind. The slightest of breezes could put it out for a thousand years. This fiasco had to carry at least the thin veneer of a trial, or they were simply playing al Asad's game. That had already happened far too many times.

And I intend to burn him alive and call it justice. The world has gone mad these last few years. "Amin al Asad, you have been found guilty of treason and crimes against humanity. For these crimes, you have been sentenced to death."

Carsogenicus laughed again. "You seem to be having some problems carrying out the sentence."

Amrath's smile was gone now. "Rest assured, we have plenty of ideas."

"You talk as if you are the victor here, sorcerer."

"You'll be dead soon. I think that counts as at least a small victory."

"My life has meant nothing since Alexander drove me out. I merely had debts to pay." Carsogenicus raised a hand to Amrath and clenched into a fist. "I have torn from my enemies that which they most loved, as they once did to me and my men." He swept them all with his impossible gaze, his empty sockets like cold, black holes in the fabric of the world. "*I* am the victor here. I *welcome* oblivion. I take your honor and your pride with me as sweet spoils."

He grinned at Xanthius, exposing bloody teeth. "The great Imperator Xanthius, guilty of war crimes, sentenced to death. They hate you even more than they hate me. Now you're a traitor for defying the Senate. How does that sit with the great and honorable hero of Laurea?"

Xanthius ignored the barbs and the question. Engaging in conversation with this man was not merely pointless, it was dangerous. "Have you anything else to say in your defense, anything that might sway the judgment of this court?"

"I deny this court. The Senate has ruled."

Amrath snickered, then laughed out loud. "The cowards behind the wall haven't the authority to rule a cabbage patch. The Council of Twelve is the true authority of Laurea, by right of conquest."

Carsogenicus chuckled again. "You, too, are conquered now, Meite."

"By Xanthius, not the Senate. My allegiance is to him."

"Xanthius wields the sword, but he lacks the will to swing it. He is a groveling toad in the end." He turned to leer at Husam. "As I always told you."

Husam's sword flashed in the light, too quick for Xanthius to countermand, and buried itself in the prisoner's shoulder.

Carsogenicus, instead of crying out in agony, calmly turned his head to look at the wound, a dark, malevolent grin spreading across his face. The muscles in his arms bulged with sudden effort, and the rope binding his wrists parted with a snap.

Gods! I had no idea he had that sort of strength!

Carsogenicus grabbed Husam's blade and held it in place, cackling as black blood oozed from the wound, bubbling and eating at Husam's weapon like acid, sending tiny streamers of smoke into the air as it worked at the metal.

"I gave you this blade," Carsogenicus hissed at Husam. "A poor strike, brother, but your hate is strong. Why did you turn from us? From *me*?"

Husam struggled with both hands to free the sword, but Carsogenicus held it fast with a grip of iron. The weakened blade parted with a snap, and Husam staggered backward, breathing heavily. "You turned from me, brother," he growled and tossed the useless hilt to the ground.

"Elgar loves you still. A hate such as yours cannot be denied, even when turned against him."

Husam spat in Carsogenicus's face. "I serve Ilaweh now. I renounce Elgar. I renounce *you*."

Carsogenicus flashed a cruel smile as he wiped the spittle from his face. "How can such righteous fury be anything but Elgar's?"

"I *deny* you!" Husam roared.

Carsogenicus turned his back to Husam. "You delude yourself. You are one of us still." Husam cried out and rushed toward Carsogenicus, his face twisted in fury.

Amrath cocked his head, and the very air between the two men rippled as an invisible wave of force exploded between them. Husam stopped mid-charge and rebounded as if he had tried to tackle a brick wall. He fell in a heap, cursing, as Carsogenicus staggered and dropped to his knees.

"Enough," Amrath commanded. His eyes were cold, merciless, almost inhumanly bright and alive. He regarded Carsogenicus as he might a bug pinned in a collection. "Don't make the mistake of assuming that because I choose to sheathe my sword, I am unarmed."

"The much-vaunted will of the Meites," Carsogenicus sneered as he rose to his feet again. "So why do you stand here trembling like a cringing lapdog, taking orders from the great Xanthius, while the fools within the wall spit on you?"

"Mei hates waste. This war is over."

"Liar! I *know* you, rabble-rouser. You broke the both of us from their prison for a reason. You are not here to kneel."

Amrath shrugged, inscrutable. "I am here because Tasinal sent me."

"More lies!" Carsogenicus pointed an accusing finger at Amrath. "Tasinal is *your* creature, not the reverse."

"He is the leader of our order."

"A *puppet* leader," Carsogenicus said. "And you pull his strings. What's your game, sorcerer? Do you work for the fools inside the wall? Perhaps you were allowed to free us. Perhaps they asked you to carry out their sentence so they could avoid the blame?"

Amrath shook his head, his eyes twinkling with mirth. "A fine attempt, that tale, but flawed at the core. My fight is with those spineless vermin hiding behind that wall, as it has always been. Now that they have made an enemy of Xanthius, I would suddenly befriend them instead of allying myself with him? Preposterous."

Xanthius gestured to Amrath to stand aside. If there were but one truth about Meites, it was that they would argue until the end of time, at least until one or the other decided bloodshed was in order. *The will of the Meites is indeed the stuff of legend, but Carsogenicus could provoke a saint.* The sorcerer nodded and stepped back, and Xanthius moved to stand before his prisoner.

"Amin al Asad, for your villainy, I hereby sentence you to death by fire. Have you any last words?"

Al Asad turned from Xanthius to Husam. For a brief moment, the hate faded from him, leaving only a gaping chasm of pain and sorrow. "Will you light the flame yourself? Do you not owe me that at least?"

Husam clenched his jaw, biting back more words, and nodded.

Carsogenicus seemed to relax at this. He turned his eyeless gaze back to Xanthius. "I have been cold for so long," he said, his voice almost wistful. "You can't begin to imagine how it feels." He wrenched the broken blade from his shoulder with a grunt and cast it down. A trail of black droplets followed it to the ground, and where they fell, the dirt smoked and crackled in protest. "I welcome your flame, Imperator. I would be warm one last time."

Outside the Praetorium, Xanthius's men bound the Monster to the central pole of the gallows, then tore down the rest and used the wood to build a pyre. Husam stood in brooding silence, observing, unlit torch in hand, as the banners of Xanthius's legions flapped in the growing wind. *An ill wind, it feels.* The gathering shadows hid Husam's expression, making him seem a huge, man-shaped pool of ink blotting out the last rays of the rapidly setting sun.

When the pyre was ready, Xanthius called anyone within shouting distance to attention as witnesses, and Husam did as he had promised. He lit his torch from the large brazier outside the praetorium and laid to the mound of wood as Carsogenicus stood mute, refusing to even meet Husam's gaze. The silence, Xanthius thought, seemed to cause Husam even worse pain than being cursed as a traitor. For all his rage and talk earlier, Husam was clearly shouldering a burden that was almost more than he could bear. There had been something between those two once, though it was difficult to know truth from rumor. Some claimed they were brothers, others that they were lovers, but whatever the case, clearly, the bond had been strong. And Husam now ended it with fire.

Amrath stood alongside Xanthius, sniffing the air, his lips pressed in a thin frown. "I don't like this."

Xanthius nodded. "Aye, it is ugly business, but we do what we must."

Amrath's eyes narrowed as he shifted his gaze toward Xanthius. "I could dance a jig to see that bastard burn," he snapped. "Look there." He pointed to the line of trees just beyond the praetorium. Xanthius turned, following the gesture, and barely suppressed a gasp.

Xanthius felt himself slipping into some surreal, half sanity. How could this be? But in the end, the mind of a soldier does not have the luxury of denial. The word 'crow' bubbled in his thoughts, over and over. *Such a small word. It doesn't actually apply to this.* They were everywhere, thousands even *hundreds* of thousands, covering the trees like black snow, silent, unmoving. *Watching.*

"How—"

"In the normal way," Amrath said softly. "They've been pouring in since the gallows were struck. Just damned quiet about it."

"And you didn't see fit to mention it?"

Amrath stared at the mass of birds, his brow furrowed. "It

seemed normal at first. And then mesmerizing. Then sinister. I decided to talk about it at 'sinister.'"

"It's unusual," Xanthius allowed, already recovering from the shock. "But they carry no swords. I see no reason to fear them."

"Don't be foolish. This is dark sorcery, make no mistake."

"I see only one sorcerer," Xanthius said.

Amrath's eyes widened in anger. "Will you let him provoke us even from the flames?"

Xanthius chuckled. "A jest, Amrath. You said it yourself, we could use some good humor."

"This is not the time."

"You should have been born a woman, Amrath. It would suit your moods better."

Amrath glared at his old enemy briefly, then softened. "And you should have been born a mole. It would suit your vision better."

Xanthius shrugged. "Fine. I confess, it's disturbing. But what would you have me do? Order an advance on their position?"

"I would not dare."

Xanthius raised an eyebrow at this. "An unusual stance for a Meite."

"It is an unusual circumstance."

"You have not seen things like this before?"

"If we could charm beasts, we could charm men. Free will is precious, aye, but perhaps it's more the pity. What would the cost of a few minds be compared to the blood we've shed?" He swept the idea aside with a wave of his hand. "This is something else, something…primal."

"The Torians?"

"I think not. I suppose their methods could produce a beast master, but why would one be here? And in any event, Torium was in no condition after…." Amrath let the comment hang. "As I said, I will spare you the details."

Xanthius snorted. "More gods nonsense?"

Amrath waved a hand toward the army of crows. "Explain it to me, then."

Xanthius stood a long moment, watching them, considering. "In Prima, I once survived an earthquake." He stroked his chin. "There's no warning, you know. Suddenly, the land just swats men and their works aside like gnats. There is little you can do. You live or die according to your luck and your reflexes. This seems like that."

"Yes," Amrath murmured. "Implacable. Elemental. That is just how they felt, in Torium."

Xanthius sighed and clasped his hands behind his back. *I will try to be open-minded.* "You truly believe you saw *gods* there?"

"Aye. I know we did."

"But even if I accept that there are gods, why would they be here?"

Amrath, suddenly haggard, turned a weary gaze to Xanthius. "For the third time, I tell you, I would spare you the nightmares."

"And you should stop with such foolishness. I am not a child."

Amrath looked back at the army of crows, his brow furrowing. "Why would gods walk the earth?" he asked softly. "*When* would they? It is not the beginning. What else can it be?"

Xanthius stood in grim silence, staring at the sorcerer, his jaw clenched. "Madness."

"Find me another answer then, if you can. I would welcome a pleasant delusion to warm me against cold certainty."

Xanthius pondered the question for a while, the rational part of his mind rejecting notions of gods walking the earth, of the end of the world. And yet, as he watched the silent, unmoving crows, he knew this was beyond his experience. Amrath was the closest thing at hand to an expert on such things.

"I have seen no gods," Xanthius said at last. "But if I do, and they would make war on me, I will oblige them."

"Bold," Amrath said, smiling. "Futile, but bold."

"If I am to die, I would as soon have it be as I have lived."

"Aye," Amrath said. "It is the same for me."

Al Asad's cry cut through the night, drawing their attention back to more immediate concerns. It was not, Xanthius noted, a cry of pain. It was long and low, a rumbling moan of release, almost sexual. The wood had taken some time to truly catch, but now the fire was blazing, the flames just beginning to lick at the Monster's flesh. His sandals were smoldering, and his ashen skin was darkening to an almost healthy color.

"The road to oblivion is warm!" Carsogenicus shouted. "This is no punishment! This is a reward!"

One of the witness soldiers, an Ilawehan, hurled a curse at the condemned man and followed up with a stone. The rock hit Carsogenicus in the forehead with a dull thud, splitting the skin. White bone peeked from the ragged gash. Black, dead blood ran down his cheeks like tears and dripped into the flames, popping and spitting as Carsogenicus cackled like a madman.

Xanthius bristled as he suddenly realized the grave danger this spectacle posed. *I am a damned fool!* He had to take control of the situation quickly, before Carsogenicus could provoke his men further. A failure of discipline now could be the end of civilization, a fact which Carsogenicus knew as well as Xanthius. The Monster might still take them to the grave with him. *I should have cut out his tongue.* Xanthius cursed the oversight under his breath as he strode quickly to the entrance of the praetorium. "I will have order!" he roared in his best battlefield voice. "The next man to break discipline will join the Monster!"

Carsogenicus howled in amusement as the flames rose higher. His pants were afire now. More black blood oozed from his split, charred legs, dripping into the hissing fire, and the flames surged with each drop, growing and feeding on the vitriolic liquid rather than being driven back. Xanthius cursed himself again for ever agreeing to this madness. He should have known this would happen. The man was already dead! There would be no passing out from smoke or heat. The Monster would taunt them until his tongue burned away, and the memory of this horror, this inhuman act, would haunt them to their deaths.

Xanthius longed to turn away from the sight, but he could not have his men see him deny the very thing he had commanded them to do. Nor would he spare himself the ugliness of watching his sentence carried out. A leader who flinched from his own justice was not just at all. He ground his teeth and made his face a stone mask. He would not turn from this.

Amrath appeared at Xanthius's side and placed a steadying hand on his shoulder. "Strength, soldier. It is nearly done."

The smell of cooking meat rolled over them, as tantalizing as it was foul. Xanthius was ravenous, as were all his men. This great host, this prodigious force of destruction that Alexander had forged with the Eye, was now a headless juggernaut, lashing out in its death throes. The supply lines had been the first organs to fail. Since Alexander's fall, few had eaten well but the crows. This smell was as cruel a revenge as any the Monster might have devised. The only good thing it brought was perspective. The memory of months of butchery, the rivers of blood they had spilled, made even this pale in comparison. Truly, what was burning the Monster compared to butchering the world?

"Elgar!" Carsogenicus screamed, his voice ragged but still manic. His dreadlocks were beginning to burn now, the ends curling inward, tiny bits of them breaking off and floating upward in the draft of the fire. They spiraled above his head, fading as they drifted, like a crown of falling stars. "Grant me prophecy, that I might show these fools their fate!"

The response was immediate. The crows, hundreds of thousands of them, took flight at once, the beating of their wings pounding like a hurricane. The witnesses looked to the sky in awe and terror as the great flight of crows rose, cawing, individual birds losing shape as they flocked. Black dots melded into groups, groups into lines, at last, forming a cohesive, moving, three-dimensional image of a clenched gauntlet in the sky above Carsogenicus. As Xanthius watched, several other flocks shaped themselves into huge spikes and flew at the gauntlet, penetrating it, leaving it with the appearance of the fingers having been nailed into a permanently clenched fist. The birds continued to twirl and spin in the air, holding the pattern as they rose and dove.

"I believe you now," Xanthius muttered to Amrath.

"I see it!" Carsogenicus cried in a wet, choking voice. His hair was gone now, and the flesh on his face was melting and burning. The fire spat and popped as the black blood rained down from his ruined frame. His body was little but charred ruins, bone, and viscera blackening under the heat of the flame as he struggled against his bonds. He turned his face toward the heavens, his cracked and bleeding lips twisting into a smile of sublime elation.

"The years run before me as the rivers!" he screamed. "I see it all! All your deaths! All your works laid to ruin! A world of ash! All! *All* unmade!"

Carsogenicus's body gave a sudden spasm. His lips were gone, exposing blackened teeth that chattered and clacked briefly, then shattered. The Monster howled his protest. "No! I served you well! I was to rest! You promised me oblivion!"

The flames erupted suddenly, shooting toward the sky, and Carsogenicus screamed again as they burned the rest of his flesh away, leaving only a grinning skull atop blackened bones.

"I submit to your will, Elgar!" it cried, the voice no longer that of a man, but now the keening wail of a banshee, shaped by forces other than flesh. "Hear me, mortals! This is the prophecy of Elgar! One thousand years do the gods grant for the Sleeper to dream! One hundred decades does the Eye of the Lion lie sundered! Ten centuries does Torium rot and fester! Then will the Sleeper awake, the Eye be made whole, and the chancre of Torium burst to spill its corruption upon the world! The scion of Elgar will rise from the blood of Tasinal, the Eye about his neck, in the City of Nothing, and the world shall become as ash! So says the Destroyer!"

The crows circling overhead broke their pattern and dove down toward the fire, the beating of their wings pushing the flames back. A single crow leaped toward Carsogenicus's skull and hooked talons into an eye socket. Another crow followed and took hold of the other socket. The pair rose on dark wings, feathers smoldering from the heat, and lifted the skull into the darkening sky, smoke and sparks trailing behind them. One after another they came, dismantling Carsogenicus's skeleton bone by bone, then circled overhead, waiting, as the others continued the process. When it was done, the entire flock rose again, screaming as they bore their grisly cargo southward.

Amrath broke the stunned silence. "That was quite a funeral procession," he said.

Xanthius glared at him briefly, then shouted to his men, "The Monster is dead! But we are still at war! All centurions will conduct readiness inspections in one hour! Those centuries not passing will be disciplined severely! Fall out and make ready!"

Xanthius looked on with satisfaction as his soldiers quickly dispersed and made themselves busy. If they were a bit slower than usual, it made no matter. He was proud of them. Even a prophecy from a god did little to sway them from their discipline. Of course, most of those lacking proper military bearing had died in Prima. Survival was always a strong motivator.

"An inspection?" Amrath asked, aghast. "At a time like this?"

"Most especially at a time like this. Clear orders let them fall back on their training, instead of their fear."

"And us? Have you some feat of leadership to blot this spectacle from our minds, as well?"

"We are leaders, Amrath. We do not have the luxury of forgetting."

"No," Amrath agreed. "We surely do not. This will all need to be considered as we move forward."

Xanthius looked at his former enemy and wondered just how much weight he should give to the 'former' part. As the Monster had noted, Amrath was *not* here to kneel. Certainly, for now, their interests were aligned against the likes of the Monster, but at some point, the sorcerer would want to resume his war against the lawyers and politicians. He could no more lay down that cause than Xanthius could take it up.

The war was far from over. That much was certain.

CHAPTER 1
PRINCES AND PROPHESY

P RELATE YAZID VALERIAN, soldier of Ilaweh, glowered at the bare, stone walls of the sparse reception area, awaiting the arrival of his prince. He had long since passed the point of anger at the wait. In other circumstances, he might well have stormed out in an indignant huff, casting a few loud curses in his wake to make his displeasure clear, but not this time. His business was too urgent to permit such indulgence. It had taken some measure of arm twisting, once quite literally, to arrange the meeting, and he had no intention of allowing his pride to undo that work.

Besides, it was becoming all too clear that this delay was deliberate, and leaving now would be surrender. Michael had been curiously unavailable since Yazid had delivered his treatise three weeks prior, and almost certainly, this situation was calculated to use up what little patience Yazid might still retain. It was, he conceded, a damnably effective maneuver. He tried to soothe his growing fury with the thought that this was Ilaweh's way of teaching him patience, but the truth had a way of peeking through that bit of self-delusion every few minutes, to prod at him like a mean child with a wooden sword might torment a caged beast.

Still, he had little choice, and so he continued to wait, the seconds slouching by, shuffling and dragging their feet in the sand instead of marching onward with precision and grace. He stared out of the single, tiny window. Below, the city of Bagdreme sprawled before him like a jewel, its minarets gleaming in the bright morning sun, and beyond, the burning desert. He tried to see the city as a visitor might, to trick himself into being fascinated by the solid, stoic architecture that had stood against the sands of centuries, impressed by the solidity of its fortifications, but it was useless. He was a native, and no amount of clever thought would change that.

For a while, he passed the time examining the scant decorations in the room, but there were precious few to take in. The Rock of Xanthia was a fine fortress, but it was short on aesthetics, as it should be. Who could see a king who lived in opulence as anything but a weakling who should be overthrown? Yazid admired a well-crafted sword that hung on the wall above a long, wooden bench, noting with satisfaction that it was no simple showpiece, but had seen actual combat. He tried searching for inspiration in a painting of Xanthius that hung on the opposite wall, telling himself that surely that proud warrior would have stood here for a month, if that was what was necessary.

At last, he turned to examine himself, cataloging the origins of the various dents and marks on his own armor and sword, and the scars that he had earned over the years. He was surprised, as he always was when he stopped to consider them, at just how many there were, remembering how he had received this one fighting a Laurean somewhere in Gruppenwald, and that one when he had fallen under the heels of a horse and had barely survived. There were hours of tales in those blemishes.

Hours, in fact, were just what he needed. He waited three before he was finally rewarded. He broke from his reminiscence at the sound of the latch, and shifted himself to a parade rest stance, forcing his face into a passive, disinterested expression, one more suitable for meeting with a prince.

Michael entered without ceremony. He was a fairly tall man, though not as tall as Yazid, and rail thin, with the hawkish features and dark, brooding stare that all of the line of Remilius bore. He was dressed in simple black pants and shirt, unarmed, his long dark hair loose and flowing halfway down his back. His pointed, well-trimmed beard fairly bristled as he glared at Yazid with undisguised annoyance.

"You're a tenacious bastard, Yazid," he said by way of greeting and extended a dark, calloused hand.

Yazid extended his own even darker and larger hand and gripped Michael's firmly. "Ilaweh teaches us patience through frustration," he said with a smile, pleased with his victory.

Michael withdrew his hand with a nod and took up his own parade rest stance. "What is it you want, Prelate?"

"You are avoiding me."

"So I am. But only because I have no time, and your wild fantasies take away from more important things."

Yazid scowled at Michael. "That much is clear from your dress. What could be more pressing than my 'fantasy,' as you call it? Is not warfare a matter of import to you, these days?"

"Aye, warfare is of greatest import. *Real* warfare, not this half-baked prophecy of dead gods and emperors walking the earth again." Michael's gaze shifted to the window, his eyes scanning the burning sands as if searching for hidden enemies. "You know damned well that the Jacynth issue is at a boiling point. If my father does not act soon—"

"It is a matter of proportion, surely."

"Proportion?" Michael snapped his attention back to Yazid. "I'll tell you about proportion. The women are in revolt! My own wife has banned me from our marriage bed as a coward. She'll not have me return while a single Jacynthi dog still rules!"

Michael pounded his fist against his chest to emphasize his point. "And I am a prince! Never mind that the Jacynthi are evil and *deserve* what they get. What will you do to sway the masses of sex-starved soldiers?" He turned away and began pacing, glaring at the floor, the walls, his gaze anywhere but on Yazid. "I tell you, it's inevitable, and it will be *soon*. My father knows it, and still he drags his feet. It's madness!"

Yazid drew in a deep breath and let it out slowly, determined not to be drawn off topic. "Michael, you *must* listen! This is not some fevered zealotry, it is hard fact. These are not religious writings I put before you, they are historical documents. Xanthius *himself* wrote of this!"

"You interpret them zealously," Michael said with a snort as he continued pacing the cool stone floor. Yazid's heart pounded loud in his ears as he waited, hoping against hope, but it was in vain. Michael stopped pacing, looked him in the eye, and declared, "This is a fool's errand."

Yazid opened his mouth to protest, but Michael stopped him with a raised hand and a face of stone. "My decision is made. If you are set to go traipsing off to Prima chasing myths and legends, most likely to die, then you'll do it on your own, with your own men. Xanthia's soldiers are *all* needed here."

"You could spare a single century!"

"I cannot. They would be noticed leaving, and it would raise questions that I cannot address at the moment."

"But Michael—"

"Enough!" Michael shouted, dismissing Yazid's attempts to protest with a slash of his hand through the air. "Try not to break anyone else's arm on your way out, Prelate."

With that, Michael turned and left, leaving the door open behind him.

Yazid struggled to constrain his anger and failed. He smashed a mailed fist into the bench, splintering the wood, then, as an afterthought, lifted the bench into the air and hurled it against the wall, sending debris flying in all directions.

As he stood, chest heaving, tears of frustration welling in his eyes, he heard motion in the doorway behind him. Reaching for his sword out of instinct, he spun, to find himself face to face with a second chance.

Philip, Michael's younger brother, stood in the door frame, armed and armored, hair bound and tucked against his head as was proper for a warrior, his expression grim. He was considerably larger and more powerfully built than Michael, but shared the same features, the same smoldering stare, the same skin colored slightly lighter than Yazid's. "It must be important, indeed, that your passion would move you to destroy my furniture."

Yazid bowed his head in shame. "Forgive me, my prince," he said softly. "I insult your home. I will repay you ten times for it, I swear."

"It's nothing." Philip strode into the room, his feet ringing heavily on the stonework, and closed the door behind him. "And I am no politician. I leave that to my brother. If you must use an honorific, I prefer Imperator."

"Imperator," Yazid said with a nod. "I thought you were—"

"In Erikar, yes. I was, but matters here require my presence." Philip looked toward the painting of Xanthius, his eyes clouded and distant, and said, half to himself, "My father is becoming an impediment that Xanthia can ill afford."

Yazid nodded his understanding. "He is of the old ways. He provokes you deliberately."

"Aye." Philip's expression grew wistful, and his eyes distant. "Still, it is a difficult thing to raise my hand against him. The beatings he gave me as a boy when I dared such things ..." The prince allowed himself a slight smile. "He will always be a titan in my mind, I think, even after this." Philip grew somber once again as he focused on Yazid. "But that is not why I am here with you."

"You heard our conversation?"

"And I read your treatise. I find it compelling."

"Would that I had known you were here. I would have placed it in your hands instead of Michael's."

"No matter. It comes to the same end. My brother is right. He can ill afford to have any appearance of instability when we … convince my father to retire." Philip paused, staring out the window as his brother had, contemplating the same matters. For a moment, Yazid's heart sank, certain that he had already seen the end of this play. "But he is also ignorant of some things," Philip continued, and Yazid dared to hope. "Your treatise rings true to me. In Erikar, we encountered a small village of Elgar cultists, who spouted much the same things you note in your work."

"Indeed? What did they say?"

"The end of the millennium, Elgar rising, that sort of thing."

"Xanthius wrote of Carsogenicus saying the same things before his execution," Yazid said, excited now. "'The scion of Elgar will rise from the blood of Tasinal, the Eye about his neck, in the City of Nothing, and the world shall become as ash.' Can there be any doubt, now?"

Philip answered with a grunt. "There is always doubt." He drummed his fingers against the windowsill, his square jaw working as he considered. "Knowledge is a weapon, and I am a warrior. I will have all the weapons I can find. If I give you the century you asked for, will you lead it?"

"I will! I will leave this very moment! But how will you avoid the questions Michael worries about?"

"I have men in Aviar, my personal retinue, on leave since we returned. You will not find finer soldiers or more devout servants of Ilaweh in all of Xanthia. And you will, as you say, go now. I will prepare a letter. I expect you to depart by sunset, and be quiet about it. I can beat my brother into agreement if he hears of our arrangement, but I'd prefer to avoid it." Philip flashed a broad, honest grin. "He's thin, but he's quick, and he hits harder than you would expect."

"I will tell no one until I reach Aviar," Yazid promised.

Philip turned as if to leave, then paused, and turned back. "Perhaps Michael is right, and this is a fool's errand. So be it. I will expect a map of the entire coast of Prima. But if he is wrong, I will expect more." He began counting on his fingers as he spoke, tapping each one as he listed his points. "I will expect a map of this 'city of nothing,' and I will expect troop strengths, defenses, the disposition of the civilian populace, the strength of their resolve, how much hardship they will endure in defending their city. I will know the political factions, who they hate, who they are allied with. I will know the weapons they can bring to bear." Finished with his counting, Philip pointed a single finger at Yazid. "And understand this: you are all expendable, save the man who brings me that information. Do not waste your lives, but do not hesitate to give them up if necessary. Ilaweh be with you."

"Ilaweh is great," Yazid said with a slight bow. He hammered a fist against his breastplate and left without another word.

The desert sun gathered him in a warm, comforting embrace as he exited the long, narrow gatehouse of the Rock of Xanthia. His young acolyte, Ahmed Justinius, was waiting for him on the steps outside, prowling back and forth like a caged lion, his white tunic darkened and clingy with sweat. Hard muscle rippled beneath his almost black skin as he paced, impatience radiating from him like heat wavering on the sand. His right hand hovered close to the hilt of the sword at his belt as if battle might be joined at any moment. *We will fight soon enough, boy.*

But, no, 'boy' was the wrong word anymore. Yazid felt both the swell of pride and the emptiness of loss in his chest to look upon his young ward, the sense of inevitability as his heart acknowledged what his eyes could not deny: the boy he had raised was truly gone forever. Here, in his place, was as strong a warrior as Ilaweh had ever caused to spring from the sands. It was a good exchange, a wise one, Yazid knew, but surely, it was a painful one as well. And it seemed so sudden. *No, it is just the right time. He is needed now. Ilaweh is great.*

Yazid's sense of loss passed quickly into wry amusement as he realized he was not the only one contemplating Ahmed's physique. Near the bottom of the stairs, three young women, resplendent and alluring in sheer silks, had gathered to admire his student, considerably less conflicted than Yazid in their appreciation. The strike Michael had mentioned would be taking its toll upon them as well as the men. They struck poses, competing to see which would first attract their target's attention, but it was in vain. Ahmed continued to pace, jaw clenched, oblivious, brooding. After a few moments, they turned back toward the forum, clearly disappointed. Doubtless, their diatribes against the Jacynthi would have an even more savage edge this afternoon when they had their turn to speak.

Yazid smiled. There were still a few things the boy would need to be taught, it seemed.

Ahmed looked up at the sound of approaching footsteps. "Yazid!" he called, his dark face brightening as he closed the distance between them in three huge bounds. "What does the prince say?"

Yazid laid an arm around his ward's shoulders, turning him back down the steps as he continued downward, feeling considerably older than he had when he entered the Rock. "He says we must go to Aviar. We will find men there to aid us in our cause."

Ahmed froze in mid-stride, gaping in astonishment. "Truly? We journey to barbarian lands?"

"Aye."

Ahmed placed a hand upon his sword, and his eyes grew hard and grim. "Will we slay them?"

"If they give us cause," Yazid laughed. "But they won't, most likely. Most of them fear us."

"And well they should!"

Yazid nodded agreement. "But first, we must make ready for the journey. Come, we have much work to do."

The trip to Aviar was not nearly as exciting as Ahmed had hoped, and less than comfortable in armor, especially with the constant grit from sand that inevitably made its way inside his tunic. Yazid had promised that the journey would have its share of wonders to a young man who had never left the desert, but Ahmed was beginning to have doubts. There had been no sandstorm, no raider attack, merely mile after monotonous mile over the desert, the clopping of the horses' hooves on the stonework road growing ever more maddening. Ahmed began to look forward to the brief respites when they traveled over sections buried by shifting dunes. How could a warrior bear such drudgery?

"A warrior must be patient," Yazid counseled. "Impatience leads to mistakes. Mistakes lead to death."

Ahmed tried to accept the lesson, but the impatience was like a devil within him. It was not so easy to exorcize as Yazid suggested. At best, he could silence it, so that Yazid would not know. That, he supposed, was a good start.

Many miles from Bagdreme, the landscape began to change. The sand grew more densely packed and rose toward distant mountains.

"Talifa's Teeth," Yazid declared, pointing.

"Why are they white at the top?"

Snow was a difficult concept to grasp and a somewhat unnerving one, but it was, as Yazid had promised, a wonder. Ahmed had been looking forward to the opportunities that climbing the mountains would bring, chances to prove himself against the elements, or perhaps even fighting a dread beast like a hippopotamus, a creature he had heard of only in books. But the prospect of traveling in snow was a daunting one. Ice should no more fall from the sky than gold. It was unnatural. He was as relieved as he was disappointed to learn that they would not be climbing the towering mountains at all, but would instead make use of a pass. He would only see snow at a distance. Someday, he promised himself, he would walk upon it. Someday.

On the other side of the pass, the land changed again, and Ahmed gasped in amazement. There was grass and growing things everywhere he looked. There were entire map grids covered with so many trees that Ahmed could not see through to the other side. Creatures stirred within the foliage and flew overhead. It was like the great gardens of Bagdreme, but without walls!

"Who could tend such a garden, Yazid?" he asked in awe. "It would take an army!"

"There is no gardener. Such is nature in the barbarian lands."

"It is like the work of a god!"

"Aye," Yazid agreed. "More than like."

They traveled many miles through the great garden, at last emerging onto a rolling savannah. It, too, was green, but the trees were fewer. Many more miles passed in this flat land before Yazid pointed to a darkening on the horizon. "Aviar."

As they approached, Ahmed conceded with chagrin that it did indeed appear to truly be a *city*, not a pathetic village as he had imagined. It was not as large as Bagdreme, and it had no wall, but it was still very considerable. "Are the Aviarans mad?" Ahmed wondered out loud. "Why is there no wall, no fortifications?"

Yazid nodded, smiling, clearly pleased with the question. "It is a free city. They cannot stand against the might of a nation, so they do not bother to try."

"But there are other threats. Bandits. Rebels. Pirates."

Yazid raised an eyebrow, his smile broadening. "What do you know of pirates?"

"Nothing. But the sea is near. Perhaps we will kill some on the trip to Prima, eh?"

"You speak more truth than you realize," Yazid said, growing somber again. "But as for why there is no wall, you must understand that Aviar provides certain things to the nations, and she is in turn protected by them." He paused a moment, then muttered, "Usually."

"A port city left free? Hard to believe. What does she offer that holds the nations at bay?"

"Entertainment. Neutral ground. A place to hide. And then there is the history of it. Alexander launched his ships from here. If Xanthia tried to seize Aviar, we would be at war with Gruppenwald, Laurea, and Alexandria, all at once. And the same would go for any of the others."

Ahmed nodded. It made sense. "Now explain the 'usually.'"

Yazid turned and cast a cool glance at his student. "I thought perhaps you had missed that. I will answer your question, but you must see some things within the city first to understand."

They came upon a small caravan as their path converged with what appeared to be a main thoroughfare. Ahmed stared shamelessly at the occupants of five small wagons ferrying tobacco and cotton, trying to absorb the essence of the barbarians, to understand them and reconcile the reality with his own childish notions. A pale barbarian child in one of the wagons stuck out his tongue at Ahmed. Ahmed twisted his own face into a fierce mask, and the child ducked beneath a tarp, squealing in fear.

As they rode onward, they met more and different travelers, ranging from dirty foot-travelers in clothes barely better than rags, to men clearly rich, born in carriages and dressed in fine colored silk, festooned with jewelry. *They must be fools. Who would announce his wealth to bandits so?*

Ahmed felt more and more ignorant at the sight of each new stranger. He had imagined the barbarian lands filled with pale-skinned men in poorly cured animal hides, armed with spears or stone axes. And yet it was not so. They were pale enough, it was true, but they wore clothes the same as any Xanthian. As for weapons, he was shocked to see that no more than one in ten even went armed, but those that did, carried steel, not wood or stone. They were, Ahmed thought, curiously normal looking, save for their deathly pallor.

Yazid pointed at a guard station of sorts as he and Ahmed approached it. Several obviously bored sentries surveyed the crowd, stopping this or that group, waving some through. A group of armed and armored men on horseback, bearing a black banner with a red dagger piercing a crown, passed without raising any notice at all. A group of women and children, following closely behind the men, were stopped and questioned. To Ahmed's eye, there seemed no rhyme or reason to their choices. He wondered what questions the barbarian guards would ask, but they chose not to ask anything at all, waving Ahmed and Yazid past with barely a second glance.

As they rode deeper into the city, Yazid leading down worn cobblestone streets and past throngs of pale, hairy, brutish people, Ahmed tried to make sense of everything about him, to under-stand these barbarians who did not seem so barbaric. Their build-ings, mostly two stories and built close together, were hardly primitive. The roads might have been better maintained, cleared of horse droppings more regularly, perhaps, but the fact that there were roads at all was problematic. How could barbarians have built roads? How could they build houses of wood and stone? Should not barbarians live in hovels of straw and wattle, dirt floors and glassless windows, and walk poorly marked trails?

Even the air was unnatural, it seemed. It carried a strange scent, salty and decaying, yet fresh. Ahmed found it simultaneously exhilarating and foul. "What is it?" he asked, sniffing.

"The sea," Yazid answered.

Ahmed felt as if his heart skipped a beat at this. "I would see it!"

"Soon. It is close. And we will answer your question, too."

Ahmed waited in silence, knowing from experience that it was useless to pressure Yazid for details. At best, he would achieve nothing. More likely, if he made a nuisance of himself, he'd wind up carrying an imprint of Yazid's palm burning on his cheek for hours. He passed the time by watching the people, marveling at how similar they were, and yet how different. Here, too, most of the men went without arms or armor. "Why are they unarmed? Are they cowards?"

"They are a superstitious lot," Yazid replied. "They look to talismans and rituals to keep themselves safe. They write how they wish for men to behave upon special paper, mark it with a seal of power, and wave their hands about as if this would compel all men to obey. They call it law."

Ahmed laughed out loud. "But that is madness!"

"And yet it works for them, much of the time. Even the Laureans practice such rituals, and they are civilized men, cowards though they be."

"But it is not true sorcery?"

"No," Yazid said. "It is mass delusion. But they believe in it, so it has power over them. It is much the same way with many primitive beliefs. True sorcery is a rare thing."

"Rare, but it exists? You have seen such things?"

Yazid's face hardened briefly. "Aye, once, in Rellith. I went fists against a Gruppenwalder while we were both riding in a rented carriage. Can't even remember the reason, now, but we both fell from the thing and were trampled by horses. He was killed, and I was near death. They brought me to a healer, but I did not know at the time that the man was a *sorcerer*." He shuddered at the memory. "I should almost have preferred to die. One look in that man's eyes was all it took to see he was half mad and losing his grip on what sanity remained. There was little I could recognize as human in that gaze. I heard later that he killed a lot of people before being put down."

Yazid said nothing for a long while, and Ahmed asked no more questions. It was only as they approached the end of the road they were on that Yazid broke the silence. "There," he said, pointing. "Do you see it?"

At first, Ahmed saw nothing. A line of buildings stood at the end of the road, nothing remarkable. Then he saw it, sun glinting between two buildings, and he could not suppress a gasp. "The sea!"

"Aye. Come, we are going to a market there. There is something I would show you."

They continued past the end of the road, cutting down an alley between two buildings to reach the shore. A frail, white-haired barbarian leaned from a window in one of the buildings and showered them with curses, shaking his fist in impotent fury, but Yazid ignored him.

Ahmed dismounted and walked slowly and deliberately across the stretch of sandy beach, trying to take in the magnitude of the great body of water. He removed his boots and walked into the surf, letting it lap at his feet. It was inconceivable that so much water could exist, and yet it did, stretching to the horizon. Like sand, Ahmed thought. Like the desert, but in motion. They were opposites, and yet the same. Fascinated, he cupped his hands and brought some of the water to his lips, then spat it back out, shocked. "It tastes of salt! Why?"

Yazid shrugged. "All seas are so." He beckoned for Ahmed to come out of the water. "There is one more thing I would show you. You will have long to look at the sea, boy, longer than you will want, I promise."

Ahmed knew it was true, but it pained him to leave, just the same. He marveled at the circling, crying gulls overhead as he made his way back to his horse, wondering what it must be like to live in such an amazing place. "How far?" he asked as he brushed the sand from his feet then pulled on his boots.

"Not far. You can see it, the building at the end of that pier."

Ahmed mounted his horse and snapped the reigns. "And what is there that is so important?"

Yazid answered him with silence. Ahmed scowled at the older man's back, feeling the impulse to curse him for his cryptic showmanship, but he was well aware of the price he would pay for such insolence. He waited for Yazid to lead, but Yazid simply turned back and looked at him. "Go."

"I am following you."

Yazid pointed down the beach, past several groups of pale barbarians strolling on the wet sand. "I said go, boy. Alone. See."

"How can I go on when I don't know what I am supposed to see?"

"You will know. Now go." Yazid raised a fist, no real threat since Ahmed was out of arm's reach, but a clear indication that further debate was not going to be productive.

Ahmed's horse surged forward at his urging, eager to run. Sand flew from hooves as Ahmed pushed the beast to a full gallop. He laughed out loud as beachgoers scattered, many screaming curses as he thundered by.

In the distance, he could see that the 'building' was, in fact, some sort of bazaar, with many people wandering about. Another hundred yards, and it became clearer: it was a prison on the beach side of a pier, open to the air, with many captives inside, shuffling back and forth. Ahmed reined in his horse, fairly certain that this was the lesson Yazid intended for him. He watched quietly, trying to understand what was going on.

There was a ship moored along the pier. A long line of small, brown people, men, women, even a few children, were being escorted by armed, pale-skinned barbarians into the prison. The prisoners looked a bit like some of the lighter Xanthians in skin tone and hair, but they were shorter, with flatter features. Most were naked, and the few who weren't wore little more than rags. Some wept or struggled, but most shuffled along, eyes dull and staring at their feet. *Defeated. But that is the nature of war.*

At the head of the pier, many barbarians were gathering about a long platform of dark, well-worn wood. There was a podium at the front. Along the back of the platform, running along its length, was a waist-high rail. Ten sets of chains hung from it at evenly spaced intervals, each a spot where a prisoner might be held fast. Clearly, Ahmed thought, this was a courtroom, where prisoners of war were judged. That would explain the outdoor prison. It was but a temporary thing, and the prisoners would soon be freed or put to death.

This should be a most interesting lesson. He had not even known the barbarians were at war. It would be good to see how they judged their enemies, to see if they had the stomach to do what was necessary. He looked about for a gallows or a heads-man, but none was in evidence. Perhaps they had some taboo against public executions.

Long minutes passed as the prisoners continued to file off the ship in chains. The crowd continued to grow, and Ahmed's discomfort grew along with it. It was not rational, he knew, but to be surrounded by so many pale barbarians troubled him. How could he tell if such men were friendly or hostile? Perhaps a toothy grin meant intent to kill, among them. He could barely tell one from another. They all looked alike, a sea of similar, alien faces differing only in their bizarre variance in hair color. How could a man have yellow or brown hair? It was beastly, and having them near him made him feel unclean. He would not say such a thing to Yazid when he told him of the lesson, though. That would surely earn him a cuff to the head and a pronouncement that men should be judged by their deeds. Still, he could not help but think it.

His gut rumbled more warnings, the sort a warrior learned to heed if he wanted to survive. Something was not right, something other than the company of barbarians. Ahmed went over things in his head, trying to isolate the problem, as the man on the platform began to take prisoners from the cage. One, a woman, wept pitifully, trying to cover her breasts and crotch in shame, but the man would have none of it. He forced her arms and legs apart and clamped the chains upon her to keep her that way. A man chained beside her turned his head away and wept.

Why would an army surrender, if it would not spare the women and children such treatment? It made no sense. A man would fight to the death to stop such a thing. And what sort of people would treat a conquered foe as such? The pale barbarians were cruel, indeed. But perhaps the brown men were cruel, too, and this was revenge? Ahmed had heard of barbarian tribes that practiced cannibalism. Could that explain this?

His stomach twisted in knots as he tried to fit the pieces together. He scanned the crowd again, searching for something in their eyes, but it was of no use. It was like trying to read the faces of dogs. The pale barbarians remained inscrutable as they waited for the man on the platform, each wearing the same cryptic face.

No, Ahmed corrected himself. There was one that did not confuse him, one near the back of the crowd, hiding his eyes beneath a hood and his face beneath a mask of brown hair, a large man, broad of shoulder and round of gut, though older, perhaps forty or fifty. That one's intentions were as clear as any Xanthian's might have been: he was here to do battle. His eyes, a bizarre shade of green, blazed with purpose, and there was, Ahmed could tell, a sword beneath his cloak.

Now that Ahmed had seen him, he saw the other, too: a small, wiry barbarian with dirty yellow hair standing beside the larger man. Like his companion, he was older, but hale enough. He, too, was here to do battle it seemed, though perhaps of a different sort. His eyes spoke less of rage than of pain and sorrow.

Ahmed nudged his horse forward, moving toward them. The crowd parted before him, most barely acknowledging his presence, though a few looked up at him with fear, loathing, or perhaps both. It would be safer to stand at the periphery if things turned violent, he thought. With any luck, he could eavesdrop on the barbarians, and perhaps make sense of things.

"Ladies and gentlemen!" the man on the podium cried. He waved a hand at one of the chained prisoners. "For our first sale today, I have a man of approximately twenty years. He is healthy and strong. What am I bid?"

The large barbarian shook his head and spat on the ground. He glanced up at Ahmed as the horse settled in behind them, but either didn't realize or didn't care that Ahmed was listening. "That rat bastard," the large barbarian muttered to his companion. "No mercy in him. We should stick a sword in his gut and treat his people to the same."

The skinny barbarian shook his head and sighed. "It wouldn't make a difference, Marcus. It's so much bigger than the traders. It's a political problem. It will take a political solution."

"Interdiction. That will change things. Kill the traders. Hit the ships before they pull in. They'll blame pirates."

"It's not that simple. It would take *years* of working with the powers that be."

"My way would take weeks."

Ahmed could resist no longer. He had to understand. "You," he called to the yellow-haired barbarian. "I do not understand this. Tell me of the war where you captured these brown men."

The barbarian looked up at Ahmed, shaking his head in amusement. "It is always war with you Xanthians," he said. "And my name is Tyler. Not 'you.'"

"Forgive me, I forget my manners in my curiosity. I am Ahmed Justinius. I have come to Aviar with my teacher to learn, but I am confused by much."

"Xanthians would have solved this slavery problem a lot sooner," Marcus grumbled. "And better."

Ahmed's eyebrow rose in surprise. "You make slaves of your conquests, then? I am surprised. I know little of barbarian ways. I thought it would be a trial until he began calling for bids."

Marcus tried to stifle a laugh and mostly failed. Tyler, however, seemed to grow even sadder. "There is no war."

Ahmed stared at the barbarians in confusion. "Then how are there prisoners?"

Marcus grew somber. "No need for a war to take prisoners, boy. Not if you're in the business of trading slaves. You just need to find people who can't do anything about it."

Ahmed answered with a grim nod, understanding now. "How is it that this can even be done?"

Tyler pointed to the ship. "They take them from Prima or islands nearby. They slip up on them in the night. Even if they didn't, it's steel against stone and wood. It's all too easy."

Ahmed waved a hand in derision. "I know well the arts of war, barbarian. I ask how this can be *done* to a man?"

"Aye. I cannot understand such cruelty either."

Ahmed rolled his eyes in frustration. "Still, your uncivilized mind cannot grasp my meaning." He pointed at the brown man on the platform who was even now the subject of much shouting and bidding amongst the barbarians. "What makes you certain that he is a man and not a beast to be subjugated as any other?"

Marcus shook his head, a wry smile on his lips as Tyler struggled for words. "Gods, Xanthian, are you so arrogant that you cannot see they are men just like yourself?"

Ahmed nodded and looked at the chained man, considering the point. "He looks like a man, aye, but men are judged by deeds, not appearance." He turned back to Tyler. "A true man would die before allowing himself to be a slave. These men live. I say they are not men at all, but beasts."

Tyler was angry now, his eyes blazing. "A cruel and ignorant judgment made by a cruel and ignorant young man!"

"Is it so?" Ahmed gestured to Marcus. "Tell me, would you surrender to such men, or fight to the death?"

Marcus grinned. "I would fight. And I would die. But all men do."

Ahmed turned back to Tyler, beaming with triumph. "What say you now?"

Tyler glared up at Ahmed. "I say that you have much gall to call *me* a barbarian."

Ahmed waved Tyler's comment aside as if it were a gnat flying in his face. "I will call you that again. Any man who will not fight and die if need be for his freedom does not deserve it."

"*All* men deserve freedom!"

"A lie! It is like saying all men deserve food, even the ones who do no work. How will they have it? If they will not take it for themselves, who will? If someone else does, are they not still beholden to him? No man is free unless he makes *himself* so!"

Tyler glared back and forth between them, appalled, as Marcus nodded and said, "It's what I've been telling you all along. It may need politicking *too*, but politicking alone won't do it. At some point, it comes to steel. It always does with these sorts." He cast a murderous glare at the man on the platform. "They'll spread that woman in chains up there for the money, and not feel a thing while she cries. You'd better believe they'll stick a knife in you if you get close to shutting them down. Trust me, there *will* be blood. It's just a matter of whose."

Tyler stared at the ground, his shoulders sagging. "I swore I would never turn to violence again after…."

Marcus put a hand on the smaller man's shoulder. "So did I. But we were young. If there's one thing I've learned over the years, Tyler, it's that there is a time and place for everything. Men like us, if we want to make a difference, we have to be prepared to fight. And we'd better be prepared to work with some hard men."

Tyler nodded, clearly miserable.

Ahmed scowled down at them. "I think you are too soft-hearted. Why would you take up the cause for men who will not fight for themselves?"

"Could be they didn't understand what would happen to them until it was too late," Marcus ventured. "Maybe if they had the chance to fight now, they would."

Ahmed looked back at the prisoners, considering. *It is possible.* He turned back to Marcus and demanded, "Give me your sword. We will see who will fight."

Marcus sighed and reached beneath his cloak as Tyler turned a shocked stare toward him. "You came armed? Just what did you intend to do here?"

Marcus handed the blade to Ahmed. "I don't know. Something. I hadn't got that far yet. But I think he'll do it better than me, anyway."

Ahmed nodded and gave his horse a kick. The beast reared and gave a loud neigh, and Ahmed joined in with his own battle cry. The barbarians immediately scattered, screaming as he and his mount surged forward and leaped onto the platform, barely missing the slaver.

Ahmed drew his own blade and tossed Marcus's on the platform before the slaver. Below, the crowd had stopped screaming and was watching in fascination.

"Pick it up, dog."

The slaver looked back and forth between the crowd and Ahmed, as if he expected salvation and was frustrated that it was not forthcoming. "You get down from here right now!" he cried as he backed away. "This is against the law! I have rights!"

Ahmed grinned as he dismounted, and kicked the blade toward the slaver. "I know *my* rights. I think you are very confused about yours."

The slaver backed up again and stood at the edge of the platform. "This is *my* property! You're trespassing. That's against the law!"

Ahmed laughed out loud. "Ah, I have heard of your law. I do not believe in your primitive superstition. It has no power over me."

Panicked, the slaver tried to step back again, felt his foot contact nothing at all, and put it back on the platform. "You're crazy!"

"You're the crazy ones, barbarian. *Pick it up!*"

"No!" The slaver kicked the sword back toward Ahmed.

Ahmed glared at him for a moment, then nodded. "Take off your clothes."

"What—?"

Ahmed brought the tip of his sword to the man's throat. "Take off your clothes. All of them. Don't make me tell you again."

The slaver stared at Ahmed in shock for a moment longer, and then, in a sudden burst of energy, began tearing off his clothes as if they were on fire. Some of the crowd made catcalls. A bottle came sailing from the crowd, aimed directly for Ahmed, but he ducked the missile.

"Will you take the blade?" Ahmed called, pointing at the thrower. The man spun and quickly vanished into the crowd without a word. "Coward! Dog!" Ahmed cried after him, but his taunts were ignored. He turned back to the slaver. "Against the bar."

The slaver, now fully naked, looked much like his slaves as he tried to cover himself. "Fine! Just don't kill me!" The slaver meekly shuffled to the bar and made no move to resist as Ahmed shackled him, though his eyes were full of fear and loathing. *You should fear me, barbarian dog. I am your better.*

Ahmed turned back to the crowd and raised his arms in a victory pose. "There is one man who will not fight!" he shouted. "Two, if you count the bottle thrower!" He grinned at the crowd. They seemed to be enjoying the spectacle well enough. Perhaps barbarians were much like civilized men after all, at least when they were amused. He bowed with a flourish, then bent to rifle through the slaver's clothes. He stood again, held up a set of keys for the crowd to see, then turned to the brown man chained to the bar. "Will you pick up the sword?"

The slave looked at him, confused, terrified. "And fight you?"

"Aye. To the death. Agree, and I will unchain you."

"You're crazy!" the man hissed. "You will kill me!"

"Would you die a man or live on as a slave? You might get lucky."

"No!"

Ahmed stepped back and cast a glance toward Marcus, but the big barbarian would not meet his gaze. The crowd booed. Ahmed turned next to the woman. "And you? Do you cling to life above dignity, too? Or would you risk your life, knowing that if nothing else, you would die free?"

The woman tried to speak, but could only choke out a sob. She nodded and raised a hand.

Ahmed shuffled through the various keys until he found the right one, and unlocked her legs and one arm. She rushed forward, lunging for the sword, but it was just out of her reach. Ahmed inserted the key into the final lock. The woman glanced at Ahmed briefly, her gaze one of infinite distance, a hundred-yard stare, the contemplation of eternity and a single, slim chance. She strained toward the weapon, pulling at her last bond, knowing that steel in her hand was the best she could hope for. Ahmed nodded and turned the key.

The woman dove for the blade, and Ahmed kicked her in the face. She staggered, blood pouring from her nose and mouth, but she did not turn aside. Her small hands closed on the hilt and swung it full force toward her opponent.

Ahmed parried her attacks, nodding, grinning. "Fight harder!"

The crowd was deathly silent now as the naked woman hurled herself at the Xanthian. She was no warrior, nor was she hard of body, yet her muscles obeyed her will. Her shame had vanished. Blow after blow she hurled at Ahmed, screaming in defiance and hatred for all that she had endured. *If sheer will could kill a man, I would already be dead.*

"Enough!" he shouted. "I yield!"

The woman seemed not to hear him. She continued swinging, and he continued parrying until the message in her eyes and ears, at last, reached her mind. She stopped mid-strike, chest heaving, spittle dripping from her lips, fury blazing in her eyes. She did not lower the blade, but she took two steps back, never letting her gaze wander from Ahmed, and keeping the blade at the ready. *Good. Stay alert, now. Forever.*

Ahmed tossed the key ring to the platform in front of her and mounted his horse. He waved at Marcus and Tyler, then snapped the reigns and sent the horse over the side of the platform. The crowd moved quickly to clear a path for him.

Ahmed sent his horse galloping down the beach as the slaver began to scream.

Yazid was staring out over the waves patiently, eyes squinting against the glare of the setting sun off the water. He turned and waved as Ahmed approached, and stared at him in silence for long moments. "Do you see, now?"

Ahmed nodded. "The barbarians trade other barbarians like beasts."

"And what do you think of such things?"

Ahmed shrugged. "I think little of cowards."

Yazid's eyes narrowed in suspicion. "I have seen this too-innocent look on your face many times, boy. I am no fool. You have done more than observe. What trouble have you been up to?"

Ahmed pursed his lips and shrugged again. "I put some of them to the test."

Yazid glared at him a moment, then shook his head, a broad smile on his face. "Then we should be off. The barbarians will be after us for violating their law, and they will come in numbers, for they fear us greatly."

"Aye, no doubt it is true."

"One question, boy. Do you understand now why I said 'usually'?"

"I think so. Some of the barbarians do not like selling men as beasts. The nations squabble amongst themselves over it, yes?"

"Indeed. There is bloodshed from time to time, covert forces with deniability. There will be war proper over it soon enough, mark my words."

"And Xanthia? Where would we stand?"

"In Jacynth, I suspect, while the rest focus here."

Ahmed laughed out loud. "Then may the barbarians go to war soon!"

"Aye. But enough talk. Let's board our ship and be off before the barbarians clap us in irons."

CHAPTER 2
THE SORCERER'S SONS

THE LIBRARY in the ancestral home of House Amrath was one of the most revered locations in all of Nihlos, rivaled only by Tasinal's courtroom, and perhaps not even by that. A millennium past, Amrath had written his great book and many of his most moving treatises in this very room. Here, behind the great oaken desk, Amrath had put quill to parchment and created the law. Here, before the enormous stone fireplace, Amrath had held forth to the other founders on philosophy, no doubt shaking his fist and shouting with a passion that was legend as he hammered home his arguments.

Unlike the courtroom, the library was no huge edifice, merely a comfortable room where the Great Father had found inspiration and, on occasion, peace. The floor was smooth marble, the walls lined with shelves of black, polished wood, each holding books of inestimable value, some hundreds of years old. There was no room for ornamentation on the walls, nor even sconces: all of the space was for the books.

Aiul rose from the couch and stared in silence at the lifelike statue of his ancestor, Amrath, a man he thought of as having been like unto a god, and bowed his head in respect. "Great

Father," he said softly, "Before I tell the others, I would tell you." He bent toward the statue and whispered in its ear, then stepped back and smiled, imagining he saw the emerald eyes twinkling with pleasure at the news.

"Fair enough," called a familiar, aged voice. "But wait not too long, boy. Some of us will be with him before long, and he will deprive you of the chance to tell us first, you know!"

Aiul turned quickly to the library's entrance, his smile broadening into a grin. "Maranath!"

The ancient fellow stood framed by the entryway, his head almost touching the lintel as he held one of the heavy, oaken doors open. He smiled broadly beneath his wild, white beard and stepped slowly into the room. At his age, his once formidable height worked against him, making balance difficult. He leaned heavily on his cane as he entered, watching his feet carefully so as not to trip over his long, brown robe. "And friend."

A woman, as old as Maranath but spry and tiny like a doll, pushed open the other door and entered behind him. She wore flowing silks that made her look as if she might blow away in a strong breeze and a huge ruby about her neck that might well have been an anchor against just such an occurrence.

Aiul's grin grew even broader. "Ariano! I am honored, indeed!"

"You honor us, child," she replied, her voice strong and smooth, betraying not even a hint of her age. The aged pair regarded him for a moment with eyes that seemed far too young and full of life for their wrinkled faces.

"Well?" Maranath asked. "Out with it! I'm tired of pretending that I have no idea what you intend to say."

Ariano punched him in the arm. "Impatient goat! He's waiting for his mother."

"Is he, now?" Maranath chuckled and flashed her a knowing grin. "I think he won't have to wait long."

Ariano glared at her companion for a moment, then turned back to Aiul, her face sweet and gentle once again, and mock-whispered, "He's always in a hurry these days. Not much time left, you know!"

"It's hardly a new thing," Maranath sighed. "It is a curse of the blood. Aswan himself was the very icon of impatience."

Ariano tittered. "Oh, don't blame Aswan for your failings!"

"I've shown remarkable patience in the past, I'll have you know."

Ariano patted his face gently and nodded agreement. "That you have, Maranath."

"Won't you have a seat?" Aiul invited the pair. "I'm sure Mother will be along any moment, and it's just we four. It's the sort of news that family should hear first."

Maranath cleared his throat, embarrassed, and Ariano blushed. "It is kind of you to call us such, child," she said. She took Maranath's arm, and the two walked slowly to the plush couch in front of the fireplace. Maranath grimaced and winced as he lowered himself to a sitting position, then sighed with relief.

Aiul was just about to offer them a drink when he heard the sound of footsteps in the foyer. Narelki, Matriarch of House Amrath stood in the doorway, a frown on her normally serene face. She wore a simple, form-fitting dress of white silk and no jewelry at all. *She is perpetually severe.* To Aiul, she seemed more sculpture than woman, a female counterpoint to the statue of Amrath: noble, aquiline face of whitest alabaster, with high, chiseled cheeks and pointed chin. Her fine hair was spun gold, not a strand out of place. Narrowed, cold eyes of pale, blue sapphire gazed at him in disapproval, and her thin, pressed, lips carved of ruby concurred.

Her heart is made of stone, so why not the rest of her?

Narelki raised an eyebrow as she surveyed the room. "I see we have guests."

Aiul flashed his most charming, confident smile at his mother. "Indeed we do. I invited them to hear my news."

"And welcome the two of you are in my humble abode," she said, nodding to the two elders. "As for me, I feel more summoned than invited, but as our Great Father told us, feelings have little to do with reality."

"It is good to see you, child," Ariano offered.

Narelki seemed to soften just the tiniest fraction at this. "It is good to see the both of you, as well. It has been some time, hasn't it?"

"You are young," Ariano said. "You have responsibilities. We understand."

Maranath rolled his eyes as if to say, "Speak for yourself," and Aiul struggled not to laugh out loud. He, too, suspected Narelki's sudden grace was more out of decorum than any real sense of ease or reunion, but he would take what he could get.

Obviously, no one was going to be surprised by Aiul's news, but it was time to make it official. "Well, you're all anxious to hear my 'secret,' so I'll go straight at it. The test was positive. Lara is pregnant! I am to be a father, and Great Father Amrath's line moves forward once again."

Ariano clapped her hands together and grinned like a child before a birthday cake, and Maranath rose with uncharacteristic speed to clap a hand against Aiul's shoulder. "Well done, boy! Well done indeed!" He gave an exaggerated wink and laughed, "We knew, of course. What else could it be? But it's good to hear it from your lips. Congratulations!"

"It's wonderful news, Aiul!" Ariano said. "I simply *must* do something to commemorate the occasion." She clasped her hands together and tilted her head, a look of pure bliss on her face, her eyes widening and seeming to lose focus as she considered. "A song? A sculpture? A painting, perhaps, of you and Lara. I have some techniques I've been wanting to try. Or a mosaic!" She spread her arms expansively, then rubbed her hands together, nodding. "Yes! I could do something grand on one of the walls in your new home! Have you any ideas on where you will live?"

"I do indeed," Aiul answered. "I think a top level suite in the Cradle of Nihlos would be appropriate."

"Oh, my, yes," Ariano agreed. "But you will need more than money for that. You will need influence as well. It's quite a difficult thing to arrange for most."

Aiul nodded, beaming. "So it is. Fortunately, I know some very influential people who—" He turned toward his mother to continue and fell speechless. The look in her eyes made him feel as if he had been doused with icy water after a long marathon. Maranath, seeing the same thing, stepped aside and leaned against the wall, a dubious expression on his face.

Narelki's face had grown rigid, making her seem even more a statue. After a moment of consternation, Aiul recovered himself and met her stare with his own, wondering if perhaps she thought of him as he did her: carved of stone, hard of heart. Both of them bore more than passing resemblance to their revered ancestor. *Only the eyes would be different. She would see emeralds.*

Narelki broke the silence. "This is a mistake, Aiul."

"Mother, we have been through this."

"We certainly have, and don't think for a moment that I don't recognize an ambush when I see one. If you imagined I would hide my disapproval of this union because of our guests, you are sadly mistaken. I will not bless foolhardiness."

Aiul sighed. "I have made my decision."

Narelki's face now showed more anger, her nostrils flaring. "It is a *foolish* decision! You are a nobleman of Nihlos. You should marry a noblewoman."

"You're a fine one to talk!" Aiul snapped, a bit more sharply than he had intended, but it was a ridiculous situation. His own father had been a commoner. "Such hypocrisy!"

"It is hardly hypocrisy to recognize the mistakes of one's youth. It is wisdom."

Aiul spread his arms wide and looked briefly to the two elders for support. "What would you have me do, mother? I *love* Lara! She carries my *child*!"

"And what of it? You needn't acknowledge the child." She folded her arms across her chest. "A commoner is fine for a mistress, but a marriage is quite another matter. They don't understand our ways, Aiul. It will go badly for you in the end, and then you will have to do very difficult things, things that will haunt you forever."

"Because it went badly for you? Because you are haunted?"

Narelki's eyes flashed in true anger now. "You go too far!"

Aiul stood a moment, silently fuming, then nodded and lowered his gaze to the floor. "You speak truth."

At this, Narelki softened a bit as well. "Oh, Aiul, I know the madness you feel. I know it well!" She walked over to her son, her head barely reaching his chin, and hugged him. "But marriage is about more than that. It is social standing, politics, and business, too. Surely those three things outweigh the one?"

Aiul shook his head and stepped apart from Narelki. "The Great Father spoke often of balance in all things. If there were a noblewoman who suited me, I would consider her, but there are none I would have as wife."

"None? Kariana is a beautiful woman! She has made no secret of her interest in you, and she is *Empress*!" Ariano's eyes grew wide at this suggestion, and Maranath was seized by a coughing fit that didn't entirely hide some choice expletives.

Aiul shook his head sadly. "Such a stupid and arrogant thing, that title. I'll always think of her as Kariana. I fail to see how my becoming one of her many toys will raise my status or that of House Amrath. Her perverse appetites are well known."

"You had no such problem with that before. You used to quite fancy her."

"Mother, you are no shrinking violet! There is a strong difference between what a man chooses for dalliance and what he chooses for wife and mother of his children!"

Narelki shook her head, unmoved. "You were very close to her since you were children yourselves. You're making excuses."

Aiul sighed, not really wanting to go here, but Narelki had him cornered. "She *changed*, mother. She was always undignified and impulsive. Those were some of the things I liked about her." He struggled against the urge to smile as one after another outrageous memory bubbled up in his mind. That would not help his argument at all. "Since she took that crown, she's become cruel and very publicly promiscuous. She would shame me, Mother, and shame House Amrath."

It was Narelki's turn to admit defeat. "You speak truth. The politics do not outweigh the cost in dignity. But surely we could find *someone*--!"

Aiul slammed a fist into his open hand. "I've made my decision, Mother!"

Narelki stared at him in silence a moment, then gave him a curt nod. "And I have made mine. As Matriarch of House Amrath, I forbid the union, as is my right."

Maranath cleared his throat, his fingers tightening on the handle of his cane. "This is unseemly." He stepped forward and gently guided Aiul aside, then faced Narelki with a scowl. "Aiul is no lovesick boy in the grip of youthful madness. He's a man in the full of his career, a respected physician, and the heir to House Amrath." Maranath tapped the cane against the ground to underscore his point. "If it is his image you are concerned with, how do you think it will seem to others that he is treated as a child?"

"Is it not also unseemly to question the judgment of a House Leader under their own roof?" Narelki snapped.

"Aye, it is," Maranath shot back. "But we Aswan are trouble-makers, eh?"

"I think we can blame your troublemaking on another name besides that of Aswan."

Maranath's face grew dark and his gaze cold. "Be careful with your words, Narelki."

"And you with yours." Her stare was just as icy as his.

He held her gaze a moment longer, grinding his teeth, then turned and strode back to the couch. He plopped down in a huff, arms folded across his chest, and glowered at the fire. Aiul almost laughed to see the old man so angry that he seemed to have forgotten, for the moment, the pain in his joints.

"Don't be upset," Ariano begged. "We are all practically family here." She smiled sweetly at Narelki. "Do you remember playing those wonderful games right here in this room with your father and me? And with Aiul, too!"

Narelki was in no mood to be soothed by reminiscing. "I remember missing my mother, and being angry at you for taking her place, if you must know the truth."

Ariano sat back, mouth gaping in shock, and gave a slight moan of dismay. At just that moment, a great cracking shot echoed from the fireplace as a knot of timber exploded, sending a stream of sparks and several large embers onto the carpet.

Narelki jumped, eyes wide and face even paler.

"Fetch water, Aiul!" Ariano cried. "Oh, hurry, dear, hurry!"

With a nod, Aiul quickly stepped into the foyer. He barely registered the doors closing behind him. Water! He needed it, and it occurred to him that he had never seen it fetched. That was slave work. But where did the slaves keep water? The kitchen, surely? Near panic, he tore down the hallway, his boots pounding on the polished hardwood, and banged a knee on a table, upsetting a vase perched upon it. The vase fell to the floor with a crash, sending shards of pottery and water all over the floor, followed by the table. Aiul grabbed at a tapestry to keep his balance, tearing it loose from the wall.

"Mei! Fool! It was right there before you!" he cursed.

The shattering vase had, fortunately, drawn the attention of the slaves. Unfortunately, that attention was from Slat, the Chief Slave, whose duties included administering whippings to the children of the household, noble and slave alike. Aiul himself had been quite unruly as a boy and had become something of a connoisseur of beatings by the time he reached manhood. Grandfather Lothrian had handled discipline before his passing, and Aiul considered his technique quite good, but once Narelki had placed Slat in charge, Aiul had begun to understand the true nature of superior quality and craftsmanship.

Slat came stalking down the hall on spindly legs, his black tunic fluttering, a scowl on his long, hairless face. His once black hair was still shoulder length, but gray now, and receding in a widow's peak. "Master Aiul, what have you done?" he called out, his deep, accusing voice sending fingers of terror up Aiul's spine, even now these long years past. "That vase was priceless!"

Part of Aiul felt compelled to shout out his innocence and flee, but it was foolish. Slat always caught runners. The truth would be best. "There's a fire in the library! I need water! *Now!*"

Slat's eyebrows rose in appreciation, and he nodded and spun on his heel. "Come with me," he called over his shoulder as he hurried back the way he had come.

Slat led him at a jog into the areas of the manse normally reserved for slaves. Even here, the place was richly appointed, though not so well as the rest of the house. It was a simple truth that form followed function, and slave areas were necessarily functional. After a few twists and turns, they came to a cistern room. Slat heaved the cistern cover aside and snatched a bucket from the floor. Aiul did likewise, provoking a harsh glare of disapproval from the Chief Slave. "Have I taught you nothing? It is inappropriate."

"Shall we let Amrath's Library burn over foolish notions of propriety? Come!"

Slat answered with a resigned nod. Together, they rushed back to the library, water sloshing from their pails, Slat muttering about the mess they were making. Aiul tried the door and cursed to find it locked. "Open the door!" he shouted. "We have water!"

"All is well," Maranath called out. Someone turned the handle from the other side, and the doors opened to reveal Ariano, Maranath, and Narelki all seated around the fireplace. Aiul did a double take and looked behind the door in shock, but there was no one there.

"What…" he began, but the words died in his throat. He had imagined it, of course. Too much stress was causing his mind to play tricks on him. The door must never have been locked at all. *Yes, it's safer to believe that, because the only other rational explanation is unthinkable.*

"Maranath stomped the coals out like roaches," Ariano said, beaming once again.

"I'll have it cleaned at once, Mistress," Slat promised, but Narelki held up a hand.

"Later. I must speak with my son now. You are dismissed."

Slat nodded and left the room, closing the doors behind him. Aiul stared at the handle briefly, then pushed his thoughts aside. It was just a moment of confusion, he assured himself.

Narelki rose and cleared her throat. "Well, that was exciting." She looked at the statue of Amrath and smiled. "Perhaps it was Great Father's way of forcing a break and letting us cool our heads, hmm?"

"I suppose," Aiul said with a nod. "But cooler head or no, I am still resolved on my choice of wife."

Narelki pursed her lips. "I suspected such. But I have reconsidered. I will not forbid you, and I will not make my disapproval known." She held up a finger of caution. "But, I will not assist you in this madness, either. If you will go against my counsel, then you will do it on your own. You have money and property aplenty. You can afford a splendid home. But I will not speak for you on the Cradle. That is asking too much of me."

Aiul clenched his teeth, biting back his anger, and nodded. It was better than the alternative, to be certain. "Very well, Mother."

"Oh, my," Ariano said. "This was too much excitement for one my age! I am suddenly very tired."

"Of course you are," Narelki said, her tone sullen and almost insulting, but Ariano seemed not to notice.

"Aiul, would you be so kind as to walk me home?" Ariano asked. "Maranath lives in the opposite direction and his legs pain him so. I couldn't ask him to walk so far just for my sake."

Maranath chuckled. "Aye. I'll be lucky to make my own trip without falling."

Aiul smiled at Maranath's wordplay a moment, then turned to Narelki. "Mother, would you have any other words with me before I go?"

Narelki shook her head, seeming very tired herself. "We've had enough words today, I think."

"Then I bid you good night, and you as well, Maranath. Thank you for coming, and forgive us for airing our private matters in front of you."

"Think nothing of it," Maranath said with a smile. "I have seen far worse. Life is full of such things. You learn to embrace even the rough spots as time passes."

Aiul offered his arm to Ariano. She reached for him gingerly and slowly pulled herself to her feet. "Oh, it's been quite some time since I walked arm in arm with such a handsome young man!"

It was a short walk to Ariano's home, and Aiul's escorting her was merely courtesy; there were no thugs or robbers in the hills of Nihlos where House Elders held their estates, though there were plenty amongst the commoners. Aiul shuddered at the thought. *Better to be a slave*. He immediately thought of Lara and felt ashamed.

Ariano seemed to sense his discomfort and patted his arm as they walked. "It was kind of you to accompany me. And it was good to see you again. We were so close when you were young, but since Lothrian died...." She trailed off and looked at the ground.

Aiul felt uncomfortable discussing his grandfather. The man was a wicked criminal, a shame on House Amrath, but Ariano clearly still loved him. Aiul would not disrespect that. "Grandfather loved you very much," he said with a sad smile.

Ariano looked up at him, her green eyes full of unidentifiable emotion. "Even after all these years, I still dream of him, of our time together." She sighed wistfully. "He was a great man, Aiul. I know you think otherwise, but you're wrong. And he loved you dearly, too."

Aiul nodded and resolved to change the subject before he said something hurtful. "*I* remember those games we played in the parlor, even if Mother doesn't." He grinned, thinking back. "What did you call that one where you would say something silly, and I was supposed to argue why you were wrong?"

"'Iconoclast.' Too big of a word for one so young to remember, I think. It's an old game. Some say Amrath invented it."

Aiul smiled at this. "It would certainly fit him, wouldn't it?"

They walked on in silence for a while, Aiul still brooding on his mother's cruelty. Below them, in the bowl of the hills that surrounded the city, lay the heart of Nihlos, a brilliant, shining jewel sparkling beneath orange clouds. Not for the first time, Aiul considered how isolated the Houses had become, sitting in their manses here upon the hill, apart from Nihlos proper.

Shimmering spires rose from the bottom of the valley, reaching for the sky with all the arrogance and power of the founders, twinkling with a million points of light. Arches and spans ran between them like spider webs, stark and limned against the luminous sky. The river Sanguinus, which surfaced only briefly near the center of the city, seemed more like a lake from afar, though its flow was the life's blood of the city. It was hard to look upon Nihlos proper and not be moved, if not for the mighty works of the ancients, then for the tragic loss of such skill and artistry over the years. *We are but frail shadows of what they were.*

When they arrived at Ariano's home, she withdrew her arm with a slight bow. The place was even larger and more ornate than House Amrath's ancestral estate, a work of art, like everything House Talus touched. Topiary beasts frolicked on the huge lawn, so true to form one could almost expect them to move. In their center sat an enormous gazebo where the musicians of the house performed shows. Flameless lights, carefully arranged to cast accenting shadows, lit the intricate landscaping. The house itself was made of white marble, fully four stories tall, each level slightly smaller than the one below. From the roof rose a great tower that was House Talus's own wonder, the highest point in Nihlos, offering spectacular views of the city.

Ariano tugged at his sleeve, bringing him back to the present. "You have grown to be quite the handsome and courteous gentleman, Aiul." Her face took on a wistful look. "Sometimes I miss the unruly boy you were."

Aiul smiled sheepishly. "My mother would argue he is still here."

"I suspect she would!" Ariano laughed, then grew serious. "You mustn't hate your mother for her decision tonight, Aiul. She's had a very hard life."

"I know. But why must she make mine so difficult? It is as

Maranath said. I am no young fool, I am a respectable man. She should support my decisions. I will be in her place someday."

"Sometimes, a mother must do what she thinks best for her child. She is wrong, but her heart is in the right place."

Aiul snorted. "She has no heart."

"It was torn from her, Aiul. She has lost more than you know, more than you can imagine. Find it in your heart to forgive her and speak of it no more. I can just as easily give you what you asked of her. It will be our secret."

"The Cradle?" Aiul gaped. "Truly?"

Ariano nodded. "House Talus will be honored to speak for you."

Aiul shook his head in wonder. "What have I done to deserve such honor from you? You treat me better than my own mother. You always have."

"You are wrong, Aiul. Your mother has always taken care of you. But there are things you don't understand. Someday, perhaps you will."

Aiul shook his head and sighed. "Is it part of the process, I wonder, of becoming a House Elder, that one master the art of speaking in riddles?"

Ariano patted him on the cheek. "There is a test you have to pass on that very subject. I'll see to the recommendation first thing in the morning. But now, I need my rest. And as for you, I think you have other things to do, things that involve a considerably younger woman, eh?" She gave him a slight wink.

Aiul blushed and nodded. "Good night, Ariano. And thank you again."

Does he love me? Lara suppressed a frown as she studied Aiul's face, searching, probing. *There must be a way to* see. The intention of forever ought to be clear in his eyes, if only she knew how and what to look for. The lust there was plain, and that pleased her well enough. *Green, like his eyes.* She ran a hand across his clean-shaven, square jaw, now grown a bit prickly in the evening, and sighed with pleasure. *But does he love me?*

She had had her share of men, of course. It would be shameful to come to a marriage bed without being skilled in lovemaking, but of love itself, she knew little. The sum of her experience was the bitter sting of not having her own returned. *It may be too much to hope for.* She tried to feel subtle differences in his touch, to hear some distinction in the sounds he made as they ground against one another, but if they existed, they were beyond her. *This is well enough, though.*

"I'm sorry," she whispered as they lay together, sweat still glistening on their bodies. "I'm not worth such trouble. Make peace with your mother, Aiul."

Aiul lifted his head from her breast and looked at her, aghast, his high cheekbones and furrowed brow making him look both fierce and noble. "Do not speak such!"

"It's true."

Aiul looked at her with a mixture of humor and disbelief. "You would have peace between me and my mother by driving a wedge between me and my child, between me and my wife to be? That sounds like sense to you?"

"I suppose not." She sighed and turned her head away. "But I'll embarrass you. I don't know the rules. I don't even know how to dance!"

"Then we shall forbid dancing in our presence!" Aiul declared, striking a lordly pose. "You think I jest? I am heir to House Amrath!" He flexed his arm to bulge the muscles and grinned. "I have that kind of power here."

Lara giggled but gave no answer, and Aiul threw the bed covers aside and rose, naked. "Garas!" he called.

Lara rolled across the bed and punched him lightly in his thigh. "What are you up to?"

"You doubt me," he answered, dancing out of her reach. "I must earn your trust."

Garas, Aiul's slave since birth, entered with Aiul's robe and a carafe of water. He was beginning to show a bit of gray in his hair but seemed young at heart, a fat, jolly, red-faced fellow. "It seems you two are well," he said with a wry smile as he offered the robe to Aiul.

Aiul slipped into the robe, then fixed Garas with a serious gaze. "We are. But there is something important we must discuss before small talk."

"Of course, my lord. What is your will?"

"There will be no more dancing in this house," Aiul declared as he pointed a finger at his slave. "None. Do you understand?"

Lara giggled and hid her face beneath the sheets. "You're mad!"

Garas regarded him quizzically. "Dancing, you say?"

"Dancing. We'll have none of it here."

Garas bowed. "We'll dispense with dancing immediately, my lord. I'll have anyone caught dancing whipped."

"Oh, no!" Lara cried. "You will not!"

"Aye, I shall, and within an inch of their life," Garas told her. "Perhaps even unto death, if it seems prudent."

Lara waved a hand in dismissal. "Mei, I will not be the cause of anyone's beatings! Take it back, Aiul! It's cruel!"

Aiul put his hands on his hips in feigned shock. "Such language, from a lady!"

Lara clapped a hand over her mouth, embarrassed, then lowered it. "You see? I'll mortify you!"

"Oh, she's taking us far too seriously, Garas."

"Indeed she is," Garas replied. "I know the answer, master."

"Do you ever not know the answer?"

"Never," Garas said, and, with a mischievous grin, broke into a silly dance.

"Stop that at once!" Aiul said, trying to suppress a grin. "Garas, do something about it!"

Lara fell backward in the bed, laughing loudly. "You're both mad!"

Garas danced his way toward where Lara lay beneath the bedclothes, still naked, and therefore quite trapped. "Only a madman would dance when the master ordered there be none! I'll beat the ruffian into submission and tie him up at once!" He began pounding his fists against his own chest in rhythm, and Aiul followed by drumming on the footboard with his hands.

"Are you sure you're beating him hard enough?" Aiul asked as Lara, tears streaming from her eyes, pulled the sheet entirely over her head.

"Oh, aye, he'll be surrendering any minute now!"

"Get away from me, you madmen, or I'll scream!" Lara cried through peals of laughter. She ducked from beneath the bedclothes and hurled a pillow at Garas before retreating into hiding once again.

"Perhaps you should take the miscreant out of the lady's sight," Aiul said. "She has very delicate sensibilities, you know."

"Mei!" Lara cursed, her voice muffled by the bedclothes over her head.

"Obviously. One can tell by her words alone that she has delicate sensibilities," Garas said still doing his odd chest thumping jig as he sidled toward the door. Aiul laughed long and hard as Garas made his exit.

Lara waited until she heard the latch click before peeking out. "You're simply dreadful, you are! The both of you!"

"It lifted your mood, didn't it?" he asked, gazing gently at her. "We've played that game many times, and it always did for me."

Lara wiped tears from her eyes and nodded. "It did."

"Then listen. I told you I have a wonderful surprise. Are you ready to hear?" He sat on the bed beside her, waiting for her to answer.

"Stop taunting me with it! Tell me!"

Aiul kissed her quickly, then held her face and gazed deeply into her eyes. "You are to be nothing less than my wife, Lara. You will have slaves and jewels and safety. And you will live in a home that befits our station. The penthouse in the Cradle!"

Lara's jaw dropped in shock. "How can that be? Your mother relented?"

Aiul cackled and shook his head. "The heartless statue wouldn't budge. But Ariano will speak for me! Isn't it amazing?"

Lara nodded in excitement, momentarily speechless.

Aiul raised an eyebrow at her silence. "Well, woman, does it please you or not?"

"Yes!" she gasped at last. "Yes, it pleases me!" She pushed her lips forward against his and took her own kiss, a longer, deeper one. She pulled back suddenly, a look of horror on her face.

"Mei, I really *will* embarrass you!"

"You will if you use that kind of language in polite places," he said with a smile.

"I'm serious, Aiul! I truly know nothing! I don't even know your father's name!"

"Neither do I," Aiul said. "He was a commoner that mother dismissed. You don't need to know the names, anyway, as long as you know a generation or two of houses." He gestured to himself with a grin. "Amrath being the most important. Me, you, our child, my Mother, and my Grandfather are all of House Amrath, so that's simple enough." Aiul rubbed a hand against his furrowed brow. "Mother's mother was House Freth, as I recall. I never knew her, to be honest. She died giving birth to Mother. By the time I came along, Grandfather Lothrian had taken up with Ariano."

"He's the great villain, yes?"

Aiul nodded, a sour look on his face. "A sorcerer. Tasinalt put him to death for it."

Lara tried to process this, but it made no sense. She squirmed, not wanting to contradict him, but she needed to understand. "She seems so young to have done so."

Aiul raised an eyebrow and stammered a moment. "Ah," he said, nodding and smiling now. "I see. You're confusing father and daughter. Not Tasinal*ta*, just Tasinalt. They like to use the house name as a kind of title for the position, but they add letters on the end as it suits them."

"Why?"

Aiul's face was perfectly blank for a moment. "I don't really know." He thought on it a moment, then shrugged again. "Arrogance, I suppose."

"Tasinalt," Lara repeated. "Tasinalt*a*'s father. And he was the lich emperor?"

Aiul's eyes grew wide in shock. "Mei, no! You really don't know anything, do you?" He shook his head in wonder. "Fine, fine, that's what we're fixing, isn't it? *Tasinal* was the lich emperor." He fixed her with a grave stare. "He was the founder of house Tasinal, as Amrath was the founder of my own house. Make sure, if nothing else, you get both of those names correct."

Lara giggled at his serious tone and poked him in the chest. "Then why are you not Amrathal or Amrathor instead of Aiul, I wonder?"

Aiul held his serious face a moment longer, then cracked a broad grin. "Because house Tasinal has the greater claim on arrogance, I suppose," he said with a laugh.

Lara, still naked, felt a sudden chill. She wrapped her arms around herself and shivered. "It's horrid, all of it, you know? Lich emperors and wicked sorcerers. You all must have nightmares most every night."

Aiul snickered at this. "Three or four times a week is about average for a noble, I suppose."

Lara could barely conceive of such madness. "How could anyone follow a lich emperor? It's insane!" The very thought made her feel as if spiders were crawling over her skin. "He'd have sat on the throne, all rotting, and not a single person would be allowed to scream or run away."

"Well, he wasn't rotten to start with, you know," Aiul said, looking a bit wounded. *I've insulted him! I am such a fool!* "He started out just fine." Aiul lay back on his pillows and sighed, smiling again now. "I don't even know that he was rotten by the end, but it was six hundred years, so I suspect he was indeed worse for wear. I wouldn't know. He disappeared four hundred years ago."

Lara gasped. "He rotted away to dust?"

Aiul rose up on his elbow and turned toward her, shaking his head back and forth. "You and this rotting! No, he simply couldn't be found."

"He finally collapsed into a heap of bones like he should have," Lara announced triumphantly. "And Elgar take him!"

Aiul rolled his eyes and lay back on the pillow. "Well, I'm sure Elgar will take all the souls he can lay hands on."

She knew she should leave it here. If she kept going, she would surely anger him, but it was all so alien, so much to think about. *If I don't talk it out, I'll never get it down.* "Sorcery! It's horrid, like the things you all eat! And your own *grandfather*! You knew him, right?"

Aiul nodded again but said nothing, just stared back at her. *Green. He'll have more soon.*

She stared at him a moment, grinning, feeling green herself. "Horrid!" she repeated, almost squeaking in distaste. "Was he very wicked, then? I suspect he must have done horrible things. Did any slaves go missing?"

Aiul laughed out loud at this. "I am surprised you commoners aren't in charge, with such active imaginations as that! No, no slaves went missing." His gaze moved to her breasts, and he ran a hand over her thigh. *Definitely green, the both of us.* "And as for wicked, he never seemed so to me. Well, except for when he took a strap to me for insolence." He paused and smiled briefly. "Which happened more often than I should care to admit."

Lara laughed. "You're bad enough. But I would have expected you to have a whipping boy or some such."

Aiul sneered at the notion. "Maybe House Veril has such idiocy, but in House Amrath, insolent children are whipped, noble or not." He ran his hand up her back, then paused. "That's not a problem, I assume?"

Lara shook her head and was about to reply when she felt her humor suddenly vanish, and her eyes swell as she made a connection. "Mei, the woman speaking for us, Ariano? She fucked a sorcerer!" Lara feigned convulsions, then scratched at her arms as if they were covered with bugs. "*Horrid*!"

Aiul grinned wickedly at her. "You'd better stop making fun of my people, or I'll have them serve something particularly disgusting at the wedding. Snails, perhaps?"

"Mei, don't you *dare*! I could never eat a snail!"

"Ah, but you'd have to, at least on that day. You'd have to show yourself worthy of being a nobleman's wife."

Lara shuddered and stuck out her tongue. "Fine, I'll say no more. It's all perfectly normal, the sorcery, the lich emperors, but snails, I simply cannot tolerate."

"Then we shall ban snails," Aiul said with a grin. He pressed her back into the pillow. "I'll quiz you on all of this tomorrow, you know."

"I think I can remember."

"Good. Because right now I have other things on my mind."

As they entwined once again, Lara felt something different, something softer, deeper, and multifaceted. She could see it, hear it, feel it, something more beautiful than she could ever have imagined, but she could find no words to describe it.

It's red.

CHAPTER 3
ILAWEH'S CHOSEN

Ahmed knew one thing very well: he hated the sea. He contemplated his new enemy as he leaned against the ship's rail, marveling at how blue the water became in the noonday sun. Oh, it was all good and well to look at it from the shore, even to bathe in it, but to ride upon it was another thing entirely.

Yazid and the Prince's men called their vessel a ship, but to Ahmed it was a cage, a prison without walls that was like as not to sink like a stone into the ever-shifting water, leaving him to drown. They promised him it was a good ship, that it would float even through a hurricane, but Ahmed had doubts and no way of knowing the truth. This was the first ship he had ever been aboard. It was made of wood. It had sails. What else was there to know about ships?

Then there was the sickness. It had begun the first day he boarded the floating prison, and he had been a laughingstock for a week before it had eased. Even now, months into their voyage, the feelings of queasiness still rose in him when the sea was rough, and it was all he could do to keep whatever meal he had last eaten. At least he had grown better at hiding it. Of all the torturous aspects of sea travel he had encountered, being mocked was the worst by far.

"Ahmed!" Yazid called in a stern voice. "Come!"

Ahmed was inclined to refuse, but he did not relish a beating, and that was just what insolence would buy him. If he were well, he would try Yazid, beating or no, and surely do some beating himself in return, but this sickness crippled him. A beating well-earned was honorable enough, but he was certain to vomit the moment he took a punch to the gut, and that would be humiliating.

He followed Yazid into the skin of the ship, silent, to the wardroom. The place was dark, lit only by a single oil lantern, and smelled of hemp, oil, and tobacco. Brutus Samir, a tribune of Prince Philip's legions, sat at a heavy, wooden table with Centurion Sandilianus al Rashid, and the ship's navigator, Tahir. Brutus was dark-skinned, bald, and powerfully built, while Sandilianus was pale, thin and wiry, with sharp features, smoldering eyes, and long, raven hair. Tahir was stranger still, his features similar to Brutus's, but lighter, and his hair was almost red. By Ahmed's reckoning, Tahir was a half-breed, a mongrel cross of true men and barbarians. Ahmed disliked him intensely, not merely for his barbarian heritage, but for his frequent blasphemies. Were it not for the seasickness, Ahmed would have offered Tahir a beating on more than one occasion.

Brutus nodded to Yazid and cast a wary eye at Ahmed. "Why bring the boy? What good is he besides fucking?"

Yazid's laughter was honest and deep. "Perhaps not even that. But he has his uses."

"You say it like you don't know," Brutus said with a leer. "I find that hard to believe. Surely you have sampled the goods from time to time?"

Yazid laughed again. "Oh, no, it is not that way with us.

Ahmed is like a son to me. But even so, we are not so fortunate as you. Our tastes are for women."

Ahmed cocked his head and grinned. "If he wants to challenge me, I would let him fuck me anyway, if he could take it by force." He laced his fingers together and cracked his knuckles, the muscles in his arms like iron bands. "And if he couldn't, then I would fuck him, eh, just because it was my due!"

Sandilianus doubled over in his seat and grunted, feigning a reaction to a gut punch as Yazid burst into howls of laughter. Tahir smiled wryly but said nothing.

Brutus raised his eyebrows and grinned, surprised. "There *is* more to this one than meets the eye!" he said. "I would take your challenge, boy, and show you a thing or two about fists and fucking, but you are tainted with woman's weakness. I cannot insult my body with such, not even second hand."

Ahmed raised an eyebrow. "Perhaps I have yet to lie with a woman."

Sandilianus snorted and leaned back in his chair against the smooth, polished wood of the bulkhead. "Then it would be a moot point. With your looks, if women have not set upon you in a pack and carried you off to have their way with you, you have no dick."

Even quiet Tahir chuckled at this one. Brutus slapped his hand hard on his own knee as the others howled in laughter once again. "You hear that, boy? If you want to fight me, you must show us you are dickless! It will be all the same to me, as long as you have no pussy."

The others roared in laughter again, and Ahmed shook his head in mock-sadness, staring at the wooden deck as if defeated, then, with a quick motion, lifted his tunic and dropped his pants. He twirled his manhood in the air, accompanied by screams of laughter, and sighed, "I am defeated, Tribune."

After long moments, Brutus caught his breath and gasped out,

"That is the wrong sword for war, boy. Put it away, so we are not distracted from Ilaweh's work."

Ahmed took a bow and covered himself again, and they all wiped tears from their eyes as the laughter faded to smiles, and, at last, to somber nods that it was time to get down to real business. Brutus rose and bowed his head in benediction. "By Ilaweh's grace, we shall begin."

Yazid, Ahmed, and Sandilianus said in unison, "Ilaweh is great." Tahir remained silent but rolled his eyes. With some effort, Ahmed suppressed the sudden urge to throttle the half-breed. *There will be a reckoning between us later, dog.*

Brutus reached into a box beside his chair and withdrew an ancient, brittle tube of rolled parchment. He unrolled it, spread it on the table and weighted down the corners with tumblers. "Here is the most recent map we have of Prima. We have puzzled over it for long, but have come to no real agreement. As first order of business, let us settle once and for all the direction on the map, and where we expect our enemy to make his home."

Ahmed studied the map before him. It depicted, in faded outline, an unfamiliar landmass. Brutus's source of confusion was clear. The map bore a stylized arrow to indicate north. Below this, another arrow, smaller and more rudimentary, pointed in the opposite direction, with the word "North" scribbled alongside in spiky script.

Tahir reached across the table and turned a knob on the oil lamp, raising the wick and brightening the room. "It's taken some time, but we have done enough mapping to come up with what I think is a match," he said. Ahmed gritted his teeth at the annoying, nasal sound of Tahir's voice. The navigator produced his own roll of paper, a partial outline of the coast, and flattened it beside the ancient map, aligning it to match. It wasn't a perfect fit, but close enough to leave no doubt as to the correct orientation. "We're about a third of the way around the continent so far, and it's clear the chicken scratch is the correct orientation."

Yazid scowled, his lips pressed flat like stacked coins as he studied the two maps. Tahir noticed his displeasure. "You disagree, Prelate?"

Yazid shook his head slowly. "I do not. Which is why I am disturbed."

Brutus looked at the others, then back at Yazid and laughed. "You are disturbed that we can find our asses without a compass?"

"You've had much experience with that!" Ahmed said with a grin, and the others laughed heartily.

Brutus grabbed at his crotch and jerked at it. "Aye, but we need only one pointer," he said, sparking more laughter from everyone but Yazid. Brutus quickly grew somber once more. "What is it, Prelate?"

The older man sighed, his face still troubled. "It would be fine if correction were wrong. But the mapmaker? It's bizarre."

Sandilianus absently polished a brightwork handhold with his sleeve. "Perhaps he was a fool."

"A fool whose work survived an eon, then?" Yazid said. "It seems unlikely."

Tahir rolled his eyes again, a gesture that Ahmed had begun to loathe. "What matter? Perhaps it was custom to indicate South in that time, rather than North. The point is, we are oriented and can make our plans."

"Aye, 'tis so," Brutus declared. "Let us move on to that. Where would our enemy make his home?"

Yazid's humor seemed all used up. His face was stern and hard. "We do not know that these people are our enemies. It has been a thousand years. Surely, enmity died with those who bore it?"

Brutus sat up in his seat, serious now. "We should be just as careful that we not think of them as friends," he noted. "In my experience, strangers are more apt to be enemies. But as you wish, Prelate. Call them whatever you like."

"They called themselves Meites at one time," Yazid said. "It is a good enough name, I think, until we find a better one."

Brutus nodded in assent. "So, where would these Meites have likely settled, that is our mystery."

"Coastal, of course," Tahir noted. "At the mouth of a river. They would have had the land to themselves, so I'd suppose we should look for the most prime spot."

Everyone nodded in agreement, but Yazid shook his head. "I think not."

Sandilianus heaved a sigh and turned from his polishing with a wry smile. "Do you truly think so, or is it habit now to tell us what fools we are?"

"Truly, I think so," Yazid said, returning the smile. "The Meites would have been very fearful at the time. They had no way of knowing when they would be attacked again, and they were surely as war-weary as the Laureans." Yazid walked to a porthole took in a great breath of fresh, salty air. "More importantly, they were powerful sorcerers. The legends say the Council of Twelve were like unto demigods, capable of facing entire armies. They would not need to settle on a river. They could have diverted one to their chosen spot." He retook his seat, considering the map. "I say defensibility would be their primary concern."

"If that is so, then we are lost," Brutus said, scowling. "If it is not coastal, we could circumnavigate the entire continent and never find them."

"Aye, but Ilaweh is with us. Now you will see why I have brought the boy." Yazid turned to Ahmed. "You must use your gift, child."

Ahmed's belligerent mood fell away in an instant. *Not in front of these men! They will think me a freak!* "Must I, Master?"

"You must. On the old map."

Brutus's face lit with sudden realization. "He has the sight?"

Yazid nodded. "He is modest about it."

"Modest?" Brutus chuckled. "This same boy who was waving his dick about like a flag?" He turned to Ahmed. "Are you mad, boy? You are touched by Ilaweh more than any of my kind to have such a gift!"

Ahmed swallowed hard. "I fear it. You don't understand."

"I understand that it is the hand of Ilaweh," Brutus replied. "That is all any of us need to know. Show us."

Tahir ran a hand over his face, obviously unimpressed. "A hundred swords says he finds nothing."

Brutus cast a baleful glare at Tahir. "Why not a thousand, heathen?"

"You don't have a thousand swords to lose."

Brutus continued his stare-down a moment, then nodded. "A hundred swords, then."

"Do not risk your money on me!" Ahmed gasped.

Brutus laughed out loud. "On you? Bah! On Ilaweh! And to shame this dog. His rare few words are blasphemies."

"Why not simply beat him, then?" Ahmed suggested.

Sandilianus flashed a cruel grin at this. "Tahir has no soul. He cannot feel pain like a man would. But part him from his gold, and he'll squeal like a little girl."

Tahir's eyes narrowed in annoyance, but his lips curled up in a smile, refusing to cooperate with the rest of his face. "The way I see it, I can't lose. Either I take Brutus's gold, or I get to go home sooner."

Brutus punched the red-haired navigator in the arm hard enough to stagger him. "I will buy myself a hard, young boy with your gold, Tahir, and fuck him in front of you just to make you ill! Eh? Will you wager that, too?"

"Only if, when you lose, you fuck my woman for me while I go out whoring," Tahir chuckled.

Brutus gave an exaggerated shudder of revulsion. "You are a monster!"

"Where is your faith, Brutus? Surely Ilaweh will save your masculinity, eh?"

"Sandi had the right of you. You have no soul."

Tahir gave Brutus a wicked leer but said nothing.

Brutus struggled with his pride a moment, then slammed a fist on the table and shouted, "Aye! Done!" He turned to Ahmed. "Do *not* fuck this up, boy!"

Ahmed felt bile rising in his throat as he lay his hands on the old map, reaching out for…something. It was a feeling for which there were no words, his gift. At times, it seemed purely guessing, at others, sure knowledge. This time? Who could know the will of Ilaweh until it was done?

He ran his hands over the old parchment, searching, feeling the grain of the material. *It is just paper. There is nothing here…no…wait…there.* He felt his hands drawn toward a point. He moved slowly, the pull growing stronger, now strong hands grasping his wrists and yanking them. The paper beneath his hands grew warm, then hot, then searing like molten lava. Visions of horror tore into his mind like daggers, brutal, unspeakable acts. Cries of agony rang in his ears.

Ahmed screamed as his hands burned and his vision flew elsewhere, showing him unspeakable things: monsters with tentacles and gibbering mouths ripping the flesh from screaming victims, blood pouring in rivers, cold, lifeless eyes glazed in unending horror. It was too much! He tore his hands from the map. "There!" he cried. He pounded a finger on the spot, feeling the heat and corruption each time his fingertip touched the parchment. "There! *There!*"

Yazid frowned and shook his head. "No. Not there."

"It *is!*" Ahmed cried. "A great evil, Yazid! *Terrible* evil!" *I can't breathe!*

Yazid nodded and placed a soothing arm upon Ahmed's shoulders. "I believe you, child. I know that place. It is called Torium, and no doubt there is *much* evil there. But this is not our destination. Look for a smaller evil."

Ahmed stared at Yazid in frustration as the other men watched the scene in grim silence. "How can I hear a whisper over that shriek?"

Yazid scowled and slapped Ahmed hard enough to rattle his teeth.

Thank you! The pain brought him back from the edge. Ahmed lowered his gaze and stared at the deck as he slowly regained his breath.

"Do you trust Ilaweh or not, boy?" Yazid asked.

"Aye, Master, I do."

"Then listen for his voice." Yazid pointed at the map. "Again. Try farther away from Torium. Perhaps it will help."

As Ahmed bent to his task once again, Brutus said, "I will not take my men there, Prelate. Even I know of Torium."

"Indeed. 'Tis a place we would do well to steer clear of," Yazid replied. "For now," he added, then held up a hand for silence.

Ahmed lay his fingers gently against the map, letting the tips just brush against the outline of the western coast. He immediately felt the pull toward Torium, a poisonous, yellow, nauseating current, a river of filth flowing to a sea of decay. It was overwhelming and disorienting, a sense of being torn in two by opposing forces of revulsion and compulsion.

Ilaweh, give me strength.

Slowly, his mind cleared, and the throbbing wound of Torium seemed to fade to a dull ache. He reached out, searching, listening.

There. A pinprick, a slight moan of pain, and yet a sense of kindred. *My brother is ill,* Ahmed thought to himself as he traced his finger along a river, up into a series of mountains. "Here."

Yazid looked at the point Ahmed indicated. It was blank, an unmarked area surrounded by mountains. "Aye," he said, smiling. "It seems just the sort of place they might have chosen. Isolated. Unexplored, even. Unapproachable without their grace. And it is very near us. It is surely the grace of Ilaweh that it should be so."

Brutus and Sandilianus nodded in appreciation as Tahir scowled stroked his chin, considering the two maps side by side. "Look here. We mapped the mouth of a river two days back. This old map shows it going inland fairly close to the mountains. Of course, how we'll get past the mountains is anyone's guess."

"If the boy's vision is right, there will be a pass," Brutus said. "And there ought to be a river."

Yazid agreed. "If there weren't, the Meites would have made one."

Brutus rose to his feet. "I'll need to prepare my men. What should we expect? What do you need?"

"This will be very dangerous," Yazid said. "We have no idea if they are hostile or not, and we can't afford to provoke them if they are inclined to be friendly." He scratched at his chin as he thought. "We go armed, but we must not look like an invading army. And we must be ready to weather an initial assault."

Brutus nodded, grim-faced. "As you say, dangerous, but I agree with your assessment." He turned to Sandilianus. "We take twenty men. You and I, and your choice of our best to fill out the other eighteen slots."

"Twenty-one then, with me," Yazid said. "A fortunate number, three times seven."

Ahmed leaped to his feet, indignant. "You would leave me behind?"

"Aye," Yazid told him, the look in his eyes suggesting that any defiance on Ahmed's part would earn him a beating. "If I fall, you must carry on this work. I will not risk the both of us."

Ahmed ground his teeth, trying to contain his anger and disappointment. There was no arguing with Yazid. Not only was he not a man to change his mind, he was *right* about this. But that didn't make it any easier to be left behind.

Ahmed nodded his assent, not trusting himself to speak. His tongue might not obey his head, and he would prefer to avoid humiliating himself in front of these accomplished warriors.

Brutus waited a moment, then nodded his admiration of Ahmed's silence. "Tahir, turn us around and let us have a look at this river. And you owe me a hundred swords."

Tahir waved a hand and sneered. "I've heard much talk, but I see no Meites."

Brutus grinned at him. "Aye. But you will."

They reconvened on the forecastle two days later. The air at the mouth of the river was thick with biting insects, the banks covered with more green than Ahmed had ever imagined. A man could be swallowed up in such a place and never find his way out.

"Can we sail the ship upriver?" Yazid asked Tahir.

The navigator scratched at his scraggly beard, considering. "Can we? Aye, but how far, I can't say. It will be slow. We'll need to stay on the sounding lines. But we could do it, at least part of the way."

Brutus shook his head. "We will anchor the ship here and proceed on foot. It's no more than twenty miles inland. I see no reason to announce our arrival any sooner than we must."

Yazid nodded. "I stand corrected."

Tahir pointed to the mountains in the distance. Dark clouds boiled over the peaks, thick and angry. "Could be trouble."

"Bad weather?" Brutus asked.

"Soon, I'd say."

Brutus eyed the distant cloud cover, scowling. "Then we'd best get started."

Ahmed watched them until they vanished into the green jungle. It made no sense, but he felt in his bones he would not see Yazid again. Other men could dismiss such notions as unfounded, but what was a man who had visions to think? How could he tell the difference? *Father, I should be at your side.*

But sons must obey fathers and men must be brave, and so Ahmed waited with his fear. There was nothing else he could do.

"I think we are ready to approach them," Yazid said.

Brutus considered, weighing things in his mind. A week ago, they had left the ship and proceeded inland on foot. Sooner than they had dared hope for, they had come upon signs of civilization, small villages with tall, thin, pale men working fields, tending animals, and otherwise going about farm business. They had given these settlements wide berth, not wanting to risk detection. Initially, Brutus had learned very little beyond what he could see through his spyglass.

Things moved quickly after that, however. They found a cave and set up a small camp from which they dispatched observers on reconnaissance missions. It was simple enough to follow the villagers when they left their homes, which led to the discovery of the pass, the road, and then the city.

The people they discovered were obviously harmless. The road to the city was patrolled, but at regular intervals, easily predictable, never more than a dozen armed men. It was a trivial matter to avoid them and slip into the city proper, a bit more challenging to blend in. The natives were tall, thin, and had a deathly pallor, but hooded robes and hands kept in pockets worked well enough as long as they were careful. No one questioned a single man who minded his own business. They were clearly more concerned about thieves than spies.

If the people were unusual, the city itself was nothing short of astounding! Brutus had never seen such great towers, so many people in one place, nor such a stark separation between the rich and the poor. When he had first entered, Brutus had thought that despite its appearance from afar, the place was little different from any other city: dirty, crowded, and occasionally requiring the use of his sword arm. Then he had looked up, and seen a true wonder: in the air above him hung *another* city, a second tier built atop the structures on the ground, actually using them and the surrounding hills as support.

Conspicuously absent were any sort of stairways or other means of connecting the levels. Another *people* occupied the second city, sharing the same land with the common folks below them. Oh, they looked similar enough and were surely the same stock, but those above lived in opulence and splendor, while the ones below lived in squalor and filth.

Everywhere on the second tier, real glass and polished steel glinted, turning the night sky into a sight to rival the very moon and stars. Indeed, it seemed whoever built this metropolis had been arrogant enough to block out the mundane lights of the heavens so that they could not possibly compete. The clouds over the city never parted, never thinned, never rained. They simply hovered, dark and brooding in the day, orange and luminous at night.

By now, Brutus knew the name of the city: Nihlos. He knew the locals spoke a variant of Priman, though a thousand years of divergence had created accents and phrases that were at times different enough to pass as another language entirely. He knew that they were relatively civilized, that there were divisions of class in a hierarchy of noble, commoner, and slave, though 'slave' meant something different here than it would in Aviar.

He knew the paths food, and other vital supplies took from the outlying villages to the city proper, and how to cut them off. He knew the city was surrounded by a ten foot stone wall, the location of the gates about its circumference, and how paltry the forces manning them were.

Most importantly, he knew that, of his estimated half million residents, less than one percent of them were under arms. They were, for all practical purposes, completely defenseless. They had no army to speak of, only police whose chief concerns were thieves and drunks.

"Approach?" He fixed Yazid with a smoldering stare and sneered. "Prelate, I begin to wonder why I listen to you and your tales. These people are weaklings. We have nothing to fear from them. This is a fool's errand."

Yazid's face grew even darker, and his right hand clenched into a fist. "Even if you do not fear them, you should fear to insult me."

Brutus held his gaze for a moment, then nodded his surrender with a laugh. "Fair enough, Yazid. I will be more respectful. But truly, these people cannot possibly be a threat to us. Bagdreme alone could field twenty legions if her need was great enough, to say nothing of all Xanthia. I think we can simply walk away from this. We know what we need to know."

Yazid shook his head. "We do not. We know nothing, truly."

"I try to be respectful, Prelate, but I try to be honest, as well. I think this prophecy business is bunk, Ilaweh be praised. It is time to admit you were wrong about this."

Yazid's fingers clenched and unclenched, and his nostrils flared wide. "If I am wrong, then how came we here? How did Ahmed and I guide you to this city that should not exist? How am

I right about everything else?" He spat on the ground. "Idiot. You think with your sword hand and your dick."

Brutus leaped to his feet. "You will go fists with me for that, old man, or you will go steel!"

Yazid answered with his right.

Sandilianus raised an eyebrow. "Just the one?"

"Aye," Brutus said with a nod. He rubbed his aching jaw absently. "Ilaweh himself struck that blow, and I struck the ground, so we do it his way. We'll hail one of the patrols."

"A dozen of them. How many of us, then?"

Brutus cast Sandilianus a gaze that seemed to question his junior's basic sanity. "All of us."

They took up a position in the middle of the road, Yazid and Brutus in the lead, all of them standing at parade rest, waiting for the noonday patrol.

Yazid watched as the strangers approached, though he heard their boots crunching on the gravel road long before they came into view. They were tall men, all over six feet, some closer to seven. At six foot four, Yazid would be counted as barely above average by these folks, but there was little substance to them. They seemed almost skeletal, not quite skin and bones, but thin and gangly, even their heads. They would have good reach in a fight, he supposed, but their blows would lack power.

The patrolmen had no discipline or military bearing. They did not march, but rather flocked, each man a separate unit in an amorphous group, ambling with his own peculiar gait along the road in a loose pack with his brethren. They wore mail of curious design, tight fitting and mostly black, with a bit of silver here and there, studs and buckles winking in the sunlight. Their helms were garish black affairs, most adorned with bat wings, though some few seemed to prefer a bird motif. Odd, spiny protrusions ran along their legs or sleeves, like teeth or claws. *It looks intimidating, to be sure, but it serves no real purpose.* On closer inspection, Yazid realized that not all of them matched, however: some had spines on only half a leg, others a quarter or the full length. Only two of them wore spines on their arms, and only quarter length. *Ah! Marks of rank.* Each carried a lasso and small sword at his belt, but no shield, no javelin, nothing with which to form a phalanx.

Brutus is right about these people, even if he is wrong about the prophecy. These men did not deserve the name soldier. Police or guardsmen, perhaps, but no more. They simply did not have the bearing.

There was a moment, as there always is in first encounters, where the surprised party realizes it is not alone, and quickly decides to flee, fight, or palaver. The strange troops staggered to a halt one by one, some in the rear actually running into the ones in the front. *Fools. Children playing at war.* After a moment of confusion, hands reached toward weapons, considering, testing.

Yazid nodded to himself. All was as expected. He raised one hand above his head in greeting, and said quietly to Brutus, "Hold your position. I will go alone."

"Don't get yourself killed, old man," Brutus replied. "I don't think I can stomach taking orders from the boy."

Yazid smiled. "I'll try to stay alive, then."

They kept their hands on their weapons as he approached, but they did not draw them, which was a good sign. Their faces looked familiar, confused like Ahmed's when he first met barbarians. Yazid was even more glad of his decision to leave the boy behind. He was still too xenophobic. Best to have him acclimate to paler faces more before allowing him into tricky situations where he could cause overmuch trouble. One side with such feelings was quite enough.

One question remained. Would they understand him? He lowered his hand and bowed. "Greetings. I am Yazid Valerian. We come in peace, if you are peaceful."

One, apparently the leader, stepped toward Yazid. He stood for a moment, icy, almond-shaped blue eyes staring from a parchment white, hairless face, suspicious, nervous. "Piss, ah?"

Yazid chuckled. "Close enough."

Brutus ground his teeth as he waited. They were too far away to hear, which left Brutus on high alert, with no way to know if he could relax. He cursed Yazid a thousand times in silence, urging him to hurry, to remember his companions.

Eons seemed to pass. Trees sprung from the ground, rose, thickened, crumbled, and died. Brutus felt senility creeping upon him as the years marched on, but he continued to stand in stoic silence at parade rest, carefully avoiding locking his knees so that he would not pass out.

At last, when enough time had passed for the old universe to die and a new one be reborn, over and over again, until one sprang into existence in which Yazid and Brutus both existed and were compatriots once again, Yazid broke from the strangers and returned. One of their number left their party and went off toward the city, which Brutus found quite alarming. He could barely contain his frustration. "Well?"

"They speak Priman. The accent is hard to understand, but your ear picks it up soon enough. It's amusing, actually. They use many archaisms. They sound like the writing in old books."

Brutus ground his teeth. "You waste my time and try my

patience, Prelate. Are we at war or not?"

"Nay. It seems we are well. They call this land Nillos, by the way. They've sent to the city for orders on how to handle the situation."

"So they say. *I say* they've sent for reinforcements, old man. We need to retreat to a defensible location *now*."

Yazid scratched at his chin, considering. "Likely. I suspect they are quite intimidated by our numbers and bearing. It is what I would do."

"Then we return to the cave."

Yazid shook his head. "It will seem hostile."

"What of it? Lie. They did. Tell them we're all going to take our afternoon nap. If they don't come back in force, then that's just what we'll do, eh? And if they do...."

Yazid laughed out loud. "A nap! I think I'll find something better than that."

"Not that it matters. It's not as if they can stop us."

"Aye. I'll think of something sensible to say."

Brutus kept his back against the cold, moss-covered surface of the cave wall as he moved toward the entrance. Slowly, carefully, he eased his head from behind the stone to catch a glimpse of the strangers advancing on his position. He guessed there were a hundred, from the quick glance he was willing to risk. One shouted something and waved a sword. Brutus heard the hum of an arrow whizzing through the air and ducked back behind the protective stone just in time. The arrow hit the cave wall and shattered.

Brutus called over his shoulder to Yazid, "I thought you said they spoke Priman."

"They *do*. How can you not understand it, oaf?" Yazid laughed. "He said come out of the cave or die."

Brutus shook his head in amusement. "Will he understand me?"

"Probably not. Can I not talk you out of this?"

"Will you surrender, Prelate? These fools cannot defeat us. Would Ilaweh approve of such cowardice?"

Yazid scowled. "No. He would not. But it may cost us dearly."

"Then we will make sure it costs our enemies even more." He leaned out of the cave, shield raised against more arrows, and shouted, "We choose death, dog! Let us see if you can deliver on that promise!"

CHAPTER 4
CLASH OF CULTURES

It was quite a lovely dream in which Caelwen Luvox found himself, one with no duties, only the company of a soft-spoken, beautiful young lady, and so he was not at all in a mood to be awakened. Had it been a woman's voice, it would have at least cushioned the blow, but it was Kelthas, his second in command.

"Commander, you must wake! There is terrible trouble!" Kelthas's voice was as young as his unshaven, boyish face, nervous and high pitched with concern.

Caelwen was the sort of man who came immediately, fully awake and wasted no time yawning and stretching or regretting lost dreams. He rose and walked naked to fetch his pants. "I'm listening."

His quarters were small and spare, though he was entitled by station to much better. It seemed silly and grasping to demand the best of the guard quarters when his own personal chambers were just across the yard of House Luvox. He had plenty of space there, whereas many of his men had only their rooms in the barracks. Even Kelthas, who was a lesser member of House Noril, had no property of his own. The Guard was home to him.

Caelwen was happy to allow Kelthas the Commander's quarters and serve his own duty in humbler accommodations.

As Caelwen finished dressing, Kelthas explained that a patrol had encountered a group of foreigners and had sent word for further instructions. "I sent Lorinal, and he's botched it badly."

Caelwen shook his head and cursed under his breath. It was indeed bad. Lorinal was as wrong a man for this job as could be found. "What is the current situation?"

"Lorinal took a hundred men with him and apparently played things wrongly. The foreigners are entrenched in a cave, and our men can't get them out." Kelthas clutched nervously at his sword hilt, his jaw clenching and relaxing several times as he searched for words. "Right now they're just holding position and keeping them pinned in, but they had several goes at them before giving up. We've got at least thirty down, don't know how many are dead or wounded."

Caelwen clenched his fists in frustration. "Mei!" He considered punching a wall but thought better of it. He had done that far too many times in the past. "You've screwed this up badly, Kelthas. Lorinal is a skull cracker, not a negotiator!"

Kelthas nodded and stared at the floor, blinking against tears, his face red with shame. "I know that now, sir."

Caelwen gave Kelthas five full seconds of glaring, to let the point sink in, then softened. *Time to train some leadership.* "So now you've the blood of some of your men on your hands. It happens to us all at some point. Learn from it and give what meaning you can to their deaths."

Kelthas clenched his teeth and blinked vigorously. "Yes, sir."

"Meanwhile, let's sort this one out. You say foreigners? From where? Barbarians from Reese?"

"No, sir. I haven't seen them, but the patrol described them as thick, dark-skinned men. I specifically asked if he meant Reesians, and he was very clear that they were not. Many of these men were darker, some almost black, and fearsome looking in their arms and demeanor, though they claimed to come in peace."

Caelwen shrugged into his mail and pulled it down at his waist, then reached for his sword belt. "I have heard of no one like this. Except…" There *was* something familiar about this. *Southlanders!* It came to him suddenly, and his blood ran cold.

"What is it, sir?"

Caelwen cursed himself for not controlling his reaction better. *We will not speak the name until I know for certain.* "Just a hunch. History. Book of Amrath, that sort of thing."

"I don't understand, sir."

Caelwen fastened his sword belt, then squeezed Kelthas's shoulder and fixed him with a sharp look. "You don't need to. Just show me where they are so I can defuse this. It could be *much* worse than you imagine."

Caelwen stood in a field atop a small, grassy hill with the remainder of Lorinal's forces, peering through his spyglass and considered the situation. The setting sun worked to the enemy's advantage, making it hard to see in the direction of the cave, a fact of which they were no doubt aware.

It was as Kelthas had said: a standoff at a cave at the foot of a small hill, thirty bodies or thereabouts lying in the grass. At best guess, he had fifteen men who were wounded but still alive. He'd also guess that number would drop to seven in short order if he didn't get them medical attention.

Caelwen lowered his glass and glared halfheartedly at the grizzled fighter who stood at his right. "Lorinal, you are an idiot," he sighed, unable to muster any real anger at him for this situation. Lorinal was a fine fighter, fiercely loyal, but common born and pig ignorant of delicate situations. His solution to everything was to hit someone in the head very hard until things changed. He excelled at handling thugs, thieves, and drunks, and that was all Nihlos had in the way of violent threats. *Well, except for Meites, but they've been quiet for years.*

Lorinal's arms were folded across his chest in defiance. "It was entirely their fault, sir! They refused to come peacefully!"

"These are not common thugs who respond well to having their heads cracked, as you've no doubt learned." Caelwen fixed Lorinal with an icy glare for a few moments, making sure his displeasure was uncomfortably clear before continuing. "Why aren't *you* lying up there bleeding or dead? As I recall, you're usually at the front of the line when there's pain to be inflicted. You're an idiot, there is no denying that, but I've never thought you a coward."

"Guess I'm getting old, sir. I just ain't as fast as I used to be. I got stuck in just in time to call a retreat." Lorinal cast a sour look toward the cave. "Them blackies is plenty tough."

"Pity. If you'd gotten yourself killed, it would save me the trouble of having you flogged for this mess."

"Aye, sir. Sorry, sir."

"I should have you flog your damned self."

Lorinal nodded his agreement. "Aye, sir."

Caelwen shook his head in wonder."You would, wouldn't you? And not hold back, I think."

"Orders is orders. Sir."

"Aye, 'orders is orders.' Give me your talker, Lorinal, and get out of my sight for a while. I've better things to do with my whips than wear them out on your scabrous hide."

Caelwen lifted the talker to his lips and pointed it toward the barbarians. "Hostiles, we would like to parley!" he shouted. "Signify you understand by waving." He raised his glass again and saw a dark, almost black arm reach from the cave mouth and wave. They understood. He raised the talker again and shouted, "Come alone, and I will do likewise." Again, the arm waved.

Caelwen turned to Kelthas. "Listen to me. If I am killed, you must contain these men at all costs, and take the matter directly to the Empress. Tell her they are *Southlanders*. Do you understand?"

"Aye, sir."

Caelwen put a hand on Kelthas's shoulder and gripped it to impress the point. "These men are no Reesian barbarians. This could start a war that could destroy Nihlos if it gets out of hand. *At all costs*. Do you understand? "

Kelthas nodded, a look of grim determination on his face. "Aye, sir."

Caelwen pulled his helmet on as an added precaution and set off alone toward the cave entrance. Shortly thereafter, a dark-skinned man stepped from the cave and did likewise. Caelwen noted his opponent was indeed armed, but his weapon was sheathed. So far, so good. They strode toward one another with purpose. Caelwen slowly raised a hand and pointed to a large oak tree as a good spot, but the stranger shook his head vigorously, pointing straight ahead to open ground. *I would have preferred a bit of shade, but I suppose it's reasonable to be suspicious.*

When they met, the dark man extended a calloused hand, and Caelwen returned the gesture. He was somewhat surprised to see that these men apparently chose to grasp at the forearm rather than at the hand, but it was easy enough to adapt.

"You understand me when I speak?" Caelwen asked.

"I do. It is difficult, but yes." The voice was shockingly deep and guttural, the accent brutal in and of itself, and yet, it seemed almost natural to Caelwen. It fit this man.

"I am Caelwen, Commander of Guards and Chief of Police of Nihlos. Identify yourself to me, please."

"Ah, someone of authority," the man said, nodding his appreciation. "It is good. I am Brutus Samir, Tribune of Prince Philip of

Xanthia. We come in peace, Caelwen of Nillos. Why do you attack us?"

Caelwen considered his opponent carefully. His limbs seemed thick as trees, the chest beneath his tunic unnaturally thick. *How in Mei's name can he even stand up?* He was armored in odd style, with a horsehair helm that covered his cheeks and nose, mail and lobstered plate at his chest, and some sort of armored skirt about his hips. Below the waist, he wore more mail, with high steel boots that came to his knees. All of it was covered with blood. *My men's blood.* This was a hard man, then, no one to trifle with. He would appreciate candor. "A foolish member of my staff made a mistake. He will be punished. But it has created a situation."

Brutus nodded. "Easily corrected by your men withdrawing."

Caelwen shrugged. "There is the difficulty, eh? I cannot simply make it disappear that twenty or thirty city guards are dead. There will be an inquiry. I am sure it can all be sorted out, but I cannot simply let you walk away."

Brutus nodded. "I understand. Now understand me. We are prepared to fight to the death."

This is a matter of pride, then. Caelwen waved the notion aside as if it were an annoying fly. "I doubt that will happen. Time is on my side." He made a show of examining his opponent. "You do indeed appear to be mighty warriors, but you must sleep some time. I can bring more and more fresh men."

"We'll fight in shifts," Brutus answered with a broad grin. "We need only a few to hold the mouth." He nodded toward the fallen men behind him. "We'll die of boredom, I think, before we fall to your swords."

"Or dehydration."

"The cave goes deep into the ground. There is an underground river, with mosses, fish, bugs. We can hold out indefinitely."

Caelwen could not suppress a wry smile at this. "A bold lie well told, but a lie nonetheless."

Brutus shrugged and smiled back, offering nothing but an enigma.

Caelwen pressed on. "We will build fires near the opening. Either you break your lines, or you pass out from the smoke. We'll get you out eventually, and alive, for the most part."

Caelwen felt victory within his grasp, only to have it torn from him by Brutus's next words. "Then we will fall upon our own swords."

Caelwen's eyes grew wide despite his best effort to suppress his shock. He hadn't seen that one coming. "You would choose death over a simple inquiry? It would be over and done with in a day or so, and you no worse for wear."

"We would choose death over being arrested and humiliated, yes."

That is truth, not bravado. Caelwen considered Brutus long and hard, trying to decide on his next thrust. At last, he said, "Here are my terms. We will not call it 'surrender.' We will call it 'cooperation.' Come peacefully and cooperate with my investigation, by your own will. We will escort your men into the city without shame, under cover of darkness, so no one even knows. I will explain to my superior. You will retain your arms, and be treated well, though you will not be allowed to leave until the matter is concluded."

It was Brutus's turn to think hard. His eyes narrowed as he considered the offer. "And this superior, he will listen to what you have to say?"

Caelwen offered a genuine smile at this. "He is my father. He will listen."

"And if we refuse?"

Caelwen's ground his teeth, angry again. *He will push to the end? Then so will I.* "I have men dying out here. The only reason

I am offering you terms is that I need this to end quickly. If you leave my men to suffer before they die, I will name you barbarians and treat you as such. I'll drag you naked through the streets, and I'll personally hang every one of you."

Brutus raised an eyebrow at this and snorted in amusement. "You are a hard man, Caelwen of Nillos. I like that. I will confer with my men. You will have your answer shortly."

Caelwen nodded. "I will wait."

Brutus turned to leave, then paused and called back, "Recover your fallen. Whatever our answer, we will not deny you that."

Caelwen watched him walk back to the cave and heaved a great sigh. *This might just end well after all.*

Sandilianus looked back and forth at Yazid and Brutus, his weathered face taut with displeasure. "Call it what you will, it seems surrender to me."

Brutus grimaced. "Aye, to me as well. And yet, if we keep our weapons, how can we be surrendered?" He spat on the cave floor. "That is what I think of diplomacy, but this Caelwen is no diplomat. His men may be soft, but he is a warrior, there is no doubt. He has the bearing."

"Does he lie?"

"No, I think he speaks honestly, but it is his father who makes the final decision. I do not like it." Brutus turned to Yazid and raised an eyebrow. "What say you, prelate?"

Yazid laid a hand on Brutus's shoulder and squeezed. "We will have many chances to die well, if that is our fate. We have our mission to consider. Philip was very clear. We are all of us expendable, save the one man who brings him back information. I think he would have us sacrifice our pride as well, if need be."

"So surrender is the only way we can complete our mission?" Sandilianus mused. "How bizarre."

Brutus shook his head in disbelief. "So it would seem."

Yazid slapped his hands on his knees and rose to his feet. "Then we are resolved."

Brutus nodded. "As you said, it is exploration, the most dangerous of missions. It would be easy to fight. It will take true bravery to place ourselves at their mercy." He thumped a fist against his chest in a perfunctory salute and turned to leave. "I will give him our answer."

Kariana Tasinal, or more formerly Tasinalta, Empress of Nihlos, was not accustomed to being awakened at odd hours. She got little enough sleep as it was, and it was difficult to be 'empressey' when she was barely able to see, much less strike a decent pose. She eyed the empty bottle on the floor beside her canopied bed. *Mei, why did I drink the whole thing?*

She was even less pleased that Caelwen should see her in such disrepair. *At least I didn't throw up in my sleep.* Not that she fancied him, at least not any more than she would fancy any other attractive man. It was that he thought himself perfect, and him seeing her in this state felt decidedly icky. Her Chief of Police loomed over the foot of her bed, armored, helmet under his left arm, his close-cropped, blond hair darkened with sweat. "What is it, Stone? Did someone spit on the sidewalk again?"

Caelwen's face hardened at this. *He's cute when he's angry.* She looked him up and down, appreciating his bulk. Most of her toys were thin and reedy, with round heads and soft features, but Caelwen was fairly bursting with lovely, muscled bits, and sported a strong, square jaw, to boot. *He's a bit swarthy, though. I bet he doesn't even shave his chest!* She imagined running her hand over his face, feeling the point of his cheekbones and the rough scratch of late day stubble. *I most certainly could get used to the idea.*

His eyes, however, were cold like winter wind on wet skin. *Perhaps 'angry' was a bit of an understatement. 'Murderous rage' might be more appropriate.* "Is war reason enough?" he growled through clenched teeth.

Kariana adjusted her shift to cover her breasts as she rose. "That's not even a little funny."

"Have you ever known me to joke with you?"

Kariana felt a chill down her spine at this, and her frivolous manner fell away with her lewd thoughts. "Why are you here, Caelwen?"

Caelwen nodded, his jaw working as he struggled for words. "This will sound mad," he began and then trailed off.

He is actually speechless! She was torn between shouting for joy at his unprecedented display of humanity and collapsing in panic at whatever could shake him like this. She settled for prodding at him. "Since when has the Stone had trouble expressing himself? Out with it!"

Caelwen shot her a glare, then squared his shoulders and said bluntly, "I believe that I have captured a scouting party of South-landers."

Kariana rubbed at her throbbing eyes, trying to understand. Southlanders were some ancient thing, evil men from...the South, somewhere. "What?" she groaned. *This must be a dream.*

"What part did you not understand, Empress?"

Kariana looked about her chambers. They *seemed* real enough, but then dreams often felt very real. She reached beneath her sheet and surreptitiously pinched her nipple to make certain. It was painful enough, but nothing changed. "The part about there being Southlanders *here*. Where are they from?"

Caelwen looked a bit uncomfortable at this and shrugged. "From the South, I suppose."

Oh, good! At least I am not the only idiot! Kariana pinched herself again, for all the good it did. "Well, what makes you think they are Southlanders, then?"

"Dark-skinned men, fierce warriors of iron will, thick men, almost misshapen. Fearsome brutes." He shrugged. "They certainly match what I learned in school."

"It cannot be true."

Caelwen's jaw bulged as he ground his teeth. "I used to try that, as a child, just deny bad things. My sorcery failed me, but perhaps yours is stronger, eh?"

"Bastard!" Kariana reached for an ashtray and hurled it at him. Caelwen stepped deftly aside, allowing the glass to shatter against the doorframe behind him in a spray of glass and cinders. "It's insane! Why would they return after so long?"

"They say they are exploring."

"They are *not* Southlanders!"

"I say they are. I have seen Talus's paintings, read Amrath's descriptions, as have you. It is simple enough for you to have a look at them and decide for yourself."

Kariana simmered in silence for a moment, absorbing the implications. Her mind was working slowly. Too many drugs, too little sleep. "Let us say you are correct. Why would you capture them? Why provoke an incident?"

Caelwen nodded, looking, to her amazement, quite abashed. "Mistakes were made. They surprised our patrol, actually introduced themselves. The sergeant in charge sent back to the city for instructions and support. I was sleeping at the time. My second sent the wrong man to handle it, and that man turned a diplomatic situation into a battle. I chose the man who gave the order. I accept full responsibility."

Kariana could feel her eyes bulging from their sockets with

fury and fear. "How could this *happen*?" she shrieked. "What were they thinking?"

"They *weren't* thinking. They were reacting as they have been trained." He shrugged. "They are commoners, Empress. They are largely idiots by design."

"Mei! How many are dead?"

"Of them? None. They crushed our people with brutal efficiency. They killed nine of ours outright and wounded another twenty-three. If I don't get my men medical attention quickly, at least ten of those will be dead by morning."

"Why are you waiting?"

"Containment, Empress. *Everyone* involved is under lockdown until you decide how to handle things." Caelwen clenched a hand into a fist and pounded at his leg. "And I beg you decide quickly. Those are young men, many with families."

Kariana breathed a sigh of relief. Then it was not yet war. For once, she was profoundly grateful for Caelwen's rigidity. "They must have ambushed our men? Or were they outnumbered?"

"Neither. There were twenty of them. Our men outnumbered them five-to-one."

"Mei!"

Caelwen nodded gravely. "Now, perhaps you understand why I believe as I do."

Kariana returned his nod, her eyes darting back and forth as she tried to make sense of things, to find a path out of this disaster. "Send to House Amrath for Aiul. Have him tend to your men. Him and no one else, do you understand? And tell him *nothing*! I need time to think."

Caelwen left quickly, concern for his men spurring him onward, no doubt. The moment her chamber door closed, she leaped from her bed and rushed to her bar. With trembling hands, she drank straight from a bottle of brandy until the burn overwhelmed her.

For a while, the panic owned her. *Southlanders!* They had defeated even the *founders*. What hope could she have against them? She could no more meet them in war than a mouse could battle a lion. Nihlos would be crushed!

Before long, the brandy had the desired effect. Her mind grew slower, calmer. She was not entirely defenseless. The Spirit Shield would keep them out, or kill them if they tried to enter the city. But it would only delay the inevitable. How long could the city last without its outlying farms?

She allowed herself a small hope. Perhaps they were not here for war? Perhaps it was true that they were exploring. Perhaps they had forgotten their old enmity. A millennium was a long time. If they had come for war, would they not have brought more than twenty? Perhaps, perhaps not. It would make sense to send an innocuous party to probe their defenses, spy upon them. And such spies would report terrible weakness, a defenseless city ripe for plucking.

She began to pace, a plan forming slowly in her mind as she weighed the possibilities and alternatives. One possibility was war with the Southlanders. This was unthinkable. At the very least, she needed time to muster an army, and even then, she doubted her chances at matching them. Under no circumstances could she take any action that might lead to war. Not yet.

Yet weakness itself might well provoke an attack, if they were hostile. If they were truly peaceful, then insult or injury could likewise trigger disaster. There had *already* been a fight. Who knew what they thought, or what the repercussions of that might be?

If they were truly here in peace, then it would be very good for Nihlos, and for her personally. And yet, how could she know? Asking would be useless. Surely, they would lie if they intended harm?

Unless, of course, she ripped the truth from them. That would solve the one problem. Their deaths would solve the other. If they were peaceful, then so be it. No one need ever know what had happened. No one in Nihlos had ever seen them.

She took another drink, feeling the pounding in her temples slowly subside. She could control this. She could reset this.

It would be easy.

Aiul woke to the sound of shouts. He was confused, sleep-addled. What was going on? Lara was just beginning to stir when Garas's cry of pain sliced through the fog in his head. Aiul leaped up and grabbed his robe, fear for Garas dancing in his chest, driving him forward.

Lara moaned softly as he shrugged his way into the robe. "What's going on?" Aiul gave no answer. Instead, he took a heavy candle holder from beside her and slipped out into the hallway.

"You have no right to be here!" Garas cried out from the front door. "There are other physicians. It's after midnight!"

"I have orders to bring *this* physician, and I follow my orders, slave. If you did the same, you should not be bleeding." Aiul's felt his guts twist in fear and confusion. He recognized that voice. What could Caelwen Luvox want here in the middle of the night? Could this be some play by his mother, having him arrested to split him from Lara?

"My master is resting!"

"Slave, you have three choices: lead, get out of my way, or pain. Think of it this way, how can he rest if he's up all night repairing what I am about to do to you, eh?"

Aiul had heard enough. If it was his mother's trap, so be it. He could not allow Garas to take a beating from the police simply to protect him. He cinched his robe and strode into the foyer.

"What is going on here?" he asked as he took in the scene. Caelwen stood in the open door, a mailed fist raised to strike. Garas, blood running freely from his nose and mouth, was doing his best to block Caelwen from entering. "You dare strike my slave?"

"It is nothing, master," Garas assured him. "Go back to sleep."

Caelwen lowered his fist and turned to Aiul. "I did. I am here under orders, as I told him."

"Orders from whom?"

Caelwen rubbed at his temple, muttered something under his breath, then nearly shouted, "Who do you think orders the Commander of the Guard to your home at such an hour, fool?"

Aiul nodded, feeling a bit staggered. This was not his mother, then. This was something serious. "That still does not give you the right to strike my slave."

"Then sue me, House Amrath. Isn't that one of your family's more disreputable arts? But for now, you'll come with me, or you'll get the same."

Aiul stared at him in shock. "You threaten me?"

"It's not a threat. It's a promise." The look in Caelwen's eyes was undeniable. He was absolutely serious. "You do not know the severity of the situation, and I am not at liberty to reveal it. Now will you come, or must I drag you?"

Aiul stammered momentarily, angry at such treatment, but knowing the only reason one summoned a physician at such an hour was that people were dying. "Let me gather my equipment."

"*Quickly*, doctor. As quickly as you possibly can!"

The imperial infirmary had been closed off to serve the wounded. Aiul had asked for assistants, but his request had been denied. "State security," was the only reason Caelwen offered. Had men not been dying in front of him, Aiul would have told Caelwen where he could stuff his state security, but for now, saving those he could took priority.

Aiul knew about triage, had been trained in how to choose who lived and died, but he had rarely needed to practice it before, and never without others skilled in medicine. Caelwen was his only helper. It was difficult, far more than he would have guessed.

This one might live, if he were the only one, if I had time, if you had gotten him to me sooner, but now I inject him with morphine to ease his passing and move on to the next. This one is already dead. Next. This one is screaming loudest. Mei, the stench! His guts are penetrated and spilling into his bloodstream. Another for morphine. Next. Mei! It's bad, blood everywhere, but it's still pumping, so maybe there is a chance. If I can just find the source. There, but Mei! I can't mend that! Fine. Morphine, but this time with purpose. Bring me a burning iron and a saw! Now!

On and on it went, too long and too urgent. When it was done, he collapsed into a corner of the royal infirmary and covered his face with bloody hands, trying not to sob. In truth, he had done much better than he had imagined. Twenty-three wounded, ten mortally so. Of these, two were dead when he arrived, another died while he was tending the others, and two were far away on clouds, awaiting their time. He had saved five (four-and-three-quarters counting the leg he had sawn off, he reminded himself). No so bad for a hopeless situation. Half was good, considering.

When he finally looked up from his minor collapse, Caelwen was standing over him, splattered with blood, yet impassive as ever. "I owe you thanks, surgeon."

"Eh? Oh, yes, of course. I wish I could have done more. If I had been here sooner, I could have saved at least two more."

Caelwen shrugged. "The situation is as it is. You did what you could, and I am grateful." He reached a bloody hand to Aiul.

Aiul accepted the help, rising on shaky legs. "And exactly what is the 'situation'?"

Caelwen stared down at Aiul with emotionless, pale blue eyes and placid face. "That is a matter of state security, on a need to know basis. You do not need to know."

"I know a sword wound when I see one!"

"I recommend you not speak of that knowledge, surgeon. I recommend it most highly."

"Or what? What will you do?"

Caelwen shook his head and sighed. "I will follow my orders and obey the law." He gently placed a hand on Aiul's shoulder. It left a mark, but there were so many others, it hardly mattered. "Listen to me. I am not your enemy."

Aiul stiffened at Caelwen's touch and stepped away. *Don't touch me, you thug. This blood is all your fault.* "I want to speak to her."

Caelwen seemed confused for a moment, then nodded as he grasped Aiul's meaning. "Tasinalta? I doubt she will see you. She is in bed."

"Why do you think she called my name in her time of trouble? She will see me. Tell her."

Caelwen nodded. "You should clean up." He cocked his head to the side, considering, and shrugged. "Then again, perhaps not. She has odd tastes."

For the second time that night, Kariana found herself in the unusual situation of having a gentleman visitor in her private chambers. Not that she didn't have many a visitor there for various debaucheries, but typically they were slaves and commoners. Most of the Housed men seemed to take little interest in her, no doubt because her power intimidated them.

This one, however, was special in any number of ways. Unlike Caelwen, the cold, cruel creature, Aiul was warm and inviting, kind, funny, appreciative. He was, in fact, everything a woman might want, save for *obedient*. What a pity. If he did as he was told, he could be the consort of an Empress. But, then, he had always resented authority. Perhaps that was what had always drawn her to him. He was safe, and yet there was the sense that if he was pushed too far, he was capable of almost anything.

"Aiul," she said softly as he entered and closed the door behind him. "It's been a long time." She let her eyes hover on him. She had always liked his body, but his hands were magical, a surgeon's hands, sensitive, dexterous, and strong. She couldn't help but smile at the traces of blood still on them. She found it quite erotic.

He smiled and ducked his head sheepishly. "It has. It's good to see you again, Kariana. I'm sorry it's under such dire circumstances."

"Oh, the situation you've dealt with is minor. We can always find more guards." The smile left his face as quickly as it had come. Why was he so damned mercurial?

"I suppose that's true enough."

"I have a bigger problem." She turned her face away and angled her shoulder, offering him a view down the front of her nightgown, but he was oblivious. He always had been, the fool. "I've captured a scouting party of Southlanders."

Aiul looked confused for a moment, then gaped as he made the connection. "Mei! Are you serious?"

She looked at him, carefully forming her expression into a mask of solemnity, hoping her eyes appeared as wide and doe-like as possible. "They are fearsome brutes."

"Aye. I've just seen their handiwork. What will you do with them?"

She said nothing for a moment, drawing things out, letting his curiosity peak before feeding it. "I must know their true intentions. And I will need your help."

Again, it took him a moment to put it together, but when he did, his face darkened with anger, and he shook his head vehemently. "I'll have no part of that! I am a healer!"

"And I want you to heal."

"To keep men alive while you torture them! I won't do it."

He was so terribly sexy when he was moralizing, and yet she knew his weaknesses, as well. Hero, healer, the need to dry tears and ease pain, these were his soft spots. She had long ago learned to cry whenever she liked. She wept for him, and he came to her, took her in his arms as she knew he would. She buried her face against his chest and delivered an admirably believable series of sobs.

"I have no *choice*, Aiul!" she said at last. "You saw what those monsters can do!"

"I did." He swallowed, hard. She was getting to him.

"Can you imagine an army of them tearing through our streets? Can you imagine them having their way with your new wife? We *must* find out what they know!"

She felt him nod against her. "Very well, then. I will help you." She smiled against his chest, knowing he could not see. He was hers, at least for this matter. And before long, perhaps in all respects, and his new wife be damned.

"Will you stay with me tonight, Aiul?" she whispered.

He shifted uncomfortably against her. "I am married now, Kariana."

A stab of anger and jealousy ripped through her. He should have been hers! The child his commoner bitch wife carried should have been in *her* belly instead. Was it not proper that Amrath and Tasinal should be together? Was it not what was always supposed to be, since they were children? He *was* hers! She had seen him first!

"What of it?" she whispered, not quite able to keep the acid from her voice. "Who pays attention to such things?"

"I do."

Of course, the hero did, the surgeon, the good and decent fool. "Then tell her I commanded it. I have that right."

Aiul was motionless for long moments. He cleared his throat before he spoke. "Then command me."

Kariana ground her teeth in rage. Not by his will, then. Not yet, anyway. "I command you," she whispered. "Stay."

CHAPTER 5

MACHINATION

It was well past two in the morning when Aiul made his way through darkened, misty streets toward the prison, medical bag in tow, his thin frame huddled in a long, black robe. Frozen breath poured from beneath his hood as he half walked, half ran, his long legs not carrying him fast enough for his comfort. His boots clicked on the cobblestones, seeming loud in his ears, the only other sound besides his steady breathing.

The route was indirect, taking him through several seedier areas of the undercity, but he had been instructed to adhere to it specifically, to avoid attracting attention. The streetlamps along the way were all conveniently unlit, which only added to his discomfort. The few people he might encounter were likely to be both hostile and emboldened by the darkness. The first time he had made the journey, nearly a week before, he had been unarmed and had it not been for his skill in running, it might well have been his last. The following night, he had fetched his old mace, the one he had used for training as a youth when he fancied that he might someday become a warrior. That dream was long gone, but the skill remained, and the second trip had been unhealthy for several would-be muggers. Since then, they had given the tall, hooded figure a wide berth when he passed.

The one advantage of making this journey at night was that Caelwen was long gone by the time he arrived at the prison. The Commander knew well what was going on, and though he said not a word in objection, Aiul knew all the same that Caelwen was furious that his promises to the Southlanders had been overruled. He would follow the law, as he always did, so Aiul had no fear of being attacked. It was just that stare, that cold, blue gaze of unswerving, uncompromising judgment. It was like ice growing over his heart. Anything to avoid it was preferable.

So much for doing no harm. He cursed silently as he walked on, furious at having been fool enough to let himself become involved in this misadventure. Kariana was rapidly approaching madness due to sleep deprivation and substance abuse. There were pills to sleep, pills to prevent sleep, pills to be happy, pills to heighten sexual pleasure, the list went on and on. And she wondered why he would never have considered her for a wife!

When she was not jamming sharp instruments into the prisoner, she was jamming them into herself, injecting Mei knew what sort of noxious potions. At other times she wept uncontrollably, demanding he stay with her and console her. This, perhaps, was more troubling than all the rest. She was simply not the same woman he had known in his youth. Where in Mei's name had she learned to torture? More importantly, *why*? She had always been indulgent and impulsive. Her wild abandon was half the reason Aiul had been fond of her in the past. But now, she was cruel as well, and frightened, paranoid. She was not Kariana anymore. The crown had changed her. She was Tasinalta, now, and his pity for her had changed, as well. It had become genuine fear.

He had, perhaps wrongly, kept things from Lara, feeling it would simply upset her for no good reason. Commoners took sexual fidelity quite seriously in marriage. And yet, Kariana had the right to command him. It was a tradition centuries old. There was nothing he or Lara could say or do about it without making themselves look terribly backward. And yet, the secret weighted upon him. He could barely look Lara in the eye. She knew something was wrong, that he left every night, and yet she demanded no answers. *Yet.*

Aiul arrived at the prison and descended the long flight of stairs into its deepest levels, beyond the sections where the stone walls were composed of actual blocks, and into the area that had been tunneled into the native granite, fully fifty feet beneath the streets above. It was a dismal place, the final destination of damned souls. The aesthetics had been carefully considered when Tasinal had commissioned it eons ago. Amrath himself had contributed greatly to the project, both as architect and consultant on the psychological effects. The design was insidious. From the seamless walls of unyielding stone; to the arrangement of sewers for maximum stench; to the deliberate acoustics that shaped and channeled sound so that screams echoed on and on; it was carefully calculated to douse the fire in a man's heart, crush the life from his soul, and leave him a pliable husk, a wretch for whom even death would be a blessing. Just being here, even as a free man, was enough to make Aiul feel ill. He could only imagine what it would be like to be an occupant.

At the bottom of the long stairs, he entered the guard post. It was a small area, more of a bulge in the corridor than an actual room, with a single, heavy iron door in the far wall. Still, it was large enough to hold a table and a few chairs, and leave enough room to allow the normal complement of six guards to fight, if need be. Aiul doubted that there had ever been reason for them to do so, certainly not in his lifetime. Most who found themselves here were generally not in a condition to ever give anyone any trouble again.

The guards ignored him, as they did every time came, continuing their card games and conversations as if he did not exist. He took a key from the wall and unlocked the heavy door, then walked through and closed it behind him. As he entered the cell block, he heard the click of the mechanism as the guards secured the door, and felt a chill run through him at the thought of being locked away in that pit of despair.

There were no bars here, because bars allowed in light, and light was hope. The cells were little more than holes blocked with the same heavy iron doors that separated the cell block from the guard post. The prisoners spent most of their lives in darkness and filth, rarely seeing another living creature. Aiul ground his teeth as he passed, steeling himself against revulsion at the sheer inhumanity of the place. He was grateful that he could not actually see the horrors that lay behind the doors, but he could still smell the stench, and hear the occasional cough, moan, or sob from the unseen wretches, and it moved him in ways he could not truly explain. He only knew he did not want to be moved in such a manner, and so he hurried,

He made his way down the block, at last reaching the interrogation room. It, too, had a door of iron, and he used his key to let himself into the large room beyond. It was little different from the other cells, its walls all seamless granite. In the center of the place stood a table stocked with various implements of torture.

Kariana, her black tresses pulled back into a tight bun beneath a tiara, stood nearby, tiny, pale, and haughty, her violet eyes locked on her victim and smoldering with barely contained rage. In her long, milk-white fingers, she held a bloody, metallic instrument, and was applying it to the prisoner's chest with great vigor. Aiul felt ill at the sight. How had they come to this?

The prisoner hung in chains, teeth bared in struggle, silent but for the occasional gasp. Blood and spittle dripped from his chin. His muscles rippled as he strained against his bonds, resolute even in the face of impossible odds. It had been nearly a week of nightly torture for him. The bright red welts on his dark skin vied for attention against the purple bruises left by clubs and boots. But still, he resisted. For all her effort, Kariana had yet to even draw a true cry of agony from him, much less any information.

"It's good you have arrived," she said to Aiul, not bothering to face him as she spoke, instead, keeping her eyes locked with her prisoner's. Hatred radiated from both tormentor and prisoner like heat. Aiul could almost see the air between them warp with the blistering emotion.

"I should have a look at him now," Aiul said.

Kariana gave the prisoner a cuff to the head, sending sweat and blood flying, and stepped back, bowing in mock deference for Aiul to come closer. "By all means."

Aiul approached the prisoner, refusing to meet the man's baleful stare as he busied himself examining the various wounds Kariana had inflicted. He struggled to keep his hands from trembling, trying to summon the steadiness he had so often taken pride in, had used to execute the most meticulous of surgeries so many times before. But that was to heal. This perversion of his skills, this preserving of life to prolong torture seemed a misuse of his gifts, a blasphemy that his hands recognized, and they refused to cooperate.

As he fumbled through his examination, he felt fear rise within him. Six days, this man had endured Kariana's depredations, and yet he had not broken. Aiul could not conceive of the sort of resolve, the well of inner strength that would carry a man through such a nightmare.

"Look at me," the prisoner rasped through cracked, bloody lips.

Kariana's ears perked up at the sound of the prisoner's voice. Aiul said nothing, fearful that he would upset some plan she had.

"I said look at me!" the prisoner shouted. "I would see the face of my enemy!"

Aiul looked toward Kariana, and she nodded. He lowered his hood and let his long, pale blond hair fall on his shoulders. He stared sadly into the proud, dark eyes of his patient, trying to say without words that this was not his will.

"You are a coward," the prisoner growled.

Kariana folded her arms across her chest and smiled. "So you would speak, now, dog?"

"Tell her," the prisoner said.

Aiul looked at Kariana, and shook his head. The prisoner was dying, and there was nothing he could do.

"So you would confess, and die easily?" she asked, magnanimous in victory.

The prisoner laughed, then coughed and spit blood. "Call it what you like," he said. "I prefer to think of it as taking your comfort with me as I depart to join Ilaweh."

"Enough games." Kariana pushed Aiul aside and stood before the prisoner again. "Who are you and why have you come?"

"You think it will change, somehow, if you ask again? I am Yazid Valerian, servant of Ilaweh, soldier of the Xanthian Empire, and herald of your doom," he said with a ghastly, bloody-toothed grin.

Kariana's face grew dark with rage, and she gave the man another cuff to the head, but his grin remained.

"You fear me, bitch," he said. "As you should."

Kariana's clutched the steel blade, momentarily speechless. Aiul could see her losing control, and considered speaking up, but thought the better of it. Six days had taken their toll on her, as well, and Aiul had no intention of making himself a target.

Kariana's face twisted in uncontrolled rage, and her voice cracked as she shrieked, "How *dare* you speak to me so! I am the blood of *Tasinal*!"

The prisoner's eyes widened briefly, but he quickly mastered himself, hiding his emotion behind a mask of contempt. "Then it is you we have come to destroy," he spat.

Kariana's eyes bulged as she struggled to master her emotion. She, too, realized she had lost the initiative. She was no longer in control of the situation.

"I can make it infinitely worse, if I don't need to worry about your survival," she said in a low, husky voice. "As I said before, you might die an easier death if you cooperate."

"Aye," Yazid replied. "I might die an old man in my bed, too, full of regret. Life is sharp and painful. It's not something a cringing lapdog like you can ever understand."

"You're a fool," Kariana hissed. "A madman, a talking ape with delusions of grandeur. Even a beast fears death!"

The prisoner snorted at this. "I see, now. You, too, are a slave. Slave to fear, slave to birth, slave to tradition and public opinion. There was never a moment in your life not planned out for you, was there?"

"I do as I will!" she shouted. "I am *Empress*!"

"You want me dead, yet you cringe in fear that killing me without breaking me would be unseemly. You lack even the freedom to choose to spare me. You dare not. It would make you seem weak. No choices for you at all, just decorum and precedent."

"Sophistry!" she cried.

"Yours. Not mine."

Kariana's eyes flared with madness, and she surged toward the prisoner, an incoherent shriek of fury on her lips. Steel glinted in the torchlight buried her blade in the prisoner's throat. Blood gushed and sprayed from the wound as the Southlander vented a gurgling, bloody wheeze that Aiul realized, to his horror, was laughter. The Southlander grinned at Kariana, pleased with his victory, which only drove her to new heights of rage. She stabbed at him over and over, until Aiul could bear it no longer. "Kariana, please! It's over!"

Kariana stood staring at the corpse for long moments, dripping blade in hand, chest heaving, eyes clouded with madness. Aiul raised a hand and ran it down his face, uncertain what to say.

Without warning, Kariana swooned and collapsed to one knee.

"Kariana!" For the moment, the grimness of the situation fled his mind. He knelt beside her and tilted her face toward the light. Her eyes seemed to react well enough, so a stroke seemed unlikely. *Who could know what's going on? She's pumped full of Mei knows what. For all I know, she's dead already.* "Kariana?" he said, softly, trying to reach her.

She moaned and fell forward into his arms, limp. She was feverish and trembling. "Mei!" Her body shook with her convulsive sobs.

"It's over," he said, even more worried now. Kariana had always been the dramatic sort. She was good at it and fooled most people, but he knew her well enough to tell this was different.

"It got out of hand," she choked out. "It all got out of hand."

He ran a soothing hand down her hair. "I know."

"It wasn't supposed to be like this."

"It was a mistake from the start, Kariana. A horrible, ugly business."

"Not just this," she sobbed. "*Everything*! This whole *life*! It wasn't supposed to be like this for me. For *us*!"

Aiul stammered briefly, blinking in shock. "What are you saying?"

Kariana looked up at him, her eyes shining with tears and wide with mad hope. "We were supposed to be together, Aiul! Mei, you were supposed to be *mine*, not hers!"

"Kariana—"

"No! Listen to me!" She tore her tiara from her head and hurled it across the room. "I hate this life! I hate it! It's wretched and horrible, and people say terrible things about me! I don't want to be empress!" Aiul tried to speak, but she clamped a hand over his mouth. "I'll give it to you, do you hear me? Leave her and come to me. You can be emperor if you want. Or we could just run away and be free! Just *stay* with me! *Please*!"

Aiul struggled to free himself from her grasp. "Kariana, you are not well! You're exhausted and in shock! What you're saying is madness!"

"It's truth!" she cried. "It's *destiny*!"

Aiul had had enough. He forcefully pulled away, and Kariana collapsed to the floor, so wracked by her sobbing.

"Don't go!" she begged.

"I must, damn it!" He hurriedly gathered his equipment. "I am married, Kariana! You must accept it."

Kariana leaped to her feet and lunged toward him, her face twisted in fury, a low, bestial snarl rising in her throat. She was on him in an instant, slashing at him with her long nails and spitting like a feral cat. "You bastard!" she shrieked. "You insufferable son of a whore! An empress on her knees offering you her crown isn't good enough for you?"

It was all Aiul could do to keep her slashing claws from his face. She was a mad tigress. He seized a flailing arm as she brought the other up and grabbed a handful of his shirt for leverage. "Stop it, Kariana!"

She spat at him and kicked savagely at his shins, punctuating each blow with a curse.

Aiul had suffered enough. He shoved her away, harder than he intended. She flew back from him, still maintaining her death grip on his shirt. The fabric tore, and she staggered back, a look of shock on her face. She teetered briefly, then fell, striking her head against the table, the Southlander's massive hand seeming to reach for her hair on her way down. She looked up at Aiul, a mixture of fear, fury, and pain on her face, the scrap of cloth from his shirt still clutched in her hand.

Aiul shook his head in consternation, torn between the contradictory urges of tending her wound and fleeing from her. "Damn you, Kariana! Why did you make me do that?"

She looked up at him, tears running down her face, no longer an empress or a savage beast, just a heartbroken little girl, exhausted and defeated. His heart went out to her.

"I'm sorry," she pleaded. "I just—" She paused and wiped at the blood on her forehead. "I never felt like this before, don't you understand? Not until you came back to me. It's too much! I can't bear it!"

"You need rest, Kariana. And you need to sober up."

She brightened. "I'll sleep, I promise! Come with me. Put me to bed."

Aiul sighed, exasperated. He had walked right into that one. "I cannot Kariana. I have a wife. I have responsibilities."

"Don't you leave me, Aiul! Not now, not tonight! I *need* you."

"My wife needs me."

"I *command* you!"

Aiul shook his head. "Not this time, Kariana. And not ever again." He turned away and walked toward the door.

"Cocksucker! Motherfucker son of a bitch bastard—" She trailed off, out of words crude enough to express her contempt. "Mei as my witness, I'll fucking *kill* you *and* that wretched whore! Do you hear me?"

Aiul hunched his shoulders against the onslaught and stepped out of the room.

"Aiul! I'm sorry! *Aiul*! *Please*!"

Aiul kept walking.

Kariana lay in a heap on the cold stone floor for some time, trembling, unable to control her warring emotions. She wept, cursed, and screamed, buffeted by rage, humiliation and deep, agonizing loss. How could this be? How had she come to this? "It isn't fair!" she screamed and tore at her hair in frustration. She tried to rise to her feet, staggered, tried again, and managed to haul herself up against the table. The dead Southlander seemed to leer at her, mocking her, drinking in her pain like a fine wine. She reached for her knife and stabbed him again, swooned, then steadied herself with both hands. Blood dripped from her gashed forehead onto the Southlander's face, ran slowly down his cheek like a tear, and mixed with the rest she had spilled from him.

"Blood calls for blood," she whispered, wondering why she should think of the phrase. She had heard it somewhere before, but why did it come to mind now?

She raised the scrap of Aiul's shirt to her forehead and daubed at the wound. It was superficial, really. She barely felt it. But then, she thought, she might not notice a sword shoved through her gut right now, not against the rest of her pain. *Well, that and the drugs.*

It was all her wretched brother's fault. If he hadn't gone and gotten himself killed, none of this would have happened. Theron would have been emperor, and she would have been happy. But instead, they had put a crown on her head, and whispered secretly that she had engineered the entire affair.

They called her murderess and whore, a poor ruler, stupid and vain. She could accept some of it. A whore? They never complained when they were with her. No, they took their pleasure and then spit on her because she took hers as well. Better a whore than a hypocrite. A poor ruler? Certainly. What had she ever been taught of such things? Who had prepared her? And yet they cursed her when the crown they placed on her head failed to magically infuse her with wisdom and knowledge. Vain? Her father had been of the mind that the entire point of her existence was to serve as decoration. She was merely what she had been groomed for, what she had been expected to be: a toy. Was it so wrong to accept her place as had been defined for her by others, to take joy in it? Stupid? Oh, yes, very, up to now, and it was high time for that to change.

But murderess? She had never hurt a soul until tonight. *Well, not without their consent and a safe word in place.* She knew how, of course. Torture was a womanly art, handed down from mother to daughter for centuries. The only use she had ever found for it was to entertain her friends who had peculiar, embarrassing tastes that their wives would not indulge. The same friends, she thought bitterly, who denounced her to hide their own shame. She was nothing but a receptacle for their vile spew.

Suddenly, everything seemed too close, too tight. She had to get out, get some air to clear her head. She looked briefly at the rapidly cooling body of the Southlander, wondering what should be done about him, then dismissed the notion.

Let someone else clean up the mess. She was empress.

Aiul spent most of the trip home cursing himself for letting things come to this. It was pure idiocy and had been from the start. He had no idea how it would play out with the Southlanders, but one thing was certain: his part in their story was over.

He was only interrupted from his brooding once when a group of three men moved toward him menacingly. Aiul hitched the edge of his cloak aside, grasped the handle of his mace, and stared at them from beneath his hood with undisguised malevolence. In truth, he would have been quite pleased to bash in some thug's skull, a fact that was apparently clear to his would-be muggers.

The men slowly backed away, then turned and fled like the cock-roaches they were.

Aiul shook his head and moved on, his mind turning back to Kariana. Damn her! He could barely contain his fury at her presumption, her selfishness, and yet he felt a deep sympathy for her, as well. He resolved not to hold it against her. She was who she had always been, and he should have known better. He would check in on her in the morning. A night's rest should clear her head of the drugs and exhaustion, and she would be in a more sensible state of mind. *Perhaps we could even be friends again,* he thought. *Mei knows, she needs some true friends.*

He found himself home before he quite realized it. His feet, apparently, knew the way well enough to take him there without his head having to be overmuch involved. He looked up briefly at the towering building, his head clouded with strange thoughts. The Cradle of Nihlos was one of the tallest buildings in the city, practically clawing at the sky. It bespoke privilege and power like little else could, a middle finger raised to the sky, defying the gods and their petty gravity. *And we who live there imagine it speaks of us in such terms, when in truth, we're all just devolved wretches, children playing with the masterworks of our betters who came before us, as the whole thing winds down like an untended clock.*

Aiul entered the Cradle's large, opulent foyer, his boots clicking against the marble tiled floor, echoing from the polished granite walls. The light from the few candles the staff kept burning at night cast a soft glow over the room, enough to see by, but not so much as to trouble the eyes of those coming in from darkness. The concierge, an elderly and dapper man with white hair, stood his usual post behind the huge reception desk. As Aiul crossed toward the elevators, the older man looked up briefly and examined a chart hanging from the wall on his left, pressed his pencil to his lip, then turned to examine a chart on his right. Satisfied, he turned back to his work. It was a practiced gesture, one that allowed him to scrutinize anyone entering the establishment without seeming to focus on any particular person. Aiul had been fooled by it for months when he had first moved in, only later did he realize the level of service and subtlety his coin had bought him. This last week, he had begun to appreciate the true value of it.

Aiul entered the elevator, giving a tired nod to the short, well-dressed attendant. The man was a commoner, of course, such menial tasks being beneath even slaves, but he still bore the air of professionalism upon which the Cradle's reputation depended.

"Twelfth floor, sir?" the attendant asked.

Aiul nodded again, and the man responded by sounding two bells, one strike against a lower pitched one, twice against a higher pitched one. The elevator jerked slightly, then began a smooth ascent.

"Still using bells?" Aiul asked.

"Aye, sir," the man answered. "Most of the residents prefer it this way, so I am told. They are more comfortable with slaves powering the elevator than with magic. The accident…"

"So the official line goes," said Aiul. "I think the truth is simpler."

The attendant stared at the floor, and repeated, "I am told the residents prefer it this way."

"Of course," Aiul said with a wry smile.

Aiul inserted his key into the lock and turned it as quietly as possible. So far, he had been lucky, and Lara had no idea how late his excursions often ran, and for her peace of mind, he wanted it to remain that way. He opened the door to find darkness and breathed a sigh of relief.

Just enough light filtered through the curtained windows to navigate by. He removed his shoes, robe, and mace, leaving them at the front door, and padded softly across the carpet to the living room. He knew he should put them away, especially the mace, so as not to provoke any questions from Lara, but his mind was in an uproar, and he needed something to calm his nerves. They could wait a few minutes, he told himself, just until his hands stopped shaking.

He took a bottle of fine whiskey from his bar, unstoppered it, and considered simply drinking from the bottle, but his manners were not so easily dismissed. He settled for four fingers in a large tumbler, neat, the first finger gulped with all the expected fire and grimacing, the remaining three to be sipped while the first worked at his nerves.

Aiul opened the heavy curtains to gaze out a huge picture window at the city below. He nursed the whiskey, his eyes roaming over the spires of the city. Everything was orange at night, tinted by the ever-present, luminous cloud cover. Nihlos knew no rain or snow, nor did she ever grow too cold or too warm, all due to those clouds. *Another miracle we will not be able to repair once it fails.*

He watched over the sleeping city for a while, seeking solace that would come only with a higher blood alcohol level. At last, the muscles in his neck began to relax, the pounding in his chest and temples subsided, and he told himself that he would, perhaps, be able to sleep.

He was jarred from his peace by the sound of movement behind him. *Luck can only hold out so long, I suppose.*

"Do you love the bitch, or is she just a fuck?" Lara's voice was higher than usual, stressed, a mixture of whisper and sob. She stepped forward from the shadows where she had been hiding, her face twisted in grief, her brown eyes brimming with tears and accusations. The light from the window was not bright, but it was enough to illuminate the sheer fabric of her sleeping gown, turning it into little more than a nimbus, a mild blur over her flesh beneath. She took her place in front of him and folded her long, pale arms over her swollen belly, waiting for him to answer.

She is so different from Kariana. Thicker, taller, stronger. Even their features were at odds: Lara was solid and broad, where Kariana was pointed and delicate. Lara's hips alone made her the better choice in a wife, but she was superior in every way. *And we dare call ourselves nobles. We have it backward. The commoners are more fit.*

Aiul stared at her for a moment, his jaw locked in place, his mind struggling to maintain cohesion as it was pulled this way and that by conflicting emotions and irreconcilable duties. As a lover, his eyes caressed the curves of her body in erotic and devoted appreciation. As a father to be, he felt giddy with pride to see the swelling of her belly, to know that his child would soon draw its first breath. As a doctor, he unconsciously scanned her for abnormalities and noted with satisfaction that all appeared to be going well with the pregnancy. But as protector and defender of his wife and unborn child, he felt bile rising in his throat. He could lie, and likely she would even believe him, but it would fester. Lies always did. They created barriers, ever-widening gaps that should not exist between two people trying to live as one.

As a doctor, he knew that a surgical scar was preferable to death, but as a husband, he could not bear to watch as he made the incision. He turned back to the window and looked out over the city as he spoke.

"It is neither. But there are things I have kept from you. It is difficult, so please, just listen until I am done. Will you do that?"

"Yes," she whispered, almost choking on the word.

He told it mechanically, a recitation of facts rather than a confession, history rather than drama. He imagined it would be easier for her, but in the end, it seemed to have simply made things worse.

She waited long in silence, weeping softly until she was certain he was done. "What is it you expect of me? What am I supposed to do? Just bear the humiliation in silence? Paint on a smile like a good noblewoman and pretend my husband hasn't betrayed me?"

Aiul turned to her, frowning. "It is not betrayal to go along with a tradition hundreds of years old."

Her face was red, her eyes bloodshot from crying. "Then why did you hide it from me?"

"To spare you this. I knew you would not understand."

Lara buried her face in her hands and said nothing, simply shook with sobs she was trying to silence. At last, she looked up again, fury in her eyes.

"I spoke to my mother about it when I first noticed. She took your side. 'He's a man, Lara,' she said. 'Men have weaknesses we have to accommodate in return for their strengths.'" Lara spat at the floor. "I thought you were different, Aiul, but you're just like my father, my brothers, like every man I ever knew!"

Aiul bit back a retort. She could not understand and did not deserve his wrath. It was not her way, and it was unfair of him to expect her to cast aside her own traditions in favor of his without time to adjust and accept. He had chosen this. He would find a way to bridge the gap. "Go to bed, Lara," he told her. "We're both exhausted. Things always seem harder to cope with when you're tired."

She nodded and dried her tears with the sleeve of her gown. "And you? Will you sleep? With me?"

Aiul shook his head. "I doubt I will sleep at all this night." He drained his glass, reached for the bottle of whiskey again, and turned back toward the window.

Lara snorted. "Feeling too guilty?"

He looked at her again, feeling haggard. "Not in the way you imagine. If only I were merely guilty of something so small as cheating on my wife." He refilled the glass and sipped at the liquor. "I am much worse," he said. He turned back to the view of the city and stared out once again. "I am a murderer now."

Caelwen stood outside the prison, armed and armored, watching the great iron doors that sealed the entrance. the Empress preferred to believe she was alone, but what she didn't know in this case would not only not hurt her, but likely keep her alive. The undercity streets were dangerous, and it was his duty to protect her.

The whole area was an embarrassment for most of those who lived on the hills, something they ignored as much as possible. Some had likely even forgotten it existed. While it was technically the very heart of Nihlos, it was now the domain of the commoners, and with commoners came crime and violence. Once, when Nihlos was younger, the Nobles had walked freely here, even at night, unafraid. *Of course, half of them were Meites at the time.* Caelwen was uncertain which was a worse plague, commoners or sorcerers. Both were sources of chaos that made life more difficult for anyone charged with maintaining order.

In the end, it hardly mattered. This was his reality, and it was best simply to deal with that, rather than waste energy imagining 'what if.' The reality was that Nihlos was permanently divided between those on the ground and those in the sky. Most of the lower entrances to the great towers had been sealed long ago, leaving access only by the bridges above. There were entire networks of roads in the spans between buildings, and the roads below lay forgotten and in disrepair. It was only natural that the prison entrance was here; this was where the criminals were.

Caelwen knew what they were up to in there, and counted it despicable, but he had no power to change it. He could only watch and wait.

At last, the iron doors swung open, and a tall, hooded figure departed, moving quickly. *What is his hurry, I wonder?*

It was another half hour before a second, smaller hooded figure exited the prison. She was addled, weaving in a drunken stupor as she made her way along the darkened, littered street. With a sigh, he fell in behind her at a discreet distance.

She could have ascended to safer levels simply by climbing within the walls of the prison, avoiding trouble altogether, but she had taken it into her head that this must all be played like some cloak and dagger farce, which led to her wandering these dangerous streets alone. *You are damned fortunate I take my duty seriously, Empress.* It was the better part of a mile to the nearest public access to the upper levels. Guards would be posted there to keep the rabble out, but between here and there, he was her only defender.

As he expected, she quickly drew unsavory attention. A dirty, grinning fool emerged from an alleyway as she passed, stroking his tangled beard. He drew his weapon and set in behind her. Caelwen dispatched the man quietly with a single thrust of his blade to the side of the thug's neck, pleased with himself that he drew no attention whatsoever. Not that even an explosion would have necessarily gotten through to Kariana, but the man might have had companions who would come running had he cried out.

A troublesome thought buzzed in his mind like an insect. Perhaps it would be better if she *were* to fall victim to some wretch. Nihlos would be better served with a competent ruler, would it not?

Wasn't everything she had done since the Southlanders arrived proof of that? *I promised they would be treated fairly!* But she had taken things out of his hands, and hidden it all from the council by invoking security protocol. *The council would never permit this if they knew. My* father *would not tolerate this.*

Perhaps it would serve some higher duty if he simply let her go on her way alone.

It was a tempting thought, but he only entertained it a moment before putting it out of his head, cursing himself for his weakness of character that such things even occurred to him. It was excuse-making, shirking of duty for personal reasons. Perhaps Nihlos *would* be better off, but it was not for him to say. Wishing her dead was nothing noble. It was simply a personal hatred, a deep disgust with her. It was shameful for a soldier to think of such treachery.

Duty demanded he follow her, protect her, even die for her if need be. But love her, even like her? Duty asked nothing there, save that he hold his tongue.

Narelki had just begun to undress for the night when there came a knock upon her private chamber door. She cursed under her breath, and called out in a stern voice, "What do you want?"

Slat's voice, muffled by the door, called back, "A visitor, mistress."

Narelki scowled and immediately regretted it. Her face scowled back at her from her vanity mirror, showing far too many lines. It was considerably more youthful and regal when she showed no expression at all. "Send them away. It is late."

Slat persisted, his voice strained. "Madam, it is the *Empress.*"

Narelki frowned at this news and saw more wrinkles at the corners of her mouth. *Mei! This can't be good.* She forced the frown away with some effort, banishing the wrinkles for the moment. *They will return soon enough.* "See that she is comfortable in the library and tell her I will be out shortly."

"It will be so, madam."

Narelki sighed and began dressing again, thankful that her hair was still proper. The timing was a nuisance, but it could have been worse. She checked her appearance in the mirror one last time, then, satisfied, made her way toward the library, her mind filled with questions about what might have led to this unannounced visit.

Nothing she imagined compared to the truth. Kariana was a wreck. *What is she wearing? It looks like something Aiul would use for surgery.* The Empress was slouched over the arm of the couch in a most undignified pose, covered in blood and sobbing. *Has she been raped?*

Slat stood by, stiff-necked and obviously irritated. Narelki was pleased to see he had, as usual, thought ahead, and covered the couch with a sheet. "She is quite inconsolable, Mistress. I can offer her no comfort. She only spoke once, when she asked for you."

Narelki waved him away. "Leave us." Slat moved to obey, but she changed her mind. "Wait. Bring water. And liquor."

"What sort?"

"I don't care. Just do it quickly."

Slat nodded and went to do as he was bid, closing the doors behind him, and Narelki turned to her visitor. "If it is something you would not speak of in front of a man, he is gone."

Kariana opened her mouth to speak, but choked on the words as she sobbed. She blew her nose into a rag she held clutched in her hand. *Please keep any bodily fluids to yourself!*

Narelki was uncertain which was more revolting, the filth or the wretched weakness. "Stop this mewling and tell me what has happened," she commanded. "Were you raped?"

Kariana shook her head. No.

"Robbed, then?"

Again, no.

"And you still don't see fit to vocalize your problem? Has your tongue been torn out, or are you really this pathetic?"

That seemed to have the desired result. Kariana's eyes flashed with rage, and she slurred, "It's your son who's pathetic!"

Narelki blinked in confusion momentarily, struggling not to reveal her shock. *Aiul? What could that even mean? And at any rate, the problem was clearly drunkenness and not assault.* "You're wasting my time. If you have something to say, then say it, or I shall return to bed."

"Wretched hag!" Kariana cried. "I am *Empress*! You dismiss me like a whore?"

Narelki felt the edges of her lips tremble as she struggled against laughing out loud, but she managed to keep her face fairly serene. "Really, dear, you *are* quite the little whore. I should think you would be used to it by now."

"I'll kill you for talking to me like that!"

That was simply too much. The laughter burst forth from Narelki's lips, a series of cruel barks with no real humor. "You are welcome to try any time you like, *child*," Narelki told her, her words hard and sharp as the edge of a blade. Kariana quailed, the fire in her eyes fading, replaced by fear. *As it should be.*

Narelki pursed her lips in disdain. *She's as bad as Aiul, though much easier to intimidate.* "Is this really what you came here to talk about? It matters not a whit to me who you fuck. I'm hardly likely to marry you. Not that anyone else is, either."

That got to her. Kariana began to bawl again. "He's already told you, and you mock me!"

Narelki raised an eyebrow, allowing her genuine surprise to show just a bit. "No one has told me anything. And as for mocking you, House Amrath has ever given true, honest counsel to House Tasinal. Calm yourself and explain." She clapped her hands and looked about in annoyance. "Slat! Where are you?"

The old slave opened the library door and entered immediately. "Awaiting your call, madam."

Narelki nodded approval. "Serve us and leave again, please. I'll call for you if I need you."

Once Slat had closed the doors behind him once again, Narelki turned an icy stare upon Kariana. "You have something to steel your nerves. Get on with it."

Kariana swigged vodka, grimaced, and cast her eyes down in shame. "I offered him everything." She turned pleading eyes toward Narelki. "*Everything*! And he turned me away."

Narelki massaged her temple with her fingertips, wondering just how well she could hide her growing frustration, both with Kariana and Aiul. "And you've come to ask for *me* to intervene? Mei, you really *are* confused."

"You're his mother! His House Elder!"

"And I have had this very discussion with him before, for all the good it did."

Kariana's face lit up with hope. "About me?"

"About anyone of some decent birth, but he would hear none of it. And, yes, your name was mentioned. He was quite clear that he would not even consider the matter."

Kariana's face fell once again. "But *why*? We loved each other before!"

Narelki rolled her eyes. *It's not an act! She really is this stupid!* "I believe it was the 'whore' thing."

Kariana leaped to her feet and hurled her disgusting rag at Narelki. It flew far wide and landed, miraculously, in the trash bin. "Fuck you!" she shouted.

Narelki allowed herself a slight smile at the serendipitous failure. *How fortunate. Now even Slat won't have to touch it.* "I shall have to decline that offer. I prefer my partners have some discretion." She suppressed a scowl of disgust as Kariana began weeping loudly once again. It wouldn't do to completely alienate her. This was important after all, and it behooved House Amrath to tolerate this nuisance for the moment.

Narelki felt a dull anger begin to creep into her mind as she listened to the Empress of Nihlos blubbering like a school girl. Even now, these long years past since Narelki's fall from grace, she still thought in old ways, still looked upon such behavior as pathetic, worse than useless. Aiul was right about Kariana. He was far too good for this creature, no matter whose blood ran through her veins. Was it any wonder he refused her?

How unfair the world was, that a beautiful, proud, brilliant man like Aiul should be condemned to the periphery while a toad like Kariana sat upon the throne. And for what? Tradition? She spat upon the notion. Tradition was a crutch for weaklings and fools.

Even as the thought occurred to her, she felt ill, knowing the source of her own deep philosophy, but unable to deny it. It was a part of her, even if she was no longer a part of it.

Her anger notched higher as Kariana prattled on. The Empress of Nihlos was on her knees, offering Aiul the throne, and he, blinded by an infatuation for a commoner, was fool enough to throw it all away. Why could he not see that once he had power, he could rid himself of this creature and take any woman he wanted? She was but a stepping stone to his destiny.

Narelki knew all too well how emotion could blind one to necessity, make one hesitate at a critical moment. And such hesitation was like a loose thread on a fine garment. Time would work at it, unravel it until there was nothing left.

She realized that she could not permit this to occur. She had ruined her own life with such idiocy. Now, these long years past, she was watching history repeat itself with Aiul, but there was a crucial difference. She had not had the benefit of a wiser soul looking out for her. Aiul did.

I am his mother. I must protect him from himself.

Kariana's memory of the trip home was as blurry as her vision. She wasn't quite certain just how she managed to find her way to her private chambers, but that is where she suddenly found herself, desperately trying to fend off wave after wave of nausea. She had just begun to master it and undress when there came a knock upon the door. "Fuck off!" she shouted.

A woman's voice, muffled by the door, answered. "Kariana? Are you all right?"

Kariana recognized the voice, and her anger fled from her in a flash. It was Marissa, her one true friend. She hurried to the door and opened it, not bothering to cover her breasts. "Oh, Marissa! I'm sorry. I didn't know it was you! I've had such a dreadful day! Come in."

Marissa was a fat, mousey girl, not the sort that anyone would call pretty, though hardly hideous. She stood in the hallway, her uncombed brown hair dangling over her hunched shoulders, hesitant. Her eyes, magnified by thick-lensed glasses, seemed uncertain as to whether she had heard correctly. After a moment, she gave Kariana a crooked-toothed smile and shuffled forward to embrace her friend.

"I heard terrible things," she sighed as she embraced Kariana. "I was so worried about you!"

Kariana felt more tears begin to well in her eyes. What a wonderful feeling it was to hear such things, to feel such regard, after all she had been through. She hugged Marissa tightly for a moment, then stepped back and took a seat on her bed, gesturing for Marissa to follow.

Kariana felt a sharp pang of guilt as Marissa joined her. She had always regarded the girl as a sister, if an ugly, ungainly one. The girl moved like a zombie at times, and Kariana had harbored any number of selfish, cruel thoughts about her. She had often counted on Marissa to make her look so much better by comparison. *I'm the ugly one, to think such things.*

Marissa looked at her in silence for a moment, then spoke. "What's wrong, Kariana?"

Kariana opened her mouth to speak, closed it again and swallowed hard, then opened it again. The words began to pour from her, a stream of pain and humiliation. Marissa stroked her hair as she told her tale, saying nothing, judging nothing.

When, at last, it was done, Marissa smiled and announced: "He's an idiot. He doesn't deserve you."

"I wish I believed that."

"You will," Marissa assured her. She smiled again and reached into her pocket. "I have something for you. Something that will help." She handed a small packet to Kariana.

Kariana smiled sadly as she opened the package to find a small cache of crystallized powder. She licked the tip of her finger, dipped it into the powder, and put her finger back in her mouth. The powder dissolved against her tongue, leaving it slightly numbed. Warmth and goodness began to seep into her troubled mind.

"Yes," she sighed. "I think it will."

Marissa waited until Kariana's eyes were dilated and her jaw slack then reached in her pocket again. "Kariana, will you do me a favor?"

"Of course!" Kariana mumbled. "Anything."

Marissa lowered her head in a practiced pose of shame and reticence. She threw in a bit of fidgeting to boot. "Maybe it's not such a good idea."

"Don't be silly. If you want it, I want it. What?"

Marissa pulled at her shirt and allowed her face to crease into a grimace. "Some of the guards…." She trailed off and let out a tiny sob.

"What?" Kariana's eyes were large and concerned. "What did they do?"

Marissa lowered her voice to a whisper. "Last time, they made me do some things while I was waiting for you. They hurt me."

Kariana's face twisted in stupefied, drug-addled rage. *Good! That's just what I need!* "Mei! Who? Who did it! I'll have them put to death!"

Marissa smiled inwardly. "I spoke to my elder about it. She wrote a death warrant, but you would have to sign it. But I don't know, now."

Kariana's eyes blazed with righteous anger, even dulled with drugs. "I'll sign it twice! Do you have it with you?"

Marissa produced a document from her pocket, silently congratulating herself at her play. *Now she thinks it is her idea.* Kariana snatched the paper from Marissa, struggled to her feet, and staggered across to her desk. She flailed about briefly for a pen, then smiled gratefully when Marissa pulled one from her pocket and presented it to her.

"Bastards!" Kariana hissed as she scratched her name on the document. "Scum! Elgar take them!"

Marissa took the signed death warrant and placed it back in her pocket, then gently guided Kariana back to her bed.

"You should rest now, Kariana." Marissa stroked Kariana's hair again as the Empress slowly settled back against her pillows. Before long, Kariana's breathing grew steady and deep. Shortly thereafter, she began to snore.

Marissa pulled a blanket over Kariana, then went back to the desk and rifled through the papers there, but found little that she did not already know about. The Empress was poor at keeping secrets. It was fortunate for Nihlos that not every House was too self-absorbed to monitor what this incompetent was up to.

Without us, the fool would have already run the city into the ground.

Marissa took the death warrant from her pocket and examined it. The signature was a scrawl, but verifiable. The three names marked for death were unimportant. They weren't even real people, as far as Marissa knew. They would be replaced in short order with the real ones: eighty-some-odd guardsmen who knew too much for their own good.

With a self-satisfied smile, Marissa slipped the death warrant back into her pocket and blew out the candles. She would receive a commendation for this, she was certain. House Prosin always took care of their own.

CHAPTER 6
CONFLAGRATION

NARELKI, seated at her desk in the library, tapped her foot on the floor, waiting for Aiul to finish his rant. This was not at all how she had planned to spend her morning, most especially after having been kept up late by Kariana's idiocy. Yet here she was. The men she had hired had obviously failed, and she would have to deal with the fallout.

Aiul's eyes flashed green fury as he roared, "This will not stand!" His throat worked, struggling to form words, his face red with fury. "Someone will die screaming for this!"

Narelki inclined her head imperiously but did not deign to stand. "You are in the Library of Amrath. You will show proper respect for the Great Father."

Aiul sneered at the notion. "The Great Father be damned!"

"I will not tolerate such talk here. If you must have a tantrum, then there are plenty of other rooms in this house." She raised an arm and pointed toward the doors. "Not here. This is a place of reason."

Aiul regarded her with a scathing glare, his hands clenched into fists. "If you define cold-blooded plotting as 'reason,' I suppose."

"You are testing my patience, child."

"And well I shall! Spare me that insipid pose. Amrath was no stranger to rage!"

"Do not presume to lecture me on the Great Father, whelp!"

"I dare what I wish! Grandfather said passion was what made the founders *truly* great!"

Narelki tensed at this but kept her fingers gently laced together in front of her. "My father was a disgrace to this House, and we will not speak of him."

"The truth does not change, even when spoken by enemies."

Narelki flashed him a condescending smile. "A ruse, quoting Amrath to me, not an actual argument. You have yet to establish truth, regardless of the speaker." She unlaced her fingers and leaned back in her chair. "The wisdom of Amrath is no bomb to be lobbed into a debate without support."

"Perhaps. But you are twisting things here, as well. I think he would find your whitewashing his humanity to be the gravest of insults!"

Narelki raised her eyebrows at this. "Now you speak for the dead, eh?"

"Would the Great Father have stood by in meek acquiescence when his family was threatened?" Aiul stepped forward and leaned in, his wild eyes inches from her own. "What would he have done, Mother?"

Narelki rose slowly and faced him, ice in her eyes. "He would have mastered his rage, gathered his thoughts, and made a rational plan. Perhaps after smashing a lamp or two, but he would have found *focus*!" She pushed at his chest, and he allowed it. "Because he understood there is a time and place for all things!"

Aiul took a deep breath. "That is so."

She stared at him, torn. He was so brash, so angry, so willful. *Perhaps Father was right. Perhaps we should have trained him, but, he has so little control! Mei, the cost if we were wrong!*

She could almost hear her father's response in her mind, his smooth, pompous baritone correcting her mistakes with merciless truth. S*afety is the creed of sheep and slaves.*

She could feel hot tears welling behind her eyes, and she crushed the weakness down with even hotter anger. She would *not* cry! "I am your Elder as well as your mother. You are obliged to hear me on both counts."

Aiul stared at the floor, his jaw still working in his barely suppressed fury. *But he is listening.*

"The truth here," she continued, "is that no harm is done—"

"Yet."

Narelki felt her anger lunging at its chains, and decided it would be appropriate to release it just a bit. "I am still speaking!" she shouted. She paused a moment for her point to sink in. "Lara is a bit worse for wear, that is all. Do you agree?"

"I agree," Aiul muttered. He looked up as he found his argument. "But as it is, she nearly lost the child. If I hadn't been close by, if I hadn't driven them away, they might well have killed her."

Narelki shrugged. "They didn't."

"*This time!* They will be back. She was targeted, Mother."

Narelki waved the notion aside. "Now you're being paranoid. What proof do you have of that? She's a commoner. Random violence is a fact of life for them. It's one of the many reasons I counseled against this whole affair."

Aiul shook his head. "In commoner areas, perhaps that is true, but not in the gardens of the Cradle! Mei!"

"Do not speak so in the Library of Amrath."

Aiul ran a hand over his face, frowning. After a moment, he continued, calmer but still aggressive. "This is what irks me with you, Mother, this retooling of history. Amrath was a Meite! They *all* were! I'm sure this chamber has heard that name from the Great Father's own lips on many occasions. It must be written at least a thousand times in his book." He turned toward the statue of Amrath and clenched his hands into fists several times. "We're all degenerates by his way of thinking, you know. Weaklings and wretches. He would have despised us as children, that we have words we dare not speak."

Narelki tightened her grip behind her back, struggling to maintain her composure. This was not the sort of conversation she could ever have with anyone, much less Aiul. He couldn't possibly understand. Better he think her a silly prude than know the truth about her. "Be that as it may, it is offensive to modern ears, and I will not have it here. If you want to discuss philosophy, I'll have Slat fetch us drinks, but I believe you have more pressing issues on your mind."

Aiul seemed to relax a bit, his scowl softening into worry. "Aye. But I am certain of it, Mother. Someone specifically targeted Lara."

Narelki pursed her lips. He was a bit too close to the truth for her liking. "I do not like indulging paranoia, but for sake of argument, we'll follow that line of reasoning. Who would do such a thing?"

Aiul eyed her gravely. "There are several people who would prefer my marriage to Lara remain without issue." He held her gaze for a moment, then turned aside, as if something had caught his eye. He walked quickly toward the trash and bent over to examine it.

Narelki bristled with outrage. "Are you accusing *me*?"

Aiul reached into the bin and pulled at a scrap of cloth. He raised it slowly, a look of horror on his face, then leaped toward her, fury in his eyes. He seized a handful of her blouse and pulled her close, then shoved the stained piece of cloth into her face.

"No, Mother," he said, his voice low and menacing. "I hadn't suspected you until just this very moment!"

Narelki felt her hands trembling. This was a dangerous situation. Aiul had always had a temper, but this was no tantrum. He was, at least for the moment, quite capable of murder. She cursed herself for making such a foolish mistake. How in Mei's name had she let that stupid whore leave incriminating evidence? And how did Aiul even know what it was? She dismissed the question. It was irrelevant. He knew, and it would have to be dealt with.

It galled her that she should actually be afraid of him. There had been a time not so long ago when she feared no one. *No! You will not go down that road! That is the way to madness!*

She laughed lightly, determined not to let her fear show, then told him in an icy tone, "If Matricide is your intent, child, then get on with it, or release me." *Mei! Even now, when I should beg for mercy or forgiveness, I can't let go of the arrogance!*

Aiul glared at her for several moments, then shoved her away, sending her sprawling on the floor. "That would be just like you, wouldn't it? 'Go ahead! Kill your mother and rule House Amrath! Forget those silly feelings and seize the opportunity!'" He spat on the floor. "If I were that sort of man, I'd have married Kariana, and we'd not be having this discussion, would we?"

Narelki rose slowly to her feet, her years weighing upon her like stones. "It's not what you think."

"No? Then tell me, Mother, what is it? That wretched bitch promised me last night she would kill Lara, just after she tore this from my shirt." He waved the filthy scrap of cloth like a flag. "So she came here, and the two of you cooked up some scheme, one that I foiled. How is it not 'that'?"

"She *was* here," Narelki conceded. "She was a wreck, blubbering like a child. I took her in because I thought she had been raped, and for a bit, I thought you might have been the one responsible for it."

"Ah, now I'm a rapist in your eyes?"

Narelki folded her arms across her chest and raised her chin. "You may have others fooled, but I know you well, Aiul. I know just what you are capable of when your blood is up. Even I am not safe from it."

Aiul snorted. "Go on, then. You're spinning quite a tale. Let's hear the end of it."

Narelki slapped him with all her might. Aiul staggered back, a look of shock on his face along with the bright red imprint of her palm. "There, now we are even. And I will not tolerate that tone from you *anymore* this night! If you will not respect me as your mother, I *command* that you respect me as Elder of House Amrath!"

Aiul stiffened and rubbed at his face. "You have that right."

"And I have responsibilities, as you well know. Advising House Tasinal has always been one of the highest duties of House Amrath. It was my duty to hear her and give her counsel as best I could." She glared at him a moment, then retook her seat, muttering, "And for this, I am manhandled and accused of treachery by my own son."

Aiul lowered his eyes to the floor, abashed. "Please, go on."

As a lawyer, Narelki was quite experienced at 'shaping' the truth, but she was not fond of outright lies. They left a foul taste in her mouth for any number of reasons, but it was simply necessary this time. "She begged me to help her, to use my influence to change your mind. I told her I had already tried and could do nothing. She blubbered a bit more, cursed, and said something about having her own means of changing things. Then she left."

Aiul's face lit with anger once again. "And you told me nothing?"

Narelki threw up her hands in exasperation. "I had no idea what she intended."

"Oh, please, Mother, you must have suspected. If nothing else, you could put two and two together. Instead, you've tried to convince me I am paranoid!"

"Of course. I knew the moment you mentioned it. That

doesn't mean I thought you should know." She waved a hand toward him. "Look at you. You're half mad with rage. She's the empress, damn you! If you move against her, she will kill you, and I won't be part of you throwing your life away. Now calm down and use your head!"

She could see the walls going up in his mind, the darkness of black hate in his eyes. She wasn't getting through to him. "Aiul!"

"There is no calming down, Mother," he said in a dull voice. "Kariana tried to kill my wife. I can't just let that pass." He turned toward the door.

Narelki rose and grabbed at his arm as he passed. "Think about what you're doing! Don't throw your life away over this!" But Aiul paid her no heed. He shrugged off her grip and walked away. He was strong, and she was weak. If only she were still strong. *If only....*

"Aiul!" But he was gone.

For long moments, she stood alone, paralyzed with fear. She'd made a terrible miscalculation. Aiul would be killed!

Calm yourself, girl, her father's voice seemed to say. *Think.*

"Damn you! Damn all Meites!" Yet, now, that way was all she had to fall back on, even if it were no longer hers. Her father's voice softened, became her own, hard, cold, clear. *Stop this pathetic weakness.*

She answered in her own voice, a warbling whisper no one outside the order had ever heard, and even then only at the end. *I can't! It's why I fell from grace! Mei, it's a thread unraveling! It's a slow, bleeding death!*

And again, what was left of her old self, her powerful, Meite self, answered, *Then admit you're pathetic nature. Call Maranath. He will know what to do.*

Narelki tore at her hair, furious at the very thought. Fire seemed to ignite within her once again, a cold flame she had not felt in many years. It would not last, she knew, but it was enough for now.

Aiul will calm. He is furious, not insane. And if, worst case, he does the unthinkable and chokes the life out of an unsuspecting Kariana? The pathetic wretch driving Nihlos into ruin? I have the political clout to smooth it over. There are many who would be glad to see her dead.

Narelki felt a cruel smile spread across her face. Things had a way of working out, in the end, if one had the will to let events run their course.

For the moment, she had will aplenty.

The palace of Nihlos served both as a living space for House Tasinal and the seat of the government. As such, it was located not in the hills of the city, but in the very center, a huge spire towering over the others. Bridges and spans along its height connected it to the rest of the city like a spider in the center of its web, sunlight glittering from metal and glass like sunlight on dewdrops.

Aiul charged up the marble steps of the main entrance two at a time. The palace gates, two huge, rune-graven iron doors, stood open to reveal a well-tended courtyard where several palace workers were having lunch. Beyond lay the main reception hall of the palace proper, glutted with commoners and slaves handling government business.

There were guards at the gates and throughout the public areas, but anyone could come and go freely. It was only as he was nearing the entrance to the private sections that he found himself chest to chest with Caelwen Luvox. The burly soldier interposed himself bodily, hand on his sheathed blade, his cold, steel-gray eyes boring into Aiul. "Stop." He said the word the like he might swing an ax.

Had Aiul not been so angry, he might have had second thoughts, but after confronting Narelki, even Caelwen was less intimidating. "Out of my way. I have no quarrel with you."

Caelwen glared back, his usual calm, cool manner missing for some reason. "Aye, is that so? I think you might, after all, House Amrath. I think you fucking well might."

"What are you talking about?"

By now, several onlookers had gathered to witness their argument. Caelwen glanced at them, hatred and disgust on his face, and gestured for Aiul to follow him into a side room.

"Oh, we don't need privacy," Aiul shouted. "I'm happy for the whole world to hear what I have to say!"

"I am not." Caelwen's hard eyes were adamant and commanding. After a moment of glaring back at him, Aiul nodded and entered.

Caelwen closed the door behind them gently, then, without warning, grabbed two hands full of Aiul's shirt and slammed him against the wall. The impact was enough to knock the breath from Aiul. Caelwen leaned closer, his eyes brimming with cold fire. "Did you know?" he asked, his voice soft and menacing.

Aiul stammered unintelligibly, still struggling to breathe. Caelwen slammed him against the wall again, then clamped one gauntleted hand around Aiul's jaw, and the other about his throat like a vise. "Did you know she was going to kill my men?"

Aiul strained against Caelwen's grasp, but it was useless. The man was strong, a trained killer. Struggling against light-headedness and black spots swarming in his vision, Aiul tried to convey that only Mei knew what Caelwen was talking about and that in short order, Aiul would be too dead to be of any use.

The message seemed, at last, to get through to Caelwen. He

relaxed his death grip on Aiul's throat slightly. "You don't know a fucking thing, do you?"

Aiul shook his head as he struggled for breath. Caelwen released him in disgust, then turned and slammed a mailed fist into one of the walls with enough force to crack the stone tiling. Aiul slid slowly to a sitting position, still wheezing.

"Why are you here, House Amrath?"

"Fuck you, House Luvox."

Caelwen laughed to himself without humor. "Just wondered if you would say. I already know. I just couldn't put it together. I thought maybe you had been the target instead of Lara."

Aiul rubbed at his aching neck. "Stop being cryptic. You've had your fun choking me, so I don't see the point of this guessing game. Get to the point or Elgar take you!"

Caelwen stared at Aiul a moment as if carefully choosing his words. "She killed them. All of them that knew about the South-landers." He looked up at the ceiling and rapped his fist against his leg. "You and I are the only ones left who know her secret."

Aiul felt suddenly and deeply ill. He stammered again, unable to find words. Somehow, the news of the guards' deaths seemed even more horrible due to his heroic efforts to save several of them. *I put them back together, and Kariana tore them to pieces again, as if they were nothing more than paper dolls.* "Mei!"

"Mei, indeed," Caelwen said. He looked back at Aiul, his eyes now watery and tired. "Are you sure she tried to kill your wife and not you?"

Aiul coughed and nodded, still rubbing at his throat. "She said she was going to last night. Promised it, actually."

"It could have been a mistake."

"They went directly for her. I heard her cries and came running with my mace. They didn't go easy, either. I damned near killed one of them before they broke and ran."

Caelwen seemed unconvinced but offered no better theory. "Still, we two are loose threads that should be burned off. No doubt, she'll slay the Southlanders too, and then we are *all* doomed."

Aiul boggled at this. "What are you saying?"

"You've seen the wounds they gave my men at five-to-one odds, and these are just scouts. How do you think we will fare when they send armies to have their revenge on us for this villainy?" He pounded a fist into a palm. "They will crush Nihlos under their boots, and they will have the right of things. This is how it all ends, and it is out of our hands." Caelwen offered Aiul a hand up. "So now we talk about you, and what you came here to do."

Aiul accepted his help and rose to his feet. His throat still hurt, but this was no time to cry like a child about it. "And?"

"Go home, Aiul. I can't let you do this."

"What? Are you mad? Now more than ever—!"

Caelwen hammered a fist against his breastplate. "I have my *duty*! I cannot simply let you walk in and stick a knife in her!"

"Elgar take your duty!"

"It serves Nihlos well, wretch. I might dance a jig to see you had stabbed her in her black heart, but I *will* kill you to prevent it."

Aiul snorted in disgust. "I say you're just weak."

"If I were weak, I'd kill you for your insults, and her for her crimes. Then I would have a go at seizing the crown myself. Who do you think would stop me?"

Aiul had no answer.

Caelwen continued, "So you understand, now. It would seem neither of us can do anything but accept our fate."

Aiul searched his mind for the right words to change Caelwen's mind, but it was pointless. The man was a rigid fool. He knew Nihlos might well be crushed by enemies if Kariana lived, and yet he would not move against her. Aiul would have to find another way.

As he neared the door, Caelwen called after him, "It's good that I stopped you here, or else you would have interrupted the Empress's preparations for her orgy. She would have been most displeased."

Aiul looked at Caelwen in confusion. "What are you talking about?"

"Just making conversation."

"Idiot!" Aiul turned to leave again.

"I hear the orgy is to be a large affair, but I won't be there, unfortunately. Ordinarily, I would be guarding the doors, but I have a more pressing duty tonight. I must bury my Lieutenant."

Aiul paused, sensing this was suddenly something more than idle conversation. "Oh?"

"Yes. His name was Kelthas. He was a good man, a father with three children." Caelwen clenched his fists. "My duty to see him off supersedes all else, you understand?"

Aiul nodded slowly, and Caelwen snapped him a salute, then turned to leave.

Tonight or never. That was the best Caelwen could offer. Aiul intended to take full advantage of the deal.

Kariana woke to what she felt certain was the impact of a sledge-hammer against her skull. It was an event worthy of a prodigious scream, but the best she could manage was a slight moan.

She rose slowly to a sitting position, raised her hands to her head with difficulty, and squeezed as if she were trying to hold back an explosion. For a few moments, there was nothing but pain and confusion. She wasn't even certain who she was, much less where. Then the memories, blurred and hazy, began to trickle in.

Mei! What did I do?

The sledgehammer struck again, and her wounded brain finally processed the fact that someone was pounding on the door. She opened her mouth to scream a curse but thought the better of it as her stomach threatened to rebel.

"Kariana! Open this door at once!"

She knew that voice, one that always made her feel like a stupid little girl. She had first heard it chastising her for entering the palace covered in mud. At the time, she had barely been old enough to understand words at all, and he, an adult, had been quite a terrifying figure. Some things never changed.

Since then, her cousin Sadrik had been her personal critic, a nettling demon who took sadistic pleasure in pointing out her mistakes. He was as bad as Caelwen, though at least he didn't bother with saccharine pleasantries. Sadrik was and always had been a sour, mean, frightening person. He had probably sprung from the womb with a frown on his face. He was the last person she wanted to see right now.

"I will break this door down, Kariana!" he shouted. "You have ten seconds!"

"I'm coming!" she answered. She had intended it as a roar, but it came out much more along the lines of a sob.

It took her some time to find her feet and shamble across the room, but she moved as quickly as she could, strongly motivated to be done with it before Sadrik resumed his pounding.

Sadrik hovered like a bird of prey, his dark eyes blazing, his raven hair a wreath of black smoke hanging low on his shoulders. Looking up at him was like looking at the larger than life-sized statues of Tasinal that one might see about Nihlos. He had the same sharp features, the same mile-high cheekbones, and commanding jawline. There was, she thought ruefully, no doubt about Sadrik's lineage. How fortunate for him.

"I am not well," she said. "What are you going on about?"

Sadrik raised a fist in which he held a crumpled document. "This death list, for starters!"

Kariana blinked in confusion. "What?"

Sadrik clenched and unclenched his hand into fists as if trying to decide whether or not he intended to punch her in the face. "Don't play coy with me!" He shoved his way past her and closed the door. "Executions in the dead of night when no one sane could breathe a word of objection!"

Kariana felt herself reeling, and steadied herself against her vanity, nearly knocking a large box of face powder to the floor. "I don't understand!"

"Do you have any idea what you've done? Mei! Eighty-seven loyal men, *good* men!"

"Stop it!" Kariana slammed a fist against the vanity, knocking bottles over with the force. "I told you I don't know what you're talking about!"

"*You* stop it! You were obviously out of control last night." Sadrik eyed a half-empty bottle of liquor on her nightstand and shook his head in disgust. "It's all over town that you arranged a botched attempt to have Aiul's wife killed, too!"

"What? That's insane!"

"Oh, yes! Quite insane! He would have likely killed you at lunch if Caelwen hadn't stopped him, and I wouldn't count on that to happen again, with you killing his men." Sadrik's face twisted in rage. He picked up the bottle of liquor and hurled it against the wall. Glass and liquid exploded; the scent of alcohol filled the room. "You're power mad, Kariana! You're going down, and you're close to dragging all of House Tasinal into the flames with you!"

Kariana shook her head over and over, feeling as if the world had suddenly slipped from beneath her feet. "It wasn't me! It *wasn't!*"

"It damned well was!"

"How *could* it have been! I could barely move! The only person I thought of killing last night was myself, and I was too drunk even to do that!" She was weeping now, confused and frightened.

He uncrumpled the paper in his hand and considered it closely, then shoved it toward her. "The signature is quite sloppy. I'd expect a forgery to be considerably cleaner. You signed this death warrant, Kariana. Go on, look at it and deny it to my face, so I have an excuse to beat you. I've been looking for one since this came to my attention."

Kariana looked at the signature, feeling ill. It was her handwriting. *But how?* She stared at the floor in silence and brushed a hand roughly over her eyes to wipe away the tears.

Sadrik nodded, satisfied. "As I thought. Now I will have an explanation, or I will call a meeting of the Elders to have you deposed."

Kariana shook her head. "I don't know, Sadrik. It's my signature, but I didn't order these men killed. I don't even know them."

Sadrik crumpled the paper, furious, then seemed to think the better of it and unrolled the ball as best he could. "You're not leaving me any options, Kariana."

Kariana glared at him with bloodshot, teary eyes. "I just don't see how, if I were so fucked up as to not even remember, if I couldn't even sign my name properly, how did I get the document written? How did I make arrangements to have someone try to kill Aiul's wife?"

Sadrik eyed her warily, the rage slowly draining from him. He gave a slight grunt. "I suppose you have a small point."

"I didn't do this, Sadrik. I *didn't!*"

"Then find me another explanation. You clearly signed the

order. If you didn't draw it up, someone else must have. Who? Did you see anyone last night?"

Kariana shook her head. "I don't remember." She paused, thinking. "I left the prison. I went to Narelki's and made a complete fool of myself. Then I came back here."

"That much we agree on. Caelwen followed you."

"He *what*?"

"And saved your life, doubtless, from muggers. Don't be an idiot. It's his duty. Go on."

"That's all. I came home. I…" She paused again, as memories slowly revealed themselves. "Marissa came."

Sadrik's scowl deepened. "Mei! You *imbecile*!"

"What? She's my friend!"

"She's House Prosin, you bleating sheep! They are *all* serpents! What did she want?"

"I was so tired. She hugged me and told me it would be okay, and she gave me something to help me sleep."

"And no doubt, you remember nothing after that."

"I must have passed out."

Sadrik rolled his eyes. "You were drugged, fool."

"No!" Kariana was reeling. "She's my friend! I've known her since we were children!"

"It is a common tactic. They have children from their House befriend children in the other houses. It's usually a source of information, but in this case, your brother's accident gave them direct access to the ruler of Nihlos! How fortunate for them!"

Kariana stood in stunned silence. Mei! Her brother's accident, the one she had been accused of engineering, was Marissa? It was unbelievable!

"It can't be," she said. "It doesn't fit. Why would Marissa try to have Aiul's wife killed?"

Sadrik shrugged. "Who knows? Perhaps to make it look like you were clearly out of your mind. Perhaps because she's not quite a perfect spy and had some genuine feelings for you, enough to seek vengeance for you. Does it really matter?" With the toe of his boot, he pushed the broken glass on the floor into a small pile as he thought. "The attempt failed, and he's out for your blood, and he may well get away with killing you. You are not well liked, cousin, and House Amrath is not to be trifled with. If Aiul manages to end you, Narelki has the clout and the skill to get him off the hook."

"No! He would never do such a thing!"

Sadrik threw up his hands. "You are *Empress*, Kariana. It is time you gave up this childish attitude. You've seen what Marissa is capable of. Keep it in mind when dealing with others." He looked at her a moment, letting his point sink in, then reached beneath his robe and produced a small, gilded dagger. "Keep this with you. You may well have need of it."

Kariana reached slowly for the weapon, feeling sicker than she had since she had awoken. The thought that she might shove this wicked piece of metal into Aiul's body was too horrific to contemplate, and yet she knew Sadrik was right. It was time to be realistic. She opened her own dirty robe and placed the knife at her belt.

It was all too much. Her life was a horrific nightmare from which she could not wake. She had no friends at all, now, no one to trust. No one except cruel, spiteful Sadrik. She could, she thought, trust him. He was simply too cruel to be manipulating her. He took too much pleasure in mocking her failures.

"I don't know what to do," she whispered.

"Eh?"

"What do I *do*, Sadrik?"

Sadrik suddenly laughed out loud. "Why, I expect you'll be assassinated in short order, most likely."

"You're horrid! I have nothing and no one! Tell me what I should do now!"

Sadrik looked at her, eyes wide, and laughed. "You don't actually think I am going to serve you like some vizier? I have affairs of my own to manage. I'm simply trying to help my eternally stupid cousin before she gets herself killed. Don't expect me to be at your beck and call."

"You *have* to help me!" she shouted. "My whole life, you've done nothing but mock me! But this isn't just me, it's House Tasinal! It's *Nihlos*! Father never taught me a damned thing about ruling. Mei, why didn't *you* take this job and I could have gone on just being pretty and having fun?"

Sadrik's cruel features wavered briefly with some undefinable emotion. *Is he feeling* guilty? *Good!* "I had another path," he answered, perhaps a bit too sharply. "A more important one."

"What could be more important than Nihlos? It's our birthright, Sadrik! It's our obligation!"

Sadrik scoffed at the notion. "*Your* obligation. I accept none of it."

"Selfish bastard!"

"Yes! Exactly!" Sadrik shouted. "I hate almost everyone I know! I despise them for their stupidity, their weakness! I will *never* accept responsibility for them! I'd be happier if they all dropped dead."

Kariana swallowed at the lump in her throat. *It's so strange when you're actually feeling what you're usually faking.* She wiped absently at sweat beading on her temple. *Why is it so hot, suddenly?* When she spoke, it was difficult to keep her voice steady. "Do you hate me? Would you laugh to see me dead, too?"

Sadrik opened his mouth to speak, appeared to reconsider, and his face softened. "Aye, you have the right of it, and I am sorry, Kariana. I will not give up my own life for you, but I will help you this once."

"Oh, thank you, Sadrik!"

"Don't thank me overmuch. I'll give you some advice, and

introduce you to some people, but I have no intention of holding your hand through this. If you can't find your own way out of this hole you've dug for yourself, I've my doubts as to whether you deserve to survive, much less rule. House Tasinal and Nihlos could be equally served by your early demise. Do we understand one another?"

Kariana nodded, dispirited and shamed by the rebuke. Sadrik was speaking truth, unpleasant though it was. This was what she most needed right now, cold, hard truth, not some toady cozening favor.

"Very well," Sadrik continued. "Let's first consider Marissa. Here is what you do about her: nothing."

"Just let her get away with this?"

"Aye. Go on about your life as if you know nothing. It can be useful to have a spy, if you are aware of what they are. She's exposed now, but until she realizes it, she will be *your* tool instead of the reverse. You can tell her what you like, and she'll dutifully report it to her masters. When the time comes to strike back at House Prosin, she will serve as an excellent delivery mechanism for misinformation."

Kariana swallowed hard again. That would be difficult, painful even, but she had always been good at lying. "Go on."

"You said before you had no one to trust. I know some people. They're loyal, as long as you pay them on time. Some of them are Housed, but their loyalty lies elsewhere."

Kariana stared at Sadrik in shock. "Assassins?"

Sadrik shrugged. "Too narrow a term, I should think. They… solve problems. Murder is just one of their methods."

"How do you know such people?"

"Does it matter? The fact is, you know them too, or you will soon, at any rate. This is not a game, Kariana. This is what it takes to rule. I say again, cousin: It's time to grow up."

Yes, she thought to herself. *It truly is.*

CHAPTER 7
TREASON

THE GUARDS at the prison didn't even look up from their evening meal as Aiul approached. They took no more notice of the silent, hooded figure than they had any other time he had come. Aiul smiled to himself, pleased at having been able to use Kariana's paranoia against her. He made his way through the cell block and beyond the torture chamber, to the true pits of Nihlos's prison. There had always been those few prisoners who could neither be killed nor ever allowed to communicate information they carried to anyone else, not even the damned, and a place had been provided for them as well. Aiul only knew it existed because he had read of the design in the Great Father's private journals.

Little had changed since Amrath had drawn his maps. There was a hidden door, just where Amrath promised it to be, and the passphrase Aiul spoke had the desired result. A vertical seam appeared in the solid rock of the wall, first a thin outline of dull, red light, rising to orange, then searing white. Aiul could feel the magic of the device crackle in the air, warm and cold at the same time, ethereal, the wondrous power the founders had commanded.

Within moments, the section separated and slid slowly into the floor.

Aiul was pleased to see that the Great Father had seen fit to care for his progeny so well. *He must have known we would come to this, blades at each other's throats.*

A rough-hewn passage lay beyond the door, wide enough for five men to stand abreast. The corridor was lit by small, glowing nodules that ran along the ceiling, odd devices like nothing Aiul had ever seen. He stepped through quickly and spoke the closing phrase. The section of wall rose once again and merged with the surrounding stone as if it had never come apart.

According to the Amrath's writings, this section of the prison was designed not to channel sound, but to seal against it. Aiul traveled perhaps a hundred feet, then passed through a series of switchbacks, where the walls changed from unfinished stone to flat, polished, rune-graven surfaces. The mark of House Yorn was etched there as well, as it was in almost every magical device of true power. *Yorn himself may have worked these walls.*

He paused in the small maze and ran a hand across the intricate patterns, marveling at the construction and the absolute silence it created. Few in Nihlos who could work such bindings as the sound wards now, perhaps none, but in the days before Tasinal had vanished, there were many skilled at such sorceries. Entire guilds had flourished in those times when sorcery had been as honorable a profession as medicine. He felt a great emptiness in his soul that such glory was long gone, squandered in feuds and vendettas until Tasinalt had taken the draconian measure of outlawing not only the craft but the very religion of the founders. Mei was hardly a god of benevolence, but what wonders his followers had brought forth following his creed! There was, Aiul considered, genuine beauty in the narcissism of the Meites.

Reluctantly, he turned from the walls and continued on his way, passing through the silent labyrinth and emerging once again into rough tunnels. Ahead, he heard shouts, and he paused a moment, the enormity of what he was doing suddenly heavy on his shoulders.

I am a traitor, he told himself. It hardly mattered if he carried out his plan or not. Merely being here was enough to damn him, but he saw no other way. Kariana would try to follow through on her threats to Lara and his unborn child, that was a certainty. He was simply playing the game that he had been forced into. Victory or death were the only choices now.

Aiul entered the holding area, making no attempt at stealth. His footsteps announced his coming long before he arrived, and the voices fell silent.

The prisoners, twenty in all, were secured in a large cage in the middle of the room. He had read of the Southlanders in Amrath's writings, seen their brutal handiwork up close, but neither had even remotely prepared him for the reality.

Their glaring, hate-filled eyes burned with contempt as he approached. The place reeked of sweat and human filth, but otherwise, the prisoners seemed well. They showed little sign of deprivation, though surely they had been fed little since their arrival a week past. Aiul shuddered to imagine what an entire nation of such warriors could accomplish.

One, a huge, bald, beast of a man presumably the leader, called out, "Where is Yazid?" The voice was deep, brutal, frightening, the accent hard to follow, but he spoke words Aiul knew.

Aiul removed his hood and moved as close to the cage as he dared, mindful to stay out of arm's reach. "The one the Empress interrogated?" *Cool and businesslike. No condolences. These are hard men. They will not appreciate a soft touch.* "He is dead."

Curses and threats erupted from the prisoners, but the leader held up his hand, and the rest grew quiet once again. "How did he die?"

With a blade in his throat, a smile on his lips, and Kariana's sanity clutched firmly between his teeth. "He died well."

The leader nodded and raised his eyebrows in wary appreciation. "I would not expect a barbarian to understand our ways." The others nodded and murmured amongst themselves.

"I am a physician and a historian. I know a little about your people. You are honorable warriors, yes?"

The prisoner nodded. "A dishonorable man has no right to call himself warrior." He slammed a fist against his chest. *Some kind of salute.* "What is your name, doctor and historian?"

"Aiul, of House Amrath." He did his best to emulate the salute, striking his own chest hard, as the prisoner had done.

The prisoner raised his eyebrows in surprise. "Truly, you are the blood of Amrath?"

"You know of him?"

"A good soldier must know history." The Southlander stretched languidly and extended his arms through the bars, smiling. *I'll want to stand well clear of his reach.* "It is said amongst our people that Amrath was as wise as he was wicked."

Aiul shrugged and gave a brief nod at this. It was a fair judgment. "You offer me no name in return."

"I am Brutus Samir, Tribune of Prince Philip's legion, and servant of Ilaweh."

Aiul nodded again, his mind racing to think of the right words that would compel these hardened warriors to work with him. "How do you feel about dying here, in this cage?" he asked at last.

Brutus spat on the floor as an answer. He drew his arms back into the cage to fold them across his chest.

"I thought as much. I have grim news. Our empress has gone completely mad since you arrived. She will likely slay you, and soon."

Brutus's face grew dark with anger. He slammed his fists against the bars of his cage. "For what crime?"

"Espionage, I presume."

"We are no spies! We deserve ransom as soldiers!"

Aiul shrugged. "You do not deserve to be imprisoned at all, that I have seen. But you must understand, Nihlos is not a place of justice now." He struggled to keep from choking as he spoke, feeling his face hardening and jaw muscles clenching. Something jagged seemed to poke at the soft places in his mind, prodding and provoking him toward deeds that, until recently, would have shocked and horrified him. "It never was."

Brutus was unimpressed. "Do you think I am an idiot? Now you will offer us mercy in exchange for cooperation, eh?" He spat through the bars at Aiul's feet. "Fool. We will die screaming before we serve you and your bitch queen. We are here to *destroy* your evil, not aid it!"

Aiul struggled against the urge to scream at the man, knowing he could not lose control, or he would lose everything. Trembling with suppressed rage, he spoke as carefully as he could. "I have just as much to fear from her. I come not to offer you mercy. I come to offer you the chance to go free, or at least die in battle, if you will join me to slay her!"

Brutus stared at Aiul in silence for several moments, gauging the sincerity of the offer. The rest of the prisoners, most of whom had only been half listening, were suddenly quite interested. They looked back and forth at one another, murmuring and exchanging subtle nods, but Brutus remained inscrutable.

"Well, damn you, would you fight with me or not?" Aiul asked at last.

"You seem very bold for a 'physician and historian,'" Brutus said. His features were still impassive, but his voice had an edge of accusation.

"I have little choice but to be bold," Aiul replied. "She tried to murder my wife and my unborn child this very morning. That motivates a man. Worse, she's had the entire contingent of guards who met you killed."

Brutus's face grew taut as he grasped the implications of the news. "So, we have become a state secret, eh? Does Caelwen live? Did he betray us?"

"He lives. For now."

"But not for long, if I understand your meaning."

"He doesn't think so, no. He called himself a loose end. And he did not betray you. As far as I know, he is incapable of such a thing. I suspect that's half the reason the Empress had his men killed."

The prisoners' seethed at this, and their curses and threats to Kariana echoed from the walls. At their outburst, Aiul felt, for all his anger, a rush of gratitude and a sense of hope that he had not expected. He was, by any reasonable definition, their enemy, and yet they felt for him, clamored to strike at Kariana as allies.

Aiul felt his cheeks burning with shame at the thought that he had come here to manipulate them, only to discover that simply asking for their help would have been enough. They were far better men than he could ever hope to be. Was it any wonder that they were so strong when they had such conviction and integrity to stand upon? He blinked back tears and cleared his throat while he waited for Brutus to answer.

"Why should we trust you?" Brutus asked once the shouting had passed.

"You shouldn't," Aiul answered, feeling his voice crack with emotion. He removed the key from his robe and stepped toward the cell door. "So I will trust you."

His hands trembled as he fumbled to place the key into the lock. Visions of all the ways things might go wrong rushed through his mind. He imagined Brutus lashing out and smashing his head against the bars. He could almost feel the heat of the

Southlander's powerful arms clamped around his throat like a python, crushing the life from him.

The door swung open, and Aiul stiffened, awaiting a charge, but none came. The Southlanders nodded approval but made no move toward him.

Aiul pulled back his robe and revealed the mace. "I have only this. I have no doubt that it will serve better in your hands than in mine."

Brutus lifted the mace from Aiul's belt and hefted it, testing its weight and balance, then nodded and took it as his own.

Aiul continued, "There are six guards at the post and a small armory. If we can take them, we'll have all the weapons we need. If not…"

With his free hand, Brutus clapped Aiul on the back hard enough to stagger him, a grim smile flickering across his lips. "This will be enough."

The guards at the outpost looked up as Aiul opened the door, then turned back to their card game. A second later, one gasped in surprise as the Southlanders burst into the room and rushed toward the table. One of the guards managed to leap to his feet and begin drawing a weapon, just as Brutus crashed the mace into the man's head, sending blood and bone flying over the stunned faces of the fellow's companions. Another Southlander flipped the table over onto the two men on the opposite side, while the remaining three scrambled to their feet and tried to flee, to no avail. Steel flashed and bit into flesh. Blood and screams filled the air.

Aiul marveled at their efficiency and teamwork. In less than ten seconds, the Southlanders had secured the area without losing even a single drop of their own blood. Standing amongst them, corpses strewn all around, Aiul suddenly felt very small. He was, to be sure, three inches taller than most of them, but they were *thick* men, he realized, dense of bone and muscle. Beside them, he felt like a fragile skeleton covered in pale skin, a shade in loose clothing, desperately trying to give the impression of substance.

The Southlanders lost no time plundering the small armory, and shouts of delight rang out amongst them as they discovered their own weapons. Most seemed to prefer a stout shield and as heavy a blade as they could swing with one hand, though the odd few had polearms or crossbows.

Brutus retrieved his own weapon, a heavy, curved blade engraved with strange symbols, and returned Aiul's mace. "You're certain there is no one above?" Brutus asked.

"Not unless someone has come since I passed. It's a skeleton crew at night."

Brutus nodded and pulled a Nihlosian chain shirt over his head experimentally. There was clearly no accommodation between his own barrel chest and the shirt that was intended for a lither figure. "I think this will not work." The others, having no more success, nodded agreement. "We will wear our own armor or none at all, and in either case, we will have to cover ourselves if we are to travel in the city. We do not look like your people."

Aiul pointed at a large rack inside the armory, where a number of rain cloaks hung. "Will those do?"

Brutus took one of the cloaks and tried it on. Closed and with the hood pulled, it covered everything but his hands. "Aye, as long as we're not observed too closely. We'll keep our hands in our pockets as much as we can, and we'll be fine. Now, have you a plan for how we reach this mad empress of yours, or do we just charge in?"

Aiul laughed nervously. "I have a desperate plan. I don't really expect us to survive. Does that qualify?"

One of the Southlanders laughed out loud. "A foolproof plan

would be too easy!" he said. "We are escapees! We *should* have a desperate plan!" More laughter rippled through the group, and Brutus, smiling, nodded for Aiul to continue.

Aiul felt awkward and self-conscious dictating strategy to these hard men. "Our empress is a libertine; she spends much of her free time in debauchery."

"What sort of debauchery?" Brutus asked.

"She is fond of orgies, wild affairs with drugs and drink," Aiul told him. "They are regular things with her. One is on this very moment."

A grim smile spread across Brutus's face. "Drunk and naked." The rest of the Southlanders nodded to each other in approval.

"Yes," Aiul said, less nervous, now, to see that they approved of his assessment. "But there is still the matter of the guards to contend with, and they will be neither drunk nor naked. We need a distraction, something to draw their attention, thin their numbers somehow. If we release the prisoner, it would cause enough chaos that they would have to send some of the palace guards to the undercity, leaving our way to the palace relatively clear."

Brutus and his men shouted roars of approval and pounded their fists against their chests in applause. "Aye, this is an evil place!" Brutus said. "It would be unseemly to take our own freedom and leave these poor wretches here to suffer! If it helps our cause, so much the better."

He turned to one of his men, the joker, and, pointing at a broom in the corner, said, "Sandilianus, take that and make us some lots to draw."

"Everyone?" the man asked.

"Aye, except for this one," he said, indicating Aiul. "One of us must return to Xanthia and bring what knowledge we have to the Prince."

Fear struck Aiul like cold water at this. "You must make certain he understands that we are not all evil, that we are oppressed! We do not need to be destroyed, we need to be liberated!"

"That is just what we will tell him," Brutus promised, laying a hand on Aiul's shoulder to steady him. "That is why one of us must escape. Otherwise, he will know only that we died here, and draw conclusions that will be bad for your people."

Sandilianus moved amongst the men, his hand full of straws. He approached Brutus and waited as the Tribune made his choice, then continued on. Brutus opened his hand and looked at the straw, cursing under his breath.

"I'm sorry," Aiul told him. "But there is honor in dying fighting, isn't there?"

Brutus gave him an annoyed look and revealed his choice to Aiul, a very short straw. "I thought you understood our ways, doctor. Is it not enough that I must flee my enemy? Will you rub my face in it, too?"

"I'm sorry," Aiul said, staring at the ground. "I didn't understand."

"I know," Brutus said. With resignation, he held up the straw and called out, "No point going further. Sandilianus, this is the lot, yes?"

"Aye, sir. You are the one."

Brutus slammed his fist into the stone wall and winced at the pain. "I know I said I would walk with you into the pit and cut off the balls of Talifa, but Ilaweh has chosen otherwise. Sandilianus, you are in command now, and I must go. There is no time to waste."

Sandilianus stepped forward and grasped Brutus's forearm. "Ilaweh be with you."

Brutus returned the gesture. "Die well, brother." Without another word, he turned and sprinted up the stairs. The rest of the Southlanders hammered their fists against their chests and watched him leave in respectful silence.

Sandilianus looked about a moment, waiting, then shouted, "Why do you delay, fools? Release the prisoners! We are to war!"

The Southlanders shouted, "To war!" and rushed into the cell block. Their battle cries and laughter were channeled and echoed back, in much the same way screams might be on some other day.

Aiul took a deep breath. The air seemed sweeter, despite the acrid scent of blood. He had once again managed to turn the enemy's weapons against them. By the time it was done, they would have an army of willing accomplices.

Perhaps there is a chance of success after all.

The prison was one of the few structures in Nihlos that connected the undercity to the upper levels. A long spiral staircase ran up through the center of the tower, allowing the occasional visit from a dignitary without forcing them to enter the undercity proper. Both entrances to the stairs were usually heavily guarded, but the escapees had quickly absorbed every bit of manpower, leaving the lower entrance abandoned.

Aiul worried as he and the Southlanders made their way up, that they might encounter guards, and indeed they came upon many, but none had the time or inclination to spare a second glance at Aiul and his band of cloaked commandos. The guards were disorganized, often alone, occasionally in small groups, and running, rather than marching, shouting alarms. Most were only half equipped, some still struggling into their mail shirts or adjusting sword belts as they rushed down the stairs. One unfortunate lost his footing on the stairs and tumbled head over heels to the ground level.

The new leader of the Southlanders, Sandilianus, grunted at this, a smile briefly softening his sharp features. "He will be glad he had his helmet on, I think," the Southlander said with a shake of his head, and Aiul chuckled in agreement. *He looks so different from that Brutus fellow, yet so different from us, too.*

The guards at the top were as distracted as the rest they had met on the stairs, shouting conflicting orders and rushing to gather equipment. No one challenged Aiul or his company as they simply walked out of the prison. It seemed almost too easy to Aiul at first, but he realized the Southlanders' natural bearing worked greatly in their favor. They were armed and marched as a matter of course. To a casual observer, what else could they be but guards? *And none of the remaining watchmen have any idea the Southlanders ever arrived, much less to be on the lookout for them.*

From a walkway outside the prison, Aiul had a clear view of the undercity. It was easy to see why the guardsmen were so disorganized and panicked. The escaped prisoners, as Aiul had expected, had thrown the entire undercity into turmoil. The commoners had taken the opportunity to riot, and the guards were engaged in a running battle with them. The streets below were dotted with fires, and smoke filled the air.

One of the few public accesses from undercity, a wide switchback staircase, was under assault. Commoners were charging in and retreating, throwing rocks as guards marched forward with shields and truncheons, cracking heads.

Aiul turned away, sickened by the sight. Many innocent people would be injured, even killed because of what he had done tonight. *I had no choice.* He nodded in the direction of the palace and said to Sandilianus, "There."

The trip was short, and with all of the guards occupied, Aiul and the Southlanders made their way unmolested. The palace gates loomed before them, closed now that night had fallen. Demonic faces leered from the empty battlements, gargoyles that for some reason Aiul had never noticed in the light of day. Five guards, bleary-eyed and surly, glared at them as they approached, clearly unenthused with their duties. Aiul could barely contain his elation. There should have been at least twenty men here!

One of the guards leaned over the ornate railing of the bridge to peer at the streets below. "I hate being stuck up here."

The sergeant in charge stepped forward and called out to them, "The palace is closed. Come again on the morrow."

Aiul raised a hand and waved. "You mistake me, sir. I am Aiul of House Amrath. I have been invited."

The sergeant nodded, then cast a wary eye toward the hooded Southlanders. "And these?"

Aiul rolled his eyes and called back, "You know her tastes. Best not to ask. She wants them hooded and cloaked until they arrive, as a surprise for her guests." He gave a slight shudder. "I don't think they're wearing anything underneath."

The guard looking over the rail dropped a coin over the edge. "Mei! Missed him!"

"Watch your language," ordered the sergeant, punctuating the remark with a cuff to the offender's head. He pointed a thumb toward Aiul. "They'll chop your head off, you say that around the wrong people."

"It's fine, really. I'm often guilty of the same sin," Aiul told him. *Open the damned gate, fool, before this comes apart!*

The sergeant shrugged and waved to the two men handling the gate. "Let them pass."

Aiul felt relief wash over him like a warm shower. *We made it.*

"Hey!" another of the guards called out, as Aiul and the Southlanders approached. "Have you guys been down in the fires?"

The sergeant held up a hand to halt them. "Just a moment, sir." Aiul felt his stomach sink as he saw one of the Southlanders quickly pocket a dark hand.

They stopped, and the sergeant looked them over more carefully. *Mei, he senses something.* By this time, the rest of the guards had grown interested as well and were pushing forward to have a look. "Lower your hoods," the sergeant ordered, his eyes narrowed in suspicion.

Aiul waved a hand imperiously. "the Empress commanded these men remain hooded. If she hears of you countermanding her order—!"

The sergeant was having none of it. He stepped forward and reached for Sandilianus's hood.

"Sword! Sword!!" one of the guards shouted, but he was far too late to warn anyone. Sandilianus's blade cleaved the sergeant's neck, sending the man's head tumbling to the ground. It bounced, then rolled over the side of the walkway and into the chaos below as the sergeant's body collapsed. *Mei, what must the fellow it landed on think?*

It was almost too quick for Aiul to follow. The Southlanders moved with the speed and surety of lions striking at deer, and with similar results. The remaining four guards reached for weapons, only to be cut down before ever clearing their scabbards.

Aiul stared at the dead men on the walkway before him, knowing that he should feel some pity for them, some remorse at having a hand in their deaths, but he could find not a drop of it in his soul. They stood between him and Kariana. He was glad that they were dead.

"Follow me," he told the Southlanders. "She is within."

The grand ballroom lay inside the secure area of the palace, just outside the kitchens. They saw plenty of servants hauling trays laden with roasted meat and steaming bread, but not a single guard until they turned the last corner.

Only two guards stood watch outside the massive ballroom

doors, both with the same sullen, inattentive attitude displayed by their counterparts at the main gate, one busy cleaning beneath his nails with a dagger, the other with closed eyes, as if he had mastered sleeping while standing up. The music and laughter from within were loud, even with the doors closed, a point in Aiul's and the Southlanders' favor.

Aiul looked up and up to the top of the doors, noting how they curved inward as they rose toward the dark ceiling some twenty feet above. They were almost pointed at the very top. *Little things seem so much more important when you suspect you're about to die. Or when you don't want to think too much about what you've done, or are about to do.* "This is it," he said softly.

Both guards snapped to attention at the sound of his voice. Aiul and the Southlanders kept moving forward.

"Stop!", one shouted.

"What is this?" the other cried.

The Southlanders shrugged out of their cloaks and drew weapons. *Aye. The time for subtly has passed.*

"Just stand aside," Aiul said, pleading with them. "It doesn't have to be this way."

The guard with the dagger in hand, eyes wide, threw his weapon at Sandilianus. The Southlander blocked it with his shield and charged forward to deliver a quick thrust with his short sword to the hapless guard's chest. The guard gasped and slowly slid to the floor as his partner fled down a side hallway toward the kitchen, shouting for help.

Aiul would have let him flee, but the Southlanders were in control. One near the back of the group unslung his crossbow and put a bolt in the back of the guard's skull, sending him down and skidding over the marble, leaving a trail of red.

Sandilianus stared hard at Aiul, his face taut, his eyes cold and wary. "It *does* have to be this way," he insisted. "Do you have the stomach for this, or do my men go in alone? I would not blame you if you stayed. You are no warrior."

Aiul grimaced, feeling close to vomiting, and shook his head vehemently. "This is my fight as much as yours."

Sandilianus gave Aiul a curt nod, then spoke to his men. "Once we enter, we bar the door against reinforcements. Kill no one who does not offer battle, but those that do, finish quickly." He turned to Aiul. "At your signal."

Aiul waved an arm at the door. "Now seems as good a time as any."

Sandilianus thrust the doors open wide on a scene of pure debauchery. The ballroom had once been considerably more austere, and host to many regal parties, but it, like everything in Nihlos, had devolved over time. Kariana had modified it to her own tastes. The smoky, patterned marble was original but the lush carpets and throw pillows were new, most occupied by one or more entangled naked bodies. The walls were decked with rich tapestries made by Nihlos's finest artisans, depicting scenes much like the one they decorated. Alongside the racy images hung Kariana's favorite toys, many and varied whips, cuffs, and razors. About the room, candelabras cast warm, flickering light and released pleasing scents to fill air already thick with 'herbal' smoke. Bars, for serving various intoxicants, circled the center-piece of the room, a great, heated bath that currently held at least a dozen revelers in its steaming waters. At the far end of the room, an enormous bed, beneath a mirrored ceiling, sat on a dais where a throne might have been, under a more mundane ruler. Kariana, herself, lay on the great bed, naked, cooing and smiling at several well-built, equally naked suitors who teased her with feathers and tempted her with grapes.

The Southlanders' entrance shattered the bliss and reverie like a brickbat hurled through a stained glass window. Screams and curses vied for supremacy with confused mumbling. Naked, drugged revelers struggled to disentangle themselves and rally against the threat as the Southlanders charged into the room.

Kariana's pushed the men away from her and sat up on the bed, eyes bulging as she sighted Aiul amongst the Southlanders. "Aiul! What are you doing?" she shrieked.

"What I must, Kariana!"

One of her partners grabbed her and hurled her over the side of the bed, shouting, "Assassins!" From across the room, Aiul saw a hand rise from behind the bed to grab a pull cord from the wall and desperately jerk it, setting an alarm bell ringing.

Most of the room's occupants were in no condition to fight and fled to cower against the walls or hide beneath furniture or pillows. A few were at just the right level of intoxication to be foolhardy and lunged for their weapons.

The majority of the naked warriors were cut down before they could bring a weapon to bear, as the Southlanders took possession of the room. Four of the defenders managed a few, halfhearted swings before going down, one even being fortunate enough to put a huge gash on Sandilianus's forehead.

And then it was done. The Southlanders still stood poised for battle, sweat trickling over their rippling muscles, eyes darting back and forth looking for more enemies. The corpses of the fallen Nihlosians twitched in death spasms. Some cowering revelers whimpered and begged for mercy. Others stared about in confusion, absently wiping away blood that had been splashed on them during the battle. A few were struggling to clothe themselves, as if their nudity were the most pressing concern of all. Behind the great bed, Kariana's lover still jerked at the bell cord in furious spasms, the ringing seeming much louder to Aiul now that the battle was over and the musicians had quit the stage to cower in the far corner of the room. Kariana herself stared at him in shock, seemingly unable to believe what was happening.

Sandilianus wiped blood from his eyes, then turned to Aiul

and pounded his fist against his chest. "By the grace of Ilaweh, we are victorious," he announced. He waved a hand toward the bed. "Your prize, doctor."

Aiul stood a moment, uncertain of what he should do. He had never really expected to succeed, and now that he was here, the doctor pleaded with him to preserve life, to have mercy. But the husband would not hear of it, and the jagged thing could not even understand what the doctor proposed, much less agree. Aiul hefted the mace and stepped forward. There could be only one conclusion, now, he knew.

Kariana seemed to suddenly understand as he approached her. She drew a dagger from her robes and brandished it at him. "Don't do this, Aiul!" she shouted, her voice high and trembling, but defiant nonetheless.

"Lara might have begged similarly," he replied. "Had I not been there!"

"It wasn't me!"

"Own your sins, bitch! You'll be accounting for them soon!"

"There are things you don't know! Things I can't tell you! Damn you, Aiul, I *love* you!"

Aiul's temples throbbed as if the jagged thing were bashing the inside of his skull with a hammer. Her arrogance was inconceivable! How could she lie to his face now, when she had told him exactly what she intended to do not a day before? How could she be such a monster as to claim to love him? She would do anything to save her miserable skin. "Save your lies for Elgar!"

Kariana's ears perked up as the sound of approaching footsteps echoed through the room. "I offered you everything! And you bring enemies into my home to murder me! Elgar take *you*, monster!"

"'Ware reinforcements!" shouted one of the Southlanders, and the immense double doors shuddered with a heavy impact. The Southlanders stood ready, waiting for the door to give way.

Aiul turned, distracted for only a moment, but that was all Kariana needed. She lunged at him with her knife, aiming for his throat, but he spun at the last moment, and caught the blade in his shoulder instead, not a lethal blow, but enough to stagger him briefly.

Kariana ducked behind the bed and twisted a wall sconce. With a whoosh of inrushing air, a concealed section of wall slid back, and she darted into the darkness beyond.

Aiul cursed silently, torn between giving chase and making a final stand with the Southlanders. He should have expected something like this. Tasinal would have taken care of his own just as Amrath had.

Sandilianus spared him the decision. "Go after her!" he shouted. "We will hold them as long as we can!"

Something large and heavy, likely a battering ram, struck the doors again, and debris imploded inward. It would hold another blow or two, perhaps three, but no more.

Aiul nodded and leaped over the bed to follow Kariana.

The passage was cramped, musty, and dark, and the ceiling was quite low, forcing him to stoop as he entered. Some fifty feet ahead, he could see Kariana's silhouette, stumbling and cursing as she fled, and beyond her, a dim light. It was impossible to judge the distance, but he was certain that it was an egress leading to the palace, one he could not allow her to reach.

It took him a moment and a few painful collisions of his head against the ceiling, but he quickly adopted a shambling, lurching stance that allowed him to make better time. Kariana was less adaptable. She cursed and stumbled along, keeping her left hand low and against the stone wall, as if she feared becoming lost.

Aiul gradually closed the distance, until, at last, he could hear her panting almost as loud as his own. She spared a look back at him as he neared, and did her best to quicken her pace as he approached, but she was hampered by her cautious gait, still keeping her hand against the wall.

He reached toward her, as he struggled to close the last few feet between them, and suddenly, Kariana lurched to a stop, her body straining forward and tacking to the left with her momentum. Her hand grasped a small, innocuous lever that protruded from the cold, wet stone, and she hauled on it with all her weight. A sharp click echoed through the passageway.

Aiul felt the wispy, ethereal surge of powerful sorcery wash over him, almost a sound, not quite a breeze, and the tunnel before him melted and twisted in the current. The stone gathered and massed like a wave of liquid rock, its base rising and pushing him backward as it crested and curled over, threatening to crash down upon him and crush him as easy as an ocean wave might shatter a sandcastle.

Aiul fell to the ground and gritted his teeth, steeling himself against an impact that never came. The flow of sorcery trickled off into the ether, leaving in its wake an impassable barrier of stone.

Behind him, he heard the muffled sound of a pitched battle, steel ringing against steel, and men crying out in rage and pain. He looked back to see that another barrier, like the one before him, had erected itself to block his retreat.

He sat there in his newly formed prison, silent but for panting. He could hear Kariana gasping on the other side as well.

"Idiot," she said in a dull, emotionless voice. "Didn't you think I would have an escape plan?"

"Don't strain your arm patting yourself on the back," Aiul replied. "*Tasinal* had an escape plan. Your possession of it is just an accident of birth."

Kariana snorted. "Touché. I'm a stupid whore, a fool ruining Nihlos, a murderess, a child. But I beat you."

Aiul sighed in the darkness. *So close. So very close.* He

listened to the distant sounds of battle, wondering how long the Southlanders would hold out. At least, he imagined, they would make a nice reckoning of themselves before they fell, and that was all they had asked for.

"It's not over," he told her, his words mechanical, his muscles feeling leaden as numbness began to creep over him.

"No," she said, her voice almost a whisper. "It never even started, did it?" To Aiul's surprise, she began sobbing softly.

Aiul closed his eyes, awaiting the inevitable.

Well after midnight, Kariana sat alone in her room, trying to find a way to live with what had passed and what had to be done about it. She considered sending for Sadrik but decided against it. She had been through quite enough abuse for one day.

The guards had taken Aiul away in chains. Only one of the Southlanders had survived. There was blood and gore all over the ballroom. She had to admit, it would have been a fine show had she not been the target. Perhaps instead of orgies, she would prefer gladiators, at least on occasion. *We might even be able to combine the two.*

There was no question about how this must be resolved. She could not allow an assassin to strike at her and live. Both Aiul and the surviving Southlander would have to die in a very public manner. There was no way around it. It was what Nihlos would demand.

And did it even matter? He felt nothing for her. He wanted her dead. The thought of it was like a sharp piece of rusty metal stabbed into her gut and twisted. She could almost taste it, a mouthful of copper and sand. She loved him. She hated him.

And none of it mattered, because she had no choices left to her, and no tears left to cry.

A knock on the door interrupted her thoughts, and a familiar voice called out. "Kariana? Are you okay?"

Kariana sat bolt upright in her bed. It was Marissa! That treacherous bitch! *Mei, she will hear the screaming inside my head. Can I lie that well?*

She decided that, while she could lie just fine, she had no desire to do so. She pulled her pillow over her head and refused to answer, but Marissa was persistent and opened the door. Kariana cursed herself for being so stupid. *Mei, you just survived an assassination attempt! What does it take to make you lock your door, fool?*

Marissa cracked the door just far enough to fit her head, and peeked around it. "Kariana?"

Kariana pulled the pillow over her eyes, not wanting to see Marissa's face. It hurt too much. It was the same as if she were dead. All of her friends, anyone she trusted, anyone she actually gave a damn about, all dead or soon to be. "I don't want to talk to anyone."

"Oh, honey, you can talk to me," Marissa cooed. Kariana heard footsteps approaching, and suppressed a shudder. What a monster Marissa was. What a cold, mechanical thing, to feign friendship like this for so long.

I will not look at her. Which would have been fine, except Marissa had always been a toucher. The bed sank slightly as Marissa sat next to Kariana and began stroking her hair.

It was such an ordinary thing. It had brought her great comfort before, yet now, it was as if Marissa were rubbing shit into her hair. Her touch was repulsive beyond anything Kariana had ever known. It was all she could do not to retch.

"It will be okay," Marissa said. "Everything will be ok."

Kariana was no longer listening to her. Two voices in her head were drowning out everything else with their dispute.

Her old voice, the one she knew so well, was saying, *It will be done soon enough. Just let it happen. It's easy.*

But now there was a new voice, an angry, shrill, cruel voice in her head as well. *It's unbearable! Do something!* That voice was tired of the blame and the accusation and was ready to deserve some of the hatred directed at her.

I can't! Sadrik said not to!

Fuck Sadrik! He doesn't tell me what to do! This is all Marissa's fault! She can't get away with it!

"I have something for you," Marissa said. "Do you want some water with it?"

Kariana nodded. She could feel the cold, hardness of Sadrik's dagger against her breast. *My one friend.*

Now! the new voice screamed. *Now! Now! Now!*

Kariana let the pillow fall to the floor, and reached beneath her robe to clutch her blade. She watched as Marissa returned, a familiar small package in one hand, a glass of water in the other.

Marissa smiled and sat beside her again. "There you go. Hiding behind that pillow is no good. This will make you feel lots better,"

Kariana leaned in as if to take the glass and pulled the dagger from her robes. Marissa regarded her warmly as Kariana lunged forward and buried her blade into Marissa's sizable belly.

Marissa's smile vanished; her lips formed a perfect circle of shock. She blinked several times and moaned softly as her hands fluttered toward the blade. Kariana snatched the weapon back, and Marissa slid off the side of the bed, clutching at her wound.

Kariana stood over her, the hate so intense in her breast that she felt she would burst into flames. "Bitch! Did you really think I wouldn't find out?"

Marissa stared up at her, tears streaming down her face, breathing in short gasps. "I'm sorry, Kariana! I *had* to! They *made* me!"

"Made you?" Kariana felt a wicked smile creep across her face as she giggled like a girl. "What would they have done to you if you refused, I wonder, that made this the better choice?" She flicked the blade with her fingertips, sending droplets of blood flying. Marissa winced as they fell on her face like rain, mixing with the tears welling in her eyes.

"I wanted to be special," she sobbed. "Like you! Beautiful! Important!"

There were no words to communicate Kariana's wrath, yet she could not contain it. It burst from her throat, a roar of bestial madness as she fell upon the frightened girl.

Marissa raised her arms and grappled with Kariana, struggling to defend herself. She was considerably bulkier, but Kariana's rage made her a tigress. They rolled across the floor, screaming, Marissa in terror, Kariana in unbridled fury, knocking over Kariana's vanity. Perfume bottles rained down, exploding as they impacted the marble floor.

"Bitch!" Kariana shrieked. "You fat fucking cow!" She slashed at Marissa with mad abandon, at her face, her breasts, any exposed flesh.

Marissa wailed in agony as the blade bit into her flesh, leaving deep gashes. She rose to her knees, desperate to escape, but Kariana kicked her flat on her back, mounted her like a horse, and bludgeoned her head repeatedly with the pommel of her blade.

Marissa could no longer defend herself. Her head cracked against the floor with each blow. She mumbled through shattered lips, "Stop. *Please.*"

Kariana, exhausted, paused her attack. She sat astride Marissa's unresisting bulk, panting and gasping from her exertion. Marissa lay still, covered in blood, eyes closed. She might have been dead save for the occasional twitch or moan.

"I thought you were my friend," Kariana whispered, her vision clouding with tears.

Marissa looked up at her with dazed, unfocused eyes. "I *am*, Kariana. But I had to be loyal to my family."

"You were like a sister to me. You *were* my family."

"I'm sorry. We can fix it, can't we? Now that you know? They were just guards. You said you didn't care about them lots of times."

Kariana felt a cold hand squeeze her heart. She wanted so desperately not to be alone that she had almost been fooled again. Marissa was still trying to cover up her part in the attack on Lara.

Kariana looked down at Marissa. There was so much she wanted to say, so many words, all meaningless, all just more opportunities for a snake to slip inside her mind once again. "I never cared about the guards." Marissa's face lit with hope for a brief moment, then fell as she looked into Kariana's eyes. "Aiul tried to kill me because of your stunt with his wife. And now I have to kill *him*."

"No! It wasn't—!"

Kariana plunged her dagger into Marissa's throat. Blood fountained over her hand in warm jets. Marissa's eyes grew wide, and she clutched at her throat as her life poured out of her, turning her head back and forth in denial.

"Goodbye, sister."

Marissa's face softened from fear to sadness as she accepted the inevitable. She reached for Kariana's hand and squeezed. Kariana snatched her hand away and spit in Marissa's face. "You ruined my life. You go to Elgar alone, bitch."

Kariana rolled off her victim and lay on the bloody floor. She breathed in the bizarre mix of scents: pungent sweat, acrid blood, cloyingly sweet perfume. Exhaustion bore down on her as the adrenaline slowly ebbed away, the pounding in her temples and roaring in her ears giving way to blissful silence. *Sleep is like dying.*

She woke to shouts and the clang of armored boots on stone.

Caelwen was staring down at her, patting her face with a mailed palm. For a brief moment, she thought he was here to arrest her.

"Two assassins in one night," he noted. "I'm impressed you survived even one. You're quite the mess, Empress."

"You missed the first one," she said in a husky, sleep-dulled voice. She shrugged aside his attempt to help her to her feet. Any assistance from him was an admission of weakness. She raised herself on her arms and stood, her muscles still aching. "It was quite a show. I guess you had better things to do." She glared at him, a silent accusation.

"I had to attend a wake. Several, actually. I filed the appropriate paperwork. Perhaps you missed it in the excitement of preparing your orgy?"

Kariana considered saying something more vulgar, but she was seized by a mad impulse to laugh. The blood, the shattered glass, Marissa lying dead on the floor, it all struck her as a great, black joke. She threw back her head and cackled like a witch.

Caelwen eyed her warily. To her surprise and pleasure, he looked a bit unsettled, frightened even.

Good, she thought. *If I cannot be loved, then fear will do.*

Soon, Tasinalta would teach all Nihlos the true meaning of fear.

CHAPTER 8
ESCAPE

BRUTUS wasted no time escaping the prison. He crouched in the shadows outside the entrance, waiting for the show to start, the bizarre, orange clouds of the night sky hovering overhead like an impending rain of fire. If Sandi and the others did their part, the escapees would provide plenty of cover for exfiltration.

He pulled the cloak tighter against the cold, cursing under his breath. Of all the battlefield conditions he had ever endured, cold was the one he hated most. The flimsy wrap, designed to keep rain off, offered precious little in the way of actual insulation. *It's better than nothing.*

Before long, the prisoners came running, for the most part, loud and disorganized, many shouting threats to the skies, though the odd few had sense enough to slink away without ceremony. Brutus shook his head quietly, knowing many of them would be dead before morning. *If they die, at least they will die free.*

Imprisoning men was yet another barbaric practice the Nihlosians favored that made absolutely no sense to Brutus. For the life of him, he could think of nothing that would warrant caging a man that wouldn't also warrant putting him to the sword.

If a man couldn't be trusted to roam free, who would leave him alive to threaten others if he were to escape? And why waste resources feeding and guarding such a man? *Cruel, stupid, and wasteful, just like everything else with these pale dogs.*

Even their criminals seemed fools. Why not simply flee? Instead, half of them sprung immediately to mayhem, setting fires and breaking windows. Brutus understood, though. They were angry, after being kept in that evil place. The fires and chaos would bring the guards running, the very men responsible for much of their misery in the prison. Sometimes the need to kill a man overrode reason. Vengeance was a strong motivator.

At any rate, their foolishness was to his benefit. Soon enough, knots of guardsmen came straggling in to quell the fires, only to be surrounded and savaged by the prisoners.

Time to go.

The escapees took no notice of him as he slipped into a dark alley, moving with purpose but resisting the urge to run. *Running men draw attention.*

It quickly became apparent that there was a flaw with his escape plan: the prisoners provided cover, but they also drew more guards. Worse, the undercity population was a rebellious lot at the best of times. Many, seeing the initial chaos, saw opportunities to indulge grudges or loot. It spread like flame through kindling, slowly at first, but steadily increasing in speed until the entire undercity was blazing with chaos, and Brutus was hardly immune.

They fell in behind him, four hooligans in all, dirty and thin, their intentions as clear as the clubs they smacked against their palms. These were no pampered lordlings. They were hard men, hungry men who had done this before. *So have I, dogs.*

Brutus shrugged out of his cloak and drew his blade. The attackers paused briefly, sizing up this new wrinkle as Brutus brought his shield to bear, then charged forward as a group.

Brutus stepped to the side, raising his shield to block the closest thug's swing with a dull clang, and slashed at his throat. The would-be mugger staggered back, clutching at his neck and gurgling blood.

Brutus wasted no time with taunts. As the remaining three circled him, trying to surround him, he lunged forward and stabbed the tallest in his gut. The man dropped immediately to his knees, screeching in agony, as Brutus faced the others and waited for an opening.

The remaining two, wide-eyed, calculated their own odds and seemed to find the numbers bleak. One, an ugly fellow with a nasty scar across the bridge of his nose, cursed, then turned and fled immediately, but his skinny, rat-faced partner scuttled to the side first and scooped up the rain cloak Brutus had dropped, as if he simply could not leave the area without *some* prize to claim for his efforts.

The skinny thief cackled, his laughter echoing off the alley walls, as he fled with Brutus's only means of hiding his face. Brutus watched them go in shock, slowly realizing what had happened. He could have defended the cloak, he felt certain, if it had ever occurred to him to do so. Now, for no sensible reason, he had lost the one thing he most needed, a thing that offered little or no value at all to the men who had taken it. *I would almost prefer they had taken my damned sword!*

Pursuing them would simply make matters worse. Exfiltration had suddenly and pointlessly become ten times harder, but there was nothing for it.

He would kill whom he had to, if it came to that.

Carefully, Brutus began making his way toward the east gate of Nihlos, the only one he had actually seen. He knew the way well enough from his earlier scouting runs. The trouble was that, with the growing unrest, he had no idea which areas were now high traffic, and which would be quiet. He tried keeping to the shadows, which worked fairly well. Once, as Brutus passed what appeared to be a brewery of some sort, a single guard approached, but the man was obviously distracted and in a hurry, burdened with his own problems. Brutus turned toward the wall and began urinating, hoping that the shadows would keep his gear from standing out too much, and the guard passed him by without a word.

It took nearly an hour of skulking on a necessarily circuitous route to arrive at the gate. Brutus's heart sank to see it was heavily guarded, with at least twenty defenders surrounded by agitated commoners and weathering a barrage of thrown rocks, vegetables, and crockery. A nearby tavern had just begun to burn, filling the whole area with thick black smoke.

Brutus could think of no curse strong or vile enough to mutter, and punching the walls would simply give him away. He waited in the shadows, seething, desperately trying to formulate a plan that would get him out of this accursed city full of madmen and back to his ship.

Idiots! Why attack the gate? But even as his rational mind asked the question, his gut answered: *Because that's where the guards are.* Mobs were more like beasts than men. They lashed out without much reason beyond proximity and vague anger. One fool with a belly full of drink sees an opportunity, and the others follow.

It was a good place for even an excellent soldier to get killed on his own. To be a good soldier, one needed discipline and team-work to control not just his own weapon but the enemy as well, even the environment to a degree. Tonight, though, Brutus was merely a lone warrior, and warriors had to rely too much on fortune for his taste. Still, it was what he had to work with so it would have to do.

He turned back toward the heart of the city, trying to remember details from the reports the other scouts had filed with him. As he recalled, there were four primary entrances to the city, on at each compass point, along with a number of smaller portals that were locked at night but left unguarded. It was tempting to try the lesser access ways, but in truth, guarded or not, they were out of the question. He wasn't strong enough to bend the bars on the gates, and he wasn't going over the wall without climbing gear. He could always try liberating some rope and a grappling hook if he ran across a store that stocked them, but it seemed far easier to mug someone for their cloak and take his chances at one of the primary exits. *Assuming they're not all like the one I just left.*

As he cast about looking for a likely victim, he heard shouts nearby, cries of rage, and what sounded for all the world like his own men in the thick of battle, crying out: "Hold the line!"

Against his better judgment, Brutus moved toward the battle and peered around a corner. Before him, was one of the rare few public access-ways from the undercity to the city above, where a pack of rioters had surrounded a group of five beleaguered guardsmen. The defenders stood shoulder to shoulder, blocking the entrance to a great switchback staircase, shields up and hard pressed against the nearly twenty men trying to push past. Several guards lay in pools of blood on the platform below, dead or dying, as the commoners pushed against the shield wall, tracking bloody footprints up the stairs.

Brutus ground his teeth, knowing what he intended was madness, but for the moment, he simply could not see walking past. *Ilaweh is great, I have lived this. I have been that man holding the line.*

He charged up the stairs and slammed his shield into the back rank of the mob, bowling three men over. He planted a boot to the face of one, a sword in the chest of another, and slammed the edge of his shield down across the third man's mouth.

It took a moment for the rioters to realize they were under

attack from the rear. Brutus slashed two more across their backs, sending them down screaming.

As the mass of rioters turned, confused, slowly toward him, the guardsmen, seeing their chance, went on the offensive. From there, it was a simple task to split the mass and slaughter the individual knots of rioters.

When it was done, Brutus simply stood, catching his breath as the guards, faces masked behind visors, stared down at him.

One finally jerked off his helmet and called out, "Elgar take me, blackie, I figured you for dead!" He was an older, grizzled looking fellow with close-cropped, gray hair, a scar on one cheek and a couple of teeth missing from his grin.

Brutus was surprised to realize he recognized the man. "I know you."

One of the other men also removed his helmet and barked at the elder Nihlosian, "Lorinal! You're wanted for murder!" He pointed his blade at Lorinal. "There's a warrant for your arrest!"

Lorinal sneered at the younger man. "Me and this 'un just saved your lives, boy, and this is how you pay us back?"

The other guards were more interested in Brutus, keeping their blades pointed at him, but making no move to attack. Brutus returned the favor, but he smiled back at them, too. He was pleased to let them interpret that smile as they would.

Lorinal pushed past the younger guard's weapon and slapped him hard enough to leave a red palm print on the man's face. "What's your name, boy?"

"Tyreth, sir. Tyreth Noril."

"A goddamn *noble*, and I just walked past your sword and slapped the shit out of you. Are you a fucking idiot? What moron trained you?"

Tyreth's face grew an even brighter shade of red as he stammered, "Yes, sir. I mean, no sir. And, uh, you trained me, sir."

"*Mei's hairy ass*, did you just call me a moron, boy?"

"No, *sir*!"

"*Sir?* Are you saying I don't know both my parents, now?"

"No, s—sergeant!"

"Do you want to die tonight, Tyreth?"

"No, sergeant!"

Then maybe you ought to call your men off that black skinned devil there before he opens your guts to the elements, you think?"

Tyreth followed Lorinal's gaze and started as if he had just noticed Brutus for the first time. "Mei!" He quickly waved at the other guards to stand down. "What in Mei's name is going on tonight?"

The guards lowered their weapons. Brutus lowered his own blade and said to Lorinal, "You were at the cave."

Lorinal nodded. "Aye, I was. I tried to kill you, too, but I wasn't fast enough. Nothing personal, just business."

Brutus grinned at him. "I heard you were already dead."

Lorinal scoffed. "From Prosin trash? I smelled those fuckers from way off and put paid to them. Now they want me for murderin' nobles, like they didn't come to murder me to start with."

Brutus had no idea what a Prosin was, but the rest made sense. Lorinal had used his blade to avoid the grisly fate his companions had met. "And now you're a fugitive like me."

"Aye. You're looking for a way out of the city, I reckon. Me too. I just couldn't let these poor bastards get slaughtered."

Brutus grunted. "Same. Seems we're more alike than we might guess. Do you have a plan?"

Lorinal nodded toward the guards. "None I want to talk about in front of them."

Tyreth, nodding, put his helmet back on, and pointed to his men, then back at himself. "We never got a good look at the people who helped us, right?"

The other guards nodded, and one reached a mailed hand toward Brutus. "Good luck, friend."

Brutus grasped the man's forearm. "You, too."

"Let's move," Tyreth called, pointing up the stairway. "We'll have reinforcements up top. We won't be so lucky with passing strangers next time."

Lorinal shook his head. "If you know what's good for you, you'll break the whole damned thing loose at the top. They can fix it once this shit settles."

Brutus waited for the guards to head up the stairs before speaking. "So how do we get out of this?"

"Is it 'we,' now? No grudges?"

Brutus laughed. "Like you said, it was business. Nothing personal."

Lorinal stared at Brutus as if taking his measure, then gave a quick nod. "Good."

"Do you have a plan? I tried the east gate. We're not getting through there. It's a warzone."

"Not to mention that you stand out like a turd in the snow. Me, at least I can keep my helmet on."

Brutus nodded at this. "How would it look if you were escorting me?"

Lorinal mulled this a moment. "Like you was a prisoner? You keep your arms behind you like they was tied?"

Brutus nodded. "What about my weapons?"

Lorinal shrugged. "Might as well keep 'em on your back. Anybody looks too closely, we're screwed anyway."

"We're not getting through any of those gates like that. Leaving the city with a prisoner doesn't make sense."

Lorinal gave a sly smile. "There's a smugglers' tunnel not far from here. The crooks that run it owe me."

Brutus shrugged. "Sounds like our best bet."

The two set out, Brutus holding his hands behind his back and

Lorinal holding one of Brutus's arms. Lorinal's knowledge of the undercity streets was the sort that could only be gained by decades of experience. He guided them through a maze of streets, cutting down alleys that Brutus didn't even realize were there, carefully avoiding high traffic areas. The few guards they ran across were harried, occupied with the chaos of the rioting, and passed by with little more than a nod of recognition. They encountered even fewer locals, and those took one look at them and found other places to be.

Lorinal pointed to a small building ahead, near the wall. "There. That's the place."

Brutus was about to allow himself a sigh of relief when he heard the sound of heavy footfalls. He spun to see a group of seven guards moving toward them at a brisk pace. For a moment, Brutus thought they would pass by like the rest, but the group's leader raised a hand and called a halt, then addressed Lorinal. "You there! We're abandoning the undercity to focus our efforts on the access points up top. Fall in. We'll escort you and your prisoner to safety."

Brutus had no idea how to respond, except with violence. Nothing else made sense; no reasonable person would refuse the escort, not in this situation. He kept his hands behind his back, hoping Lorinal had a play.

Lorinal simply continued moving toward the building, as if he hadn't heard. The leader shouted out, "Halt! Identify yourself!"

Lorinal turned slowly and answered, "Sorry, sir. I got hit in the head. I'm not feeling so good. Name's Dranner, zone three, second squad."

The officer nodded and waved to one of his men. "Restlin, see to his wounds." He turned to another and ordered, "Sarath and Bralon, keep an eye on the prisoner. He looks like trouble."

"Aye, Captain," one, presumably Restlin, called as he moved toward Lorinal.

Brutus did his best to look as if his hands were bound behind his back as the other two guards approached him. He stared at the ground, hoping against hope that the guards would miss a hundred different clues. Brutus did not relish killing these men, not when their only motivation was to help a comrade in arms, but he had his orders directly from the prince. He had to get back to his ship, and if that meant some well-meaning unfortunates had to die, it was Ilaweh's will.

Sarath and Bralon eyed Brutus warily as Restlin gently guided Lorinal to a sitting position. The medic began easing Lorinal's helmet off. "There's a lot of blood here. What happened?"

Brutus tensed. If they recognized Lorinal, the game was over.

Lorinal sighed and mumbled, "Can't rightly say. I just remember getting hit. I don't even know how I got here."

The medic ran a hand over Lorinal's head. "I'm not finding a wound here."

The captain's eyes grew wide as he stared at Lorinal, and Brutus took a deep breath. *Here it comes.*

"Lorinal!" the captain shouted, pointing a finger at the grizzled veteran. "Secure the prisoner and arrest that man! He's wanted for murder!"

Lorinal shoved the medic aside and leaped to his feet. "You bunch of fucking pussies! Prosin slaughtered nearly a hundred of our brothers and you dick lickers want to arrest me for defending myself?" He drew his blade in a fluid motion and swept it about in a warning arc. "Fuck the lot of you if you think I'll go easy!"

"Drop your weapon!" the captain ordered, as he drew his own. All of the rest of the guards likewise drew their blades, except for Restlin, who was still struggling to his feet.

"Fucking traitor!" Lorinal shot back. He called to the rest, "Just walk away! Go home to your families!"

The two guards nearest Brutus were wavering back and forth between the two targets, uncertain which to engage. Restlin put a hand on his weapon but didn't draw. "Is it true? There were a lot of men missing from muster this morning, about eighty."

The captain's eyes flickered toward his medic, then back to Lorinal. "I don't know, and I don't care. I have my orders."

Lorinal spat on the ground. "Then this ends hard, boy."

Yes, it does.

Brutus swept his blade around, slashing Sarath's throat deep enough to nearly decapitate him. The man's head lolled backward on his shoulder, wide eyes seeming to stare longingly toward the lit spires of the city above, blood jetting over Bralon's shocked face. He and Restlin staggered backward, raising their hands reflexively as Brutus unslung his shield and positioned it to his front.

Lorinal charged the captain, battered the other man's blade aside, and tackled him. The captain hit the cobblestones with a thud and whoosh of outrushing breath, and Lorinal jerked a dagger from his belt and buried it in the man's chest.

One of the four nearest the captain shouted, "Fuck if I'm dying for House Prosin!" He turned and fled down the dark street, and after the briefest of hesitations, his three companions followed.

Bralon blew out a breath he had been holding for several seconds, spraying blood from his lips. He, too, turned and staggered off towards his companions.

Lorinal rose slowly to find Restlin still standing, wary, hand on hilt. The old veteran glared at him and said, "Don't tell me you're gonna be stupid."

"I have to know if it's true," the medic sighed, his voice quavering.

Lorinal sheathed his sword and bent to retrieve his dagger from the captain's corpse. "Yeah," he answered. "They came for me, too, but I knew something wasn't right, and it didn't end well for them."

"But *why*?" Restlin asked, voice quavering.

Lorinal pointed toward Brutus. "To keep people from knowing about him and his."

The medic, seeming to only really notice Brutus for the first time, gaped. "Mei! Is he—"

"A Southlander," Lorinal told him.

Brutus grunted at this. "We call ourselves *Xanthians*."

Restlin stared at Brutus a moment, then turned back to Lorinal. "I had a cousin with your unit. He didn't show up for muster, either. His name is Harwin. Harwin Luvox."

Lorinal shook his head slowly. "I knew him. Good man. But I reckon he's dead, boy. As far as I know, I'm the only one they missed, and they're on my trail."

Restlin blinked rapidly as he nodded his understanding. "Very well, and thank you for telling me." He set off after his fellows, calling over his shoulder, "I never saw either of you. Gods be with you."

Brutus tore a strip of cloth from the dead guard's blouse and wiped his blade clean. "That was a goatfuck."

Lorinal jammed his blade back into his belt. "Aye. Well, they wanted it that way. We did what we had to." He began rifling through the captain's pockets. "He won't have no use for money anymore, but we sure as shit might."

"What's next?"

Lorinal pointed to the building he had been about to enter before the fight and said sarcastically, "It's still in the same place I reckon."

Brutus glanced at the two corpses on the ground. "Leave them?"

Lorinal nodded glumly. "I hate it, but somebody will find them soon enough. Neither one of 'em deserved it, but it is what it is. Let's go. I hate looking at it. It's just a damned shame is what it is. Fucking evil nobles are the ones at fault." He waved at Brutus to follow. "It ain't far now."

From the outside, the hovel looked abandoned, windows boarded, the mortar between its bricks dark and crumbling. The interior was little better. The wooden floor was collapsed in several places, and cobwebs hung from exposed rafters. Brutus suppressed an impulse to sneeze as Lorinal reached down to haul on an iron ring embedded in the floor. The door opened in silence that belied its unused appearance, revealing a dark, hand-dug tunnel with crude stairs vanishing into the darkness. The ceiling was lower than he would have liked, but it was comfortably wide—at least six feet. *The better to move illicit cargo through, presumably.*

Lorinal pulled a small, glowing crystal from his pocket. The stone was clear, almost glasslike, similar to a rectangular prism. It cast a dim, yellow light, enough to see only a couple of feet ahead, but it would keep them from tripping over anything if they moved slowly.

Brutus followed Lorinal and the dim some thirty or forty feet below ground, where the tunnel leveled off. Ahead in the distance, Brutus could see the glow of lamplight.

Lorinal paused and whispered, "Listen, blackie, keep quiet from here, and let me do the talking. I got an arrangement with these boys down here."

Brutus grinned. "Brutus," he said.

"Huh?"

"My name. Brutus Samir."

Lorinal raised an eyebrow. "I guess we never got around to that, huh? Well, you already know my name, Brutus, on account of people screaming it out, so I reckon we're proper introduced now. You ready?"

"Indeed."

The passage widened into a cavern as they approached the

light. By the time Brutus could make out individual people, it was a full twenty feet wide. Crates and boxes of all sorts lined the walls, along with a few sparse pieces of furniture.

Brutus counted thirteen men huddled about a fire in the middle of the tunnel, some on chairs, others sprawled in the dirt. As he and Lorinal approached, the men rose and turned toward them.

"Who the fuck are you?" called a squat man as he reached for the hilt of his sword.

"Lorinal, and a friend," Lorinal answered.

Several voices murmured, and the short man stepped toward them, more visible now as he approached. "The fucking guard?"

"One and the same," Lorinal answered. "Just passing through."

"The *fuck* you are!" he spat, with all of the attitude a short stature tended to induce in a man who desperately wanted to seem large and imposing.

Lorinal glared at him. "I got an arrangement with you boys."

"You *had* an arrangement with Smotts. New management, new arrangements. You want to pass through this tunnel, you pay me."

"What's your name, you little bitch?" Lorinal demanded.

"They call me Troll, old man. You'd best remember it. Toll's a hundred nobles up front."

"You little shit!" Lorinal sneered. "I paid you a hundred times over by not hauling the lot of you in!"

"That was then. The Troll will have his toll, now. It's a hundred nobles in gold, or you can march you and your black-skinned friend the fuck back the way you came."

Brutus grinned at Lorinal, finding the old guard's growing rage tremendously amusing. Lorinal's eyes bugged as he shouted, "If we had a hundred nobles, we wouldn't be down here in the first place!"

Troll shrugged. "Not my problem. This is business."

"We're as good as dead if we turn back!"

"You're dead for sure if you keep coming without paying me."

Brutus eyed the rest of the men in the cavern. None of them seemed very excited. Their hearts didn't really seem to be with the little man. *Ilaweh, I will see you or my men soon.*

He struck swiftly, grabbed Troll by the throat, hauled him close, and clamped an arm about his neck like a steel band. "Then it is a good day to die. Do you feel like dying, dog?"

The rest of the men in the room began to laugh, some whistling or stomping their feet in approval.

"Fuck you, Troll!" one yelled.

"Twist his head off, blackie!" another shouted.

Troll turned wide, pleading eyes up at Brutus. Brutus grinned back at him. "You talk much for a man with no friends."

Lorinal began to sidle to the edge of the tunnel, and Brutus followed, dragging Troll by his head, to hoots, whistles, and peals of laughter from his men.

One stepped forward, a younger man with a cruel smile. "Do it. You'd be doing us a favor."

Brutus laughed out loud as he reached the other side of the cavern and began backing down the tunnel there. He squeezed Troll's neck until the man's eyes bulged and his face went deep red, then shoved him away. "I'm a soldier, not an assassin."

The younger thug knelt next to Troll, while the short man rubbed his neck and shouted in a raspy voice, "You're fucking *dead men,* you hear—" His threats ended with a gurgle.

Brutus watched the younger man's smile grow even more cruel as he withdrew a bloodied blade from Troll's back to even more cheers.

"You owe me, Lorinal," the young man called.

"Doubt I'll come back this way, Mohen, but I'll buy you a beer if I do."

"Make that two."

Lorinal laughed. "Two it is!"

They moved quickly, back into the darkness on the other side, once again using Lorina's crystal for light.

Brutus looked over his shoulder but saw nothing save blackness. "Will they follow?"

"Doubt it," Lorinal answered. "Troll is a new thing. Word on the streets is he was a tyrant. Mohen is solid, for a crook. He understands the rules. He's likely in charge now."

The passage narrowed and ascended again, and Brutus followed Lorinal through yet another door, which opened into a small shack. It held little in the way of furniture, but it was cover from prying eyes, and shelter from the wind. Lorinal sat on the ground in a corner and closed his eyes a moment.

Brutus spat in his palm and wiped at a dingy window. His spirits lifted to see he was indeed outside the city wall. He turned to Lorinal and asked, "Where will you go now?"

Lorinal shrugged. "I dunno. Away from here. You?"

"To my ship, and back to my prince. This is not over."

Lorinal laughed at this. "Give 'em some for me. Does a man have to be a blackie to fight with you, or would you take the likes of me?"

Brutus shook his head and laughed. "As long as you don't cry when we make fun of how ugly you are. Your sword arm is what matters. I'd fight with you at my side anytime."

Lorinal gave him a snaggle-toothed grin. "I got some business to tend to. I might not even come back, but if I do, and you make it back with an army, I'll sign on. I never did nothing but follow my orders and try to stay alive, and they'd kill me for it. I reckon I'd be happy to kill them first, just like I did with them Prosin snakes."

Brutus reached and grasped Lorinal's forearm. "You're a good man. I won't be hard to miss when I return, I promise. Good luck."

Brutus hauled open the shack door and set out through the deepening snow. It wasn't the worst forced march he had done, but it would be twenty hard miles, for all that.

One foot in front of the other, just like any other march.

CHAPTER 9
JUDGMENT

KARIANA sat alone at her desk in her private reading room, taking stock of her situation, desperate to work out a plan to move forward. The early morning sun shone from a window, blinded her briefly, until she rose and closed the heavy purple curtain against it.

Ordinarily, she wouldn't even be awake this early, but the events of last night both made sleep difficult and demanded immediate attention.

She was to hold court in less than an hour, a closed session with the house elders. It was her plan to call for the unthinkable, Aiul's execution, along with the lone surviving foreigner. How had this happened? Murders, assassination attempts, convoluted plots, *madness*! And somehow, here she was, right in the middle of it. Life was supposed to be simpler. It was supposed to be fun and carefree, not a nightmare of mistrust, intrigue, and death. What had she done to deserve this?

Nothing, of course. Nothing but be born. And for that sin, there was no forgiveness, nothing but misery and constant ratcheting of pressure. She felt as if her head would implode from it. There was no one to trust, no one at all. Well, perhaps the stone-faced, stone-hearted Commander of her Guard. He could be trusted to do his duty and to stare at her with loathing and disapproval. Even now, he stood watch over her outside the study door, doubtless praying a bolt of lightning would make an end of her and free him, but until then, still loyal.

It was, all things considered, a paltry showing.

She wracked her brain for a plan. What would she do, or say? Mei, Nihlos was a city of monsters, spiders spinning webs, and she was a fat, tasty fly buzzing about, oblivious, defenseless.

But no more.

She would find a way. She could be a monster, too. She would be the most fearsome monster of all. Fear was the true currency of Nihlos, and she would find a way to spread the wealth generously.

A knock upon the door startled her from her ruminations. Caelwen entered, casting his usual non-smirk her way. "You've a visitor, Empress. Lady Maralena of House Prosin."

Kariana felt her bowels fill with ice, but rage warmed her quickly. *That bitch has the gall to come here?* "Send her in."

Caelwen scowled, then swung the door wide, gesturing to the stately woman behind him. "You may enter."

Maralena Prosin was a pretentious elder, well-heeled and well-dressed in expensive silks and furs. She held her head high, allowing sun from the skylight to sparkle on her array of expensive chains and baubles.

Fond of diamonds, are we? Kariana glared at her, saying nothing. *Wretched bitch! I should push you in a river. You'd surely be dragged to the bottom by all of your stones.*

Maralena looked at Caelwen a moment, then sighed and turned to Kariana. "I asked for a private meeting."

Caelwen gave her a stone-faced stare. "Over my dead body."

Maralena stiffened and pursed her lips. "That could be arranged."

Caelwen stepped toward the Matriarch of House Prosin, invading her space, and allowed his hand to settle on the pommel of his blade. "No doubt. I'll rest well knowing my father will put the lot of you snakes to the sword in response. It would be a fine trade." Then, to Kariana's surprise, Caelwen actually smiled. It was a thin, humorless smile, and brief, less than a second, but it was a smile nonetheless. Truly, it was a time for miracles.

Maralena's cold demeanor cracked, and she stepped back quickly. That, too, lasted only a moment before she recovered, but it was all Kariana needed. *She's not as tough as she'd like us to think. Or as brave.*

"Call off your dog, Kariana. I'm here to talk, nothing more."

Caelwen rolled his eyes. "Oh, come now. Didn't you bring a drink for our empress, or a muffin? You'd have to have something to hide the poison."

Maralena flushed in anger but kept her tone cool. "That's quite enough."

Kariana smiled. "You may leave us, Caelwen."

Caelwen turned to her, the expression on his face as close to a wounded look as stone features could allow. "Empress? I think that unwise."

Kariana laughed, a tinkling, innocent sound she had spent years perfecting. It had a peculiar effect on men. Of course, Caelwen was not a man and was therefore at least partially immune, but it served well enough. "Oh, Caelwen, what are you worried about?" She turned to Maralena and let her little girl mask fall, staring at the Matriarch with raw hatred. "If she kills me, you'll kill her and be rid of us both."

Maralena's eyes darted nervously back and forth between the other two. She licked her lips. "Just so."

Caelwen was unconvinced but obliged to obey. "Just so, indeed." He gave Maralena a final stare, then stepped into the hallway and closed the door.

Kariana gestured toward the most uncomfortable chair in the room, a high backed wooden affair that was simply unbearable to sit in overlong. "Have a seat."

Maralena raised a hand "I'll stand."

I'm Empress. I'll keep sitting. "Fine. What brings the Matriarch of House Prosin to my humble abode?"

Maralena clenched her jaw so hard that Kariana half expected to hear the sharp report of bone cracking. The elder took a slow, deep breath. "There is no point in games. You murdered my grand-niece and accused her of being an assassin. Obviously, I know she was no such thing." She clasped her hands behind her back and cleared her throat. "We have a problem. I'm here to sort it before it gets out of hand."

Kariana laughed again, not the tinkling laugh this time, but a mocking, cruel, hateful sound that she'd never once practiced. What gall this woman had! Kariana ran a hand across her bosom, heartened by the feel of Sadrik's knife, and considered. *I could stab this bitch now, and who would do a thing about it?* It was a dark, tempting idea, but a bad one. It would make things considerably worse for her at the trial, whatever lie she might tell to cover it up.

But, then, perhaps Maralena could be useful to her there, if they could come to terms. *Not from weakness!*

Kariana let all emotion drain from her face. She stared at Maralena, and the Elder woman held her gaze with feigned disinterest, but a twitch beneath her eye betrayed her nervousness.

Kariana said, "You murdered my brother, and you slipped in to spy on me. You drugged me for years, doing Mei knows what." Kariana wanted very much to continue in a cold, collected manner, but it was all like knives stabbing into her brain. She gripped the edge of her desk, physically restraining herself from leaping upon the old woman and letting consequence be damned. Her voice rose to a shriek. "You murdered nearly a hundred men in my name! What the *fuck* do you imagine entitles you to come in here, indignant, and ask me for *anything*?"

"Calm yourself, fool! Neither of us wants this business to be public!"

Kariana struggled a moment, grinding her teeth, the urge to use her knife almost unbearable. At last, she nodded. "Go on."

"We had nothing to do with your brother's death, but it was no accident. The killer was of House Tasinal."

"Who?"

"One I would not care to anger. That information comes at a price higher than you can pay. Perhaps someday, you'll have something to trade."

Kariana shook her head in disgust. "Fine. But the rest stands."

"We did what we did for the good of Nihlos. What you lacked the intelligence or stomach to do."

"I have the stomach for a lot, as you found out!"

Maralena snorted. "Please. You murdered a fat, unsuspecting child. It's hardly a statement of resolve. It was a tantrum."

Kariana felt rage rise within her again. "I might have another, you wrinkled hag!"

"Ah, and killing an old woman will surely be a step up for you as a force to be reckoned with, eh?" Maralena waved the death threat aside with a dismissive hand.

Kariana drummed her fingers on the desk. *I can still stab her if I want to.* "What is it you want, old woman?"

Maralena sighed, a sour look on her face, as if she were contemplating eating something foul. "Peace. What will it cost?"

Kariana considered this unexpected wrinkle. "I have a real assassin to deal with in just a few moments. If I screw it up, I am likely dead, and House Tasinal and Nihlos are both wounded. Narelki will be my biggest enemy. You know things. I need to know them, too."

Maralena rewarded her with a grim smile. "You are wrong

about your greatest enemy, but there is little you can do about that. I can help with the political issues, and I can tell you much about Narelki. In fact, hearing what I have to say about her is your cost for my peace."

Kariana cocked her head in confusion.

Maralena's smile grew hard, and Kariana's confidence wavered. The old woman seemed terribly tough now, frightening. "They gave us Marissa's body for burial. I examined it myself." As quickly as it had come, Maralena's resolve seemed to melt, and she looked away, staring past Kariana, eyes unfocused. "You put her through as much pain as possible. You twisted the knife. You let her suffer long before she died, didn't you?"

Kariana felt a pang of remorse to hear it put in such terms but steeled herself against it. Marissa was a traitor, a monster. "She started all of this! She ruined my life! I'd kill her *again* if I could!"

Maralena turned her gaze back to Kariana. A single tear ran down her cheek and splattered on the marble floor, a small bomb, a precursor to a larger one. "It was Narelki who tried to have Lara killed." She swallowed hard, her gaze pinning Kariana like a dagger. "Poor Marissa had nothing to do with it. She didn't even know why she was dying."

Kariana felt her eyes begin blinking of their own accord. "You lie!" she gasped.

"Do I lie about your visiting Narelki? Or about Aiul finding a piece of his shirt in her trash, a piece you tore from it? Or perhaps the lie is in Narelki letting you take the fall for her crime because she feared Aiul's wrath? Which do you think?"

"How can you know this?" Kariana choked out.

"The same way we knew what you were doing. We have eyes and ears everywhere."

She didn't even know why she was dying. Kariana felt a tremor run down her arm and slapped at it as if it were a fly. The pain seemed a good thing; it pushed back the darkness welling in her just a bit. But it was not enough. She sat for several moments as the trembling took hold of her entire body and her vision tinted red.

Kariana leaped from her chair, lifted it overhead, and hurled it against the door. Her hands seemed to have a will of their own, taking up any fragile object she could find and smashing it on the floor: a dish from the desk, a lamp on the table beside her.

Caelwen burst in, sword in hand. Kariana hurled an ink blotter at him, barely missing his head. "Get out!" she screamed. "Get out! Get out! Get *out*!"

Caelwen flashed Maralena a questioning look. She nodded, still in tears. Caelwen shrugged and left, closing the door behind him.

Kariana's outburst ended as quickly as it had begun. She found herself on her knees in the corner, vomiting. *Oh, how dignified.*

Maralena cleared her throat. "Are you quite done?"

"Now is the wrong time to take that tone with me, bitch!" Kariana tore a curtain loose from its rod and wiped her face with it. She rose slowly, looking about for her chair, then remembered that it was in pieces against the wall. With a grunt, she swept her arm across her desk, knocking the rest of its contents to the floor, then lay down on it, staring up at the stippling on the ceiling. It almost seemed to make words, perhaps in a foreign language. After several moments, she stopped trying to decipher it and heaved a great sigh. "Do go on."

Maralena sniffed hard, then continued. "I will tell you all you need to know to bring Narelki to ruin. You were but a weapon. It was Narelki who wielded you. *She* killed my grandniece." She raised a clenched fist and shook it in the air. "We shall take her son in payment."

"Just that easy?" *I doubt your fist is going to intimidate Narelki. She'll rip your head off and hang it on her wall.*

"Easy? No. We'll have to deal with the Meites." She grimaced at this. "We have a chance to beat them politically. Let us hope they are sane enough to let our victory stand."

Kariana sat bolt upright on the desk and stared at Maralena. "*Meites?*"

"I told you, there is nothing you can do," Maralena answered as if educating a child. "I will manipulate the others, but the Meites are largely impossible to handle in such a manner."

"Who are they? How many?"

Maralena sighed, tired and seeming a bit frightened, but still angry. "That wasn't part of your price, Child Empress. If all goes well, perhaps we can negotiate for that information later."

"And if not?"

Maralena shrugged. "Why, then you'll get the information for free, for all the good it will do you. They're more than capable of killing us all if they choose to do so."

Kariana lay back down on her desk and stared up at the ceiling again. "I see."

Kariana arrived early to the courtroom, memories of her conversation with Maralena still painfully fresh in her mind. The session would start at noon, and she needed at least a little time to mentally prepare herself for the coming battle. The elders would surely be difficult, if not outright hostile. She took her place at the far end of the room, behind an enormous, mahogany and marble judge's desk, and sat in silence. *Claiming the room is the only advantage I have.*

The great courtroom of Nihlos was regarded as a magnificent work, and Kariana supposed it was so, in a cold, impersonal way.

Soaring arches lined the left and right walls of the enormous chamber, and below each lay a great, stained glass window depicting legendary exploits of the founders. Here, one showed Tasinal at the very desk Kariana now occupied, smiling down on the rebel Aswan and granting him mercy. There, Amrath, his right arm raised overhead, hand clenched into a fist, delivered some rousing speech or another. She should know what he was saying, she supposed, but really, she was having enough trouble keeping everything Maralena had crammed into her head. It was neither the time or the place to try remembering her history. *It's not as if I ever really even knew much of it.* That lack was dangerous, now. History was the realm of sorcerers.

We could practically fit the entire population in here. Everyone that matters, anyway. Most of the room was given over for a standing audience, but eleven seats sat on a raised platform facing the judge's position, places for the Elder of each House other than Tasinal. *Why do they sit higher than me?*

Meites! The very word was enough to chill her deep in her bones. Try as she might, it was impossible to separate childhood tales and likely reality. What did she actually even know about Meites, other than they were wicked sorcerers who slay unruly children? If she had paid more attention to her history lessons, and less to drink and dick, she would be in a much better position. She made a resolution to remember that bit of wisdom for later. *Assuming I survive.*

The founders had all been Meites. It was their religion. They were, by all accounts, demigods. Now the name of their god was a vile curse, and practicing their faith was a crime punishable by death. Her own father had made it so, but why? Did it even matter? Unless Maralena was lying, there were dark sorcerers amongst the elders. But who, and how many?

I'm so screwed. I should make out my will while I wait for them. I'll name Sadrik my successor and stab myself. With any luck, they'll notice it's his dagger and blame him, and he can hate the world just like I do.

She turned and looked up at the larger than life statue of Tasinal that stood behind the desk, literally watching over the current rulers of Nihlos as they conducted official business. His aquiline face seemed to glower at her in disapproval, and she suppressed a shudder. They called him the Great Tyrant, the Undying Emperor, or sometimes, outside of the earshot of his heirs, the Lich Emperor. But he was also the father of her house, the well from which her blood sprang.

In theory, he was still wandering about somewhere, doing whatever wicked, undead sorcerers do. It was possible he could show up and make everything right again. She felt anger rise in her once again as she stared at the statue. *Help me, you bastard! Come and fix this mess I've made!*

She sighed, knowing it was a lovely but hopeless fantasy. Alive, dead, or undead, Tasinal had left Nihlos long ago, walked away without explanation, and for the first time in her life, Kariana understood why. It was a thankless job only a fool would want, a tar pit that trapped anyone stupid enough to set foot inside. Once you had the power and made enemies, you *needed* the power to survive. Unless, of course, you were a wicked sorcerer who could just blast anyone who troubled you. Then you could just walk away. Kariana did not have that luxury.

The thought of sorcerers blasting their enemies brought her quickly back to her unpleasant reality: who were the Meites?

Twelve houses, twelve elders. She knew she herself wasn't a Meite, and unless Maralena was playing a very odd game, which seemed very unlikely, neither was she. People with great personal strength rarely resorted to subterfuge. They would simply hit someone very hard and take what they wanted by force. *And what a joy that would be!* No, Maralena was no Meite. So, ten possibilities, then, and all of them would be arriving in short order. Could she work out which they were, just by observing? She resolved to give it a try. *Shut up and observe!*

They filtered in slowly as noon approached. The first to arrive was Ariano of House Talus, clad in pink flowing silks. She was an aged crone with a sickeningly sweet disposition. Ariano smiled warmly at Kariana and took a seat at the front of the courtroom. Kariana returned the smile, though she had her doubts as to how convincing it was. She was simply glad the old woman didn't try to strike up a conversation. Surely not a Meite.

Next came Davron Noril, and with him Polus Luvox, Caelwen's father. Davron was openly armed with a heavy sword, and both wore that odd, spiky armor they liked so much. *Really, it just seems bad form. You're not going to be fighting anyone in here, not that you know of, anyway. I'd rather have something comfortable.* Once, Polus had been blond, like his son, and Davron black-haired, but now they were both gray. Even at their ages, they were powerfully built men, warriors, still dangerous and handsome. They looked her way briefly, acknowledging her existence and nothing more, then took seats and waited in silence. Meites? It seemed unlikely. Why bother with swords if one could blast enemies to bits with a thought?

Narelki came next, the wretched whore, dressed in pure white. Prandil Idlic, the equally wretched gadfly writer, accompanied her, waving his hands dramatically as he regaled her with some idiotic tale. Narelki's glance toward Kariana was as cold as a corpse in a blizzard. Kariana shivered at the sight. *She could be one of them.* But Maralena hadn't seemed to think so.

Prandil, ever the provocateur, winked at Kariana and grinned like a wolf, his hatchet face lit with humor and playfulness. Kariana was simultaneously outraged and titillated. The old letch actually thought to flirt with her! He'd written so many horrid things about her in his editorials, and yet she had to admit, she found his barbs hilarious when they were directed at others. *He's not so old.* Neither of them were, for that matter. Aside from Kariana, they were the youngest of the elders, and it was well known that they were at least on occasion lovers. Kariana smiled back, thinking that it would be delicious to fuck Narelki's man and rub it in her face. *No, he's not so old at all.*

But was he a Meite? Perhaps, but it seemed unlikely. She'd never thought of sorcerers as being inclined to biting wit and sarcasm, and certainly not as dirty old men flirting with women half their age. A proper sorcerer would be reading musty books and making pacts with demons or some such.

Maralena was next to arrive. Her jewels were gone now, as was her other finery. She had chosen a simple brown tunic and pants with no adornment at all. *That's supposed to make you look unassuming, eh? Are they that stupid?* Maralena was accompanied by Olemus Freth, who was as rich as an old dragon and twice as fat. *Mei, is he wearing a tent?* Sadrina Veril, the socialite, chattered at them from behind, festooned in rubies and red silks, and sporting a ridiculous hat with pink feathers that rose a foot above her head, her fiery red tresses peeking out from the edges. Kariana tittered to herself, remembering that Prandil had once written about Sadrina: "She might easily be replaced by a mannequin. It would serve just as well for displaying clothes and jewelry, and would be better company by far." They ignored her completely as they took their seats as far away from the others as possible. Meites? Not a chance.

Lucreta Strall and Maklin Yorn arrived shortly thereafter. House Strall was chiefly concerned with education in Nihlos, and Lucreta, a teacher, of course, was the archetypal blue-haired frump. She carried a blue-sequined, fish-shaped handbag, probably filled with nothing more than a few pencils and tissues to wipe children's faces. She waved at Kariana, and Kariana felt compelled to return the ridiculous gesture. Maklin, dressed in a black tunic and pants, moved slowly, a combination of his age and his intent focus on his ever-present sketchbook. His pace was a simple cycle: every few steps, he stopped, looked confused, then enlightened, and scribbled something, then started moving again. He didn't even look in Kariana's direction. She might have taken offense to it as a snub, save for the fact that it would be dishonest to accuse him of ignoring her. It was more the case that he was not even aware of her existence. Meites? Impossible.

Last, and five minutes late, came Maranath Aswan, looking haggard and disheveled. The eldest of the elders, he moved ever so slowly, his long beard swaying as he struggled forward, his gnarled hand gripping his cane as a lifeline. *Mei, did he even bother to change clothes for the trial? Or bathe?* She sighed with relief. Not so many Meites after all. Perhaps it was all a lie that Maralena had cooked up to frighten her.

But as Maranath passed and met her gaze, she felt her breath catch in her throat. His brilliant blue eyes bored into her from beneath his gray brows, fire and ice, brooding, so full of life that it made her feel weak and old. They were the eyes of a child!

He's faking it. She didn't know the source of that notion, but she knew it was true. *Old and gnarled, yes, but he doesn't need that cane. He doesn't need anything!*

Maranath smiled at her and took a seat next to Ariano. *Mei! He knows I know!*

In the end, it hardly mattered. He would be with her or against her, and she would just have to play the hand she had been dealt. Feeling slightly sick, she rose, cleared her throat, and called out, "This meeting will now come to order. Caelwen, please seal the room."

Caelwen entered from outside and hauled on the heavy doors. He cast a glare of rank disapproval her way, no doubt in regard to her 'Plan B' precautions. Once the doors were closed, a contingent of a hundred guardsmen would take up position and await her orders. If things went really awry, that should be more than enough to handle even a few sorcerers. She just hoped Caelwen's overdeveloped sense of duty would keep him from betraying her secret. There was some slight risk to his father's safety if it blew up in her face, but it might very well be a matter of her saving his life with this scheme. She was fairly certain Caelwen would keep quiet. It was just a precaution, after all.

The elders gradually grew silent, save for Sadrina, who went right on nattering away to Olemus. Polus fixed her with a withering glare, and she blanched and fell silent.

"There's no way to pretty this up," Kariana said, repeating the words she had practiced with Maralena. "You all know the situation by now. I called this closed session because I intend to execute the foreign agent as a spy, and Aiul of House Amrath for high treason." She looked pointedly at Narelki, hoping to see a reaction, but Narelki's face remained a stone mask. The rest of the elders murmured amongst themselves for several moments, and Kariana stood by, waiting for the battle to begin in earnest.

Polus Luvox was the first to speak. He rose and called out, "Insufferable fool! Our ancient enemies return to Nihlos, and you told us nothing? You told *me* nothing? By rights, we should have *you* on trial here!"

Kariana blinked a few times. *That was unexpected.* "It seemed like a good idea at the time?" She looked to Maralena to see the Elder palming her face. *I guess that was the wrong thing to say.*

Prandil tittered at this. "Do you believe in fairies, too, I wonder?"

"It was a mistake, in retrospect. All leaders make them from time to time." *There, better. She's looking less like she's having a stroke, now.*

Prandil laughed and shook his head. "You seem to be going for some sort of record here."

Kariana clenched her jaw, struggling not to respond in anger. "Be that as it may, I am trying to rectify those mistakes. That is why we are here." *There. That's sounds more like Father. I can do this.*

Prandil folded his arms across his chest and grinned like a fool. "Oh, indeed. It shall be quite interesting seeing what form that takes."

Narelki took that moment to rise, and a hush fell over the courtroom. House Amrath was well respected, and Narelki doubly so. Kariana felt as if her hatred for Narelki would burn a hole through her chest, fall onto the desk, and set it on fire, but she managed to control herself.

Narelki looked pointedly at Kariana and spoke, her voice as icy as wind blowing over a frozen lake. "This is all irrelevant. You have no authority to put any Housed citizen to death."

Kariana waited a moment for the murmuring amongst the elders to pass, then conceded, "True enough. But this is a special case of high treason, and requires a heavy hand."

Narelki looked around at the others, then back at Kariana. "There is clear precedent here," she called out in a strong, confident voice "In the case of Aswan's Rebellion, Tasinal himself established the proper punishment: imprisonment until the offending noble bends a knee. Tasinal's Mercy is well known to any who have actually made a study of the law." She looked pointedly at Kariana.

Maranath rose, and Kariana felt herself flinch. What would the Meite say?

The old man wobbled on his cane a moment, then spoke, his voice strong despite his age. "Narelki is quite correct. This is basic history. My own house would not even exist were it not for Tasinal's Mercy."

Maralena, grinning, called out, "I'm not so sure that's a compelling argument." Laughter erupted from the rest of the elders.

"Indeed!" Prandil added, chuckling. "The lot of them are

crotchety old men waving canes about and provoking scandals. They're born that way!"

Maranath took their barbs with good humor. "Aye, and House Idlic has never once provoked scandal!"

Prandil raised a hand to his cheek in feigned shock. "Never!"

Maranath aped a scowl and waved his cane at Prandil. "I'm not so old that I can't thrash you for insolence, pup! Now leave an old man to speak without heckling, if you have it in you."

Prandil mimed zipping his lips shut and nodded vigorously.

"All humor aside," Maranath continued, "This notion of executing a noble is simply not legal, and we all know it."

Kariana shook her head vehemently. *Don't screw this up. Play it like she told you!* "This case is *not* the same. Aswan led an internal rebellion. Aiul conspired with foreign nationals. This is not rebellion, it is treason, a much higher crime. There *is* no precedent."

Kariana smiled to see Narelki's jaw clench.

Maranath grunted loudly. "Tasinal was not so foolish as to force his loyal subjects into such decisions."

The rest of the elders once again broke into debate, arguing the merits of the points raised. Polus, at last, rose to speak with their consensus. "We will not judge these men without hearing them speak. Bring them before us and let them account for themselves. Then we will decide if you have the right of things."

Kariana nodded. "Very well. Caelwen, bring in the prisoners." She would have preferred carte blanche, but Maralena had told her to expect this.

Caelwen turned and opened one of the double doors. "Bring them in."

The Southlander and Aiul, flanked by four guards, entered the courtroom in chains, still wearing the bloody clothes in which they had been captured. They slowly made their way forward, their movement restricted by hobbles. The Southlander stood at attention before the elders, while Aiul stood slump-shouldered, head bowed in shame. Caelwen quickly ushered the guards out again, then closed the doors and took up station behind the prisoners.

Kariana cleared her throat and spoke. "Here stand before you a Southlander spy and a traitor who conspired with them to murder me and conquer this city." *Yes, very indignant! That should sell it well.* "What can either of these wretches possibly tell you that will vindicate them? What can this foreigner do but bring death upon us if he is released? I tell you they must die!"

The Southlander's eyes grew wide, and he struggled at his bonds. "I deny this court! Barbarians cannot sit in judgment of civilized men!"

Caelwen gave Sandilianus a cuff to the ear. "The prisoner will not speak unless spoken to."

Sandilianus turned and spat at him. "You promised us justice! You are a cowardly, lying dog! Elgar take you!"

Caelwen, his face carefully blank, raised his fist again, but Maranath called out, "Let him speak." Caelwen lowered his fist and nodded.

Maranath looked down at the prisoner, summing him up. "What is your name, Southlander?"

Sandilianus stood to attention again. "I am Centurion Sandilianus Abu al Khayr, officer in Prince Philip's personal retinue, serving under Tribune Brutus Samir, and loyal servant to Ilaweh."

"A warrior, you say?"

"Take these chains from me, and I will do more than say it."

Maranath chuckled and shook his head. "You have no idea what you're asking, boy. If you are no spy, and you did not come here for war, then why come at all?"

Kariana felt a cold chill run up her spine. *He's taunting the Southlander!*

"We are explorers," Sandilianus answered. "We followed

Yazid Valerian, a holy man, on a quest to find an ancient evil." He stared pointedly at Kariana. "But evil found Yazid, instead."

Maranath waved his hand impatiently. "Yes, yes, we know the story. She is an imbecile, that much is established. But what is the ancient evil you speak of?"

Sandilianus shook his head. "I can say no more."

Polus rose and called out, "Not even to save your life?"

Sandilianus shook his head again. "I am a warrior. I am already dead."

Polus glared at Kariana. "This man is no spy."

Kariana leaped to her feet in outrage. "Of course he is! And he must be put to death as one! He cannot be allowed to communicate our weakness to his people, or we are doomed!"

"We did not hide our faces or skulk about!" Sandilianus shouted. "Not once we knew who we were dealing with. We approached your men openly, and we were attacked and murdered!"

"You lie!" Kariana cried, pounding her fist on her desk. "You hid yourself under hoods and cloaks and slipped into this very building to murder *me*!"

Sandilianus jerked at the chains that bound his hands, as if he might break them and use them to strangle her. "By then we were at war, a war *you* began with *us*! There is no dishonor in surprising an open enemy! I deserve ransom, or at least an honorable death. I am no spy!"

Maranath sighed and turned back to the other elders. "This Empress is out of control. I propose we remove her."

Prandil chuckled. "Oh, Maranath, always so serious! She has spunk!"

Maranath did not smile. "No, I think we have made a mistake putting her on the throne."

"Just so," Polus agreed, his face stern and unforgiving. "This has gone beyond incompetence and well into power madness.

What she proposes isn't merely idiocy and dishonor, it's an outright act of war against a people who can in all likelihood raze Nihlos if provoked. I stand with Maranath."

Kariana was seething. She couldn't hold her tongue any longer. She pointed a finger of accusation at Maranath and shouted, "Bold words from a criminal, Meite!" If she was wrong, it was going to be a disaster, but it already was. She had little to lose.

Maranath looked at her with a raised eyebrow for a moment, then began to laugh softly, his beard quivering, eyes twinkling in amusement. "Mei. Prandil may have a point, for once. We underestimate you, don't we, my dear?"

Kariana turned to Polus. "Is that not a clear confession in open court? You stand with a *criminal*?"

Polus sneered at her. "The children are so weak these days, and ignorant." Lucreta squirmed uncomfortably in her seat as he looked her way for a moment, then turned back to Kariana. "Meites do not recognize law when it conflicts with their will. The law exists only to keep fools from dabbling."

Kariana felt her jaw go slack as she looked around at the rest of the elders, most of whom were nodding in agreement. Maralena, pale-faced and wide-eyed, was gesturing at her not to go down this path, but it was simply too late. "Mei! All of you? You're *all* a part of this?"

"She was far too young to have been given the crown," noted Lucreta.

"And too ignorant," Polus shot back at her.

Lucreta seemed to shrink a bit at the accusation, but muttered, "It was how Tasinalt wanted things."

Olemus nodded. "Untrained and weak, as I told you all at the start of it. It was a reckless decision."

"Don't talk about me like I'm not here!" Kariana commanded. This was all spinning out of control.

Ariano inserted herself into the silence that followed Kariana's outburst, her soft, almost musical voice at odds with her wizened, shrunken features. ""You would have us speak to you? I seem to recall that it was you who chose to ignore me when last we spoke of meaningful things. You never answered my question about your brother."

Mei, will that damned rumor never die? "Shut up, crone! You know nothing!"

Ariano smiled "Perhaps it is best if we are both silent, for now."

"An easy thing for you to say, you wrinkled old whore! You're not fighting for your life!"

Polus held up his hand for order and again spoke to Kariana. "Nihlos has ever been ruled by those with the will to do so. Laws are for those who lack initiative."

Prandil jeered, "It must gall her to know the bitter truth, that her life is a great, self-inflicted delusion."

Kariana was mildly heartened to see Caelwen's cool demeanor slip away as he glared daggers at his father. For once, she felt some empathy for her guardian. Corruption everywhere! But unlike Caelwen, she was flexible. She could play this game. She just needed to learn the rules, form some strategies. *If they have no law, then neither do* I.

"I have plenty of initiative," she growled. "I think when we are done here, I shall make it my goal to root out these criminals and put them all to the sword!"

At this, the chamber erupted in reaction from all save Maklin, who was still busily scratching away at his pad, oblivious. Maralena again looked as if she might be close to having a stroke. Sadrina cackled and punched her in the arm. Olemus rolled his eyes. Prandil, Maranath, and Polus all laughed out loud, and everyone else snickered softly.

Prandil wiped tears from his eyes and spoke for them all.

"You barely survived this one's wrath," he said, pointing to Aiul. "You think you would weather Meite assassins?" Prandil turned to Maranath. "I like this empress. She's amusing. After we spank her, I say we return her to the throne."

"Don't mock me!" Kariana fumed.

Prandil's smile vanished, and his eyes grew dark with anger. "I do what I will, *child*," he replied, the humor gone from his voice. "You would do well to remember that."

Kariana had a sinking feeling that she had just uncovered another Meite.

Maralena rose to her feet, almost stumbling. "Mind your tongue, fool, before you bring ruin on us all!"

Ariano smiled her sickeningly sweet smile again. "Aye. It is dangerous to antagonize hidden enemies."

Kariana could scarcely breathe. The throbbing in her head felt as if a spike were being driven into her skull. She was screwed, totally and utterly fucked beyond all repair. It was freeing, in a way, the realization that she had absolutely nothing left to lose. "It's dangerous to back desperate people into corners, too!"

Maralena's eyes grew wide as she looked from Kariana to Caelwen standing at the entrance, then back again.

She's worked it out! Good for her! Oh, well, they'll all know soon enough.

The matriarch of House Prosin leaped to her feet and shouted, "Mei! You *fool!* Don't!"

Kariana smiled and screamed at the top of her lungs, "Guards!"

The courtroom doors were nearly torn from their hinges as the guards burst into the room, weapons drawn. Caelwen drew his own weapon, but instead of joining them, he stood motionless, obviously conflicted. Kariana smirked at his confusion. It served him right, always being so smug and cocksure.

Her amusement was short-lived, however. Polus shouted to

his son, "Stand down and secure the prisoners!" She noted with detached amusement that Caelwen's duty to his father was likely the only handhold on sanity the poor wretch had left.

The rest of the Elders barely flinched as the guards continued to pour in. Only Lucreta gave even the slightest indication of distress, slowly closing her eyes and calling out, "Have mercy!".

Kariana laughed her new laugh, the really wicked and evil one that came so easy now. She struggled to commit the scene to memory, so she could accurately describe it later. What a grand tapestry this glorious victory would make! "Kill these traitors! Kill them all!"

As one, Maranath, Prandil, and Ariano rose.

"Have mercy!" Lucreta screamed again.

The courtroom rippled like a mirage in the burning sun as invisible waves of power erupted from the three Meites in a widening circle of swirling ether.

"Mercy is for the weak," Ariano called out in a sing-song voice.

Lucreta lowered her head and wept.

Ariano opened her mouth wide, and multiple voices in perfect harmony poured forth, so liquid they could almost be seen as well as felt and heard. The music quickly rose in pitch and volume, bouncing back and forth from the stone arches, folding upon itself and gathering power with each echo, until it was the shriek of a hurricane trapped within the confines of the courtroom.

The huge, stained glass windows imploded, the sound of their shattering like a thousand champagne flutes being dashed against the walls. Glass rained down in chaos, jagged, grisly death for all below. With a sudden jolt, the deadly shards jerked sideways, organized now into a coherent unit, gravity no longer their master. Brilliant sunlight reflected in a dazzling display from razor-like edges as they spun and leaped in unison, a school of shilling fish dancing in the air.

The missiles darted toward the entrance. The guards screamed in pain, confusion, and fear, as the fragments ripped through their ranks, trailing streamers of blood.

Beyond the entrance, more guards were rushing into the corridor, responding to the cries of their fellows. Maranath lowered one hand and reached toward the ground as if he were grasping an invisible carpet, then jerked upward. Screams of tortured metal and stonework echoed throughout the palace as the floor outside the courtroom door erupted, sending jagged spikes of stone through the approaching guards. As his hand reached shoulder height, Maranath whipped it downward again, and the floor responded in kind. The raised section surged forward like a tidal wave, stone and steel rending and exploding with shrapnel in a wave that roared down the hall, dashing hapless guards to bits against the walls and ceiling as easily as the sea breaks mighty ships of war against rocks. It struck the doors at the other end of the hall, tore them from their hinges, and kept going, leaving a trail of destruction in its wake.

Kariana flung her head back and laughed. Well, she hadn't expected to win, not really. Again, it was freeing. *I might as well die with some style.* With a cry of abandon, she jerked Sadrik's knife from her shirt, leaped from her seat, and charged headlong for Narelki.

Prandil boggled at her briefly, then backhanded the air in front of him. Invisible force hit her in the chest like a charging elephant and sent her flying backward through the air. She came down hard at the feet of the statue of Tasinal, gasping for breath.

So this is how it ends. At least they will remember Tasinalta the Mad for a long time. Maybe they will frighten children with tales about me. She smiled at the thought. *That's so much better than being a stupid whore.*

Prandil surveyed the carnage, and his face lit with a sudden realization. He turned toward the back of the courtroom. "Maklin, you lazy wretch, you might have lent a hand, you know! We could have been killed!"

Maklin didn't even look up from his sketchbook. "You're still alive," he muttered.

"We might not have been!"

Maklin grunted at this. "Can't you see I'm busy here? And it's not as if you did much yourself. Beat up a small girl, oh, very powerful indeed."

Prandil struck an indignant pose, hands on his hips and brown, pointed beard quivering with feigned outrage. "It's hardly my fault these two hams stole the show. I was quite looking forward to a fight, but it was over too quickly."

Maklin waved a hand dismissively. "Just so."

"There are always more fools," Ariano told him, her voice still edged with strange harmonics. She was no harmless little old lady anymore. That mask had slipped from her the moment the fight began. *Not really a 'fight.' More of a 'slaughter,' actually.* Now her green eyes sparkled with brilliant malevolence, and her mouth twisted in a cruel sneer.

The same was true for Maranath. His cane was gone, as was all pretense of frailty. He stalked toward her with all the vigor of a young man, his eyes windows into the heart of a storm.

In the distance, the sounds of metal shod boots echoed toward them: more guards, more unsuspecting victims.

"You have done enough!" Lucreta shouted, tears still streaming down her face. "You have the power to spare lives, too, damn you!"

Kariana spat out a mouthful of blood and stared out at the carnage. She couldn't help but chuckle at her own gross underestimation of the Meites. Who would have suspected Ariano or Maklin? Mei, it was beyond anything she had imagined, though. In a few moments, they had devastated the thousand-year-old courtroom and killed at least fifty men. *I wonder if they will get in as much trouble as I did about the guard killing thing? I doubt it.* The marble floor beneath the Meites' feet was slick with blood. She looked up at Tasinal's scowling countenance, feeling as if her face would crack open with her mad grin. *He seems...pleased.*

Prandil eyed Lucreta warily for a moment, then raised his hands and smoothed the air before him. The courtroom entrance conformed to his will, stretching and smoothing itself into a solid wall. "We'll finish our business without their interference."

Narelki shook her head in distaste. "At least there is that."

Maranath turned toward her sharply and spat, "You disapprove? We should have let this fool kill us all for sake of decorum?"

"Of course not," Narelki told him. "But it was costly. It will be hideously expensive just to replace the guards, to say nothing of the courtroom. The glass, the stonework, it was all priceless."

"Oh, my dear, you need not worry," Ariano told her, laying a hand upon her arm in sympathy. "Has not Talus always provided for the beauty and truth of Nihlos?" Narelki's eyes flickered at this, but her face remained impassive as Ariano continued. "I have several students who excel just this sort of craftsmanship. With Yorn's help, we will have the whole place repaired in a week."

Without looking up from his notebook, Maklin raised a hand and nodded agreement. "I have ideas for a few new features, as well," he said. "It won't take long to draw up the plans. I'll start as soon as I am finished with this."

"Then at least there is some good news," Narelki said in a sour tone. "Shall we resume?" She paused, waiting for objections, but none came. "Then we shall add to the agenda a discussion of Tasinalta's fitness to serve, to be determined after we settle the current business. Maranath, as eldest, it is appropriate that you conduct the proceedings."

She speaks to him, but she doesn't look at him. Why?

"Very well," Maranath agreed. He was once again a very old man, limping to take his place at the desk. He stood over Kariana, where she still lay in a heap. "Get up, you idiot," he told her. "It will go better for you if you hold your tongue until we choose to deal with you."

Kariana wasted no time in obeying. She scrambled to her feet, stood on shaky legs, and limped to a seat beside Davron, doing her best to appear as dignified as possible. Davron gave her an amused look and gestured to his lip to indicate where she was bleeding.

Maranath nodded and cleared his throat. "Caelwen, bring forth the Southlander."

Caelwen whispered something to Aiul, most likely a death threat, and stepped forward with Sandilianus. The Southlander stood silent and respectful.

"I see we have your attention," Maranath noted.

"Aye," said Sandilianus. "That display was difficult to miss."

"Intentionally so," Maranath said with a nod. "Now, where were we? Ah, yes. Spy, not a spy, attacker or not, etcetera."

Sandilianus returned his own grave nod. "We did not come as enemies."

"And yet we are enemies now, whoever is at fault."

"And I have seen too much of you to be ransomed."

"Just so," Maranath said. He stroked at his beard, thinking. "You would prefer death to prison, I presume?"

"An honorable death, yes."

"We will grant a proud warrior an honorable death, then, if there are no objections," said Maranath. He glared pointedly at Kariana, daring her to speak, but she remained quiet, eyes lowered. *I may be stupid, but I am not* that *stupid.*

Davron passed Kariana a napkin for her lip and rose to speak. "Southlander, you would die in battle?"

"Aye," Sandilianus answered.

"Then tomorrow at dawn, you will face twelve warriors, one after the other," Davron said. "You may choose the weapons."

"And if I am victorious?"

Davron's face lit with a broad grin. "Survive twelve of my best, and I will grant you my *name*, Southlander.

Several of the Elders gasped in shock. Narelki pursed her lips in disapproval. "Surely you jest?"

Davron looked toward her, obviously offended. "I do not joke about killing, lawyer."

Narelki shook her head vehemently. "You cannot name an outsider. That would be unprecedented!"

Davron pointed a finger at the Southlander, keeping his gaze on Narelki. "If he is victorious against such odds, I think we had best be prepared to surrender more than our names to his people."

Kariana's mood immediately brightened to see Narelki skewered so well. Narelki blinked as she absorbed Davron's comment, then shrugged and took her seat. Davron stood another few moments, as if waiting for her to challenge him again, then took his own seat, muttering under his breath, "Cunt."

Polus quite clearly heard the insult but made no response. *They probably agree on that.* Kariana looked at Davron in surprise, and he raised an eyebrow, the ghost of a smile on his lips. She couldn't help but grin and took the opportunity to squeeze his thigh in a gesture of camaraderie. He smiled at this, then gently but firmly removed her hand from his leg. *I should have known you preferred goats!* It was hardly the truth, but the real reason was too painful to cope with at the moment.

Maranath cleared his throat, demanding their attention. "The prisoner will be remanded to House Noril," he announced. "Caelwen, secure the Southlander and bring forth Aiul."

Kariana could not look at Aiul as he passed. It simply hurt too much. She stared at the floor, struggling against tears.

Maranath waited until Aiul was settled, then gave him a nod

of recognition. "Amrath Aiul, you stand before this council of Elders, accused of conspiring with foreign agents to assassinate Tasinalta. How do you plead?"

Aiul would not look at the old man, preferring to stare at the blood-streaked floor. "Guilty," he said, his voice numb.

"We know your tale. You are a historian as well as a physician, are you not?"

Aiul looked up at this, annoyed. "You know full well I am."

Maranath nodded and waved both hands as if to fend off a rabid beast. "Decorum, boy, decorum. Now shut up, will you, and don't bother thanking me for saving your life, eh?" He stared at Aiul until the younger man broke eye contact. "Now, as for your punishment, you know of Aswan. His sentence shall be yours."

Aiul did not answer, merely stood in silence, staring at the floor. At last, he said softly, "Aswan had to pledge loyalty to Tasinal to be forgiven. I will pledge my loyalty to you right now. I never wanted to do anything but live my life, and see my child born and grow. I am not a rebel by conviction, merely by necessity."

Prandil rose, his brow furrowed. "It is not so easy as that. Do you understand the true nature of Aswan's crime, why he was punished?"

Aiul nodded and swallowed hard. "His crime was letting his pride overrule his reason. He misjudged his strength."

"He refused to back down from a clearly superior force," Prandil said. "He fought even when he knew he could not win. His sin was waste."

"Indeed," Maranath agreed. "What Prandil is trying to say, and failing, is that your pledge is misplaced. You cannot swear allegiance to us. Tasinalta defeated you. You must swear it to *her*."

Aiul's jaw bulged as he absorbed Maranath's words. "No," he hissed through clenched teeth. "That, I will not do."

Maranath nodded, smiling despite himself. "I think none of us expected any less. Nevertheless," he said, growing somber once again, "There are well-established consequences for such defiance. You understand the choice you are making?"

"What of my property?"

"It will remain yours," Maranath told him.

Aiul nodded. "I understand my choice."

"Objections?" Maranath glanced about the room. Kariana bit her tongue, knowing that speaking up now would only make things worse for her, later. The rest of the elders nodded their agreement.

"Very well," Maranath said. "Amrath Aiul, you are sentenced to the pit until such time as your pride is outgrown by your intellect." He gestured to Caelwen. "Remove the prisoners. Our remaining business is not for their ears."

Kariana tried to gather her thoughts as she watched Caelwen march his two charges into one of the adjoining chambers. The bitter taste of fear made it difficult to concentrate.

"Tasinal Kariana," Maranath called, his voice dripping disdain. "Have you anything to say for yourself?"

Kariana shrugged and stared at the floor, emulating Aiul's manner, though inwardly, she was anything but resigned to her fate. "What is to be said?" she muttered. "Clearly, I overestimated myself. Am I permitted the same mercy as the Traitor? I won't squander it like he does."

Maranath leaned across the desk, eyes wide and amused. "Tasinalta, the 'Blood of Tasinal,' bends a knee?" he asked.

Kariana burned as if immersed bodily in acid as she choked out, "I do."

Narelki called out, "Tasinal's Mercy does not apply to her. This situation is unprecedented."

Kariana licked sweat from her lips. "Is there precedent for the removal of a ruler of Nihlos?" She asked as if it were a rhetorical question, but she honestly had no idea. It was just a die cast into the wind.

Narelki froze, considering the point.

Score!

Ariano glowered at Narelki. "There is no need for precedent where there is sufficient power and will."

Kariana didn't like the sound of that. "There *is* precedent for the *absence* of an emperor," she sighed. "And it's not good."

"You would compare yourself to Tasinal?" Prandil asked, shocked. "I am amazed at your arrogance, child. Even in defeat, you preen and strut. I think I may be in love!"

Kariana had an answer. Maralena had prepped her with any number of clever responses, though she hadn't expected them to be of much use. "'Arrogance is not merely the right, but the duty of a ruler.' So said Amrath." She stole a glance toward the Matriarch of House Prosin and couldn't help but smile at her obvious distress. *Please, have a stroke right here in the courtroom!*

Narelki inclined her head to stare down her nose at Kariana. "Quoting Amrath is far from *understanding* him," she said. "And it is unseemly, considering your recent attempt to murder his progeny."

"'The truth does not change, even when spoken by enemies,'" Kariana quoted again, grinning her hatred at Narelki and Maralena both, daring either Matriarch to take some foolish action. "Amrath's words are for everybody. You don't own them."

The raised platform creaked as Olemus Freth rose to speak. *Mei, it* is *a tent! I swear it!* "She is correct," he told them. "I care little for the politics here, only the practical results. The young people of Nihlos are quite fond of her antics, even if they hate her as a person. Kariana's appetites and behaviors have generated whole new industries. We may not have Meites battling in the streets, but we could certainly see economic chaos, perhaps even riots if she is deposed. It would be quite destructive."

Prandil scowled at Olemus. "You are a gutless worm."

Olemus shrugged at this. "You are the one who suggested putting her back on the throne."

"That was *before* she tried to kill us, idiot! Or did you take a lunch break and miss the exciting part?"

"Ah, I see," Olemus said defiantly. "You're some special kind of Meite, one without blood on his hands?"

Sadrina Veril put her fingers in her mouth and let loose with a piercing whistle. "Bravo! They're all wicked fiends!"

Prandil cast a genuinely murderous glare toward her. "The opinion of a mooning cow means nothing to me." He turned back to Olemus. "And as for you, I succeeded at any killing I ever got up to, and that is the crucial difference here."

Kariana could barely contain her elation. They were all at one another's throats. *Maybe they will kill each other! Wouldn't that be something?* "I submitted," she said. "I bow to your will! Can I not be forgiven like Aswan?"

Maranath sat back in his chair and regarded her with tired eyes. "Sparing your life is a far cry from returning a madwoman to power."

She had something perfectly calm and reasonable to say, but couldn't for the life of her remember it now. "Who, then, old man?" she shouted. "After your 'demonstration,' only a madwoman would *want* the job!"

Maranath sat in silence, a smile flickering about his lips.

Kariana leaped to her feet. *Here I go again. I really should make out a will sometime.* "Go on!" she shouted. "Say it! Kariana the stupid whore, good for nothing but being a lightning rod for assassins!" She walked to the judge's desk, stood in front of it, and turned back to the Elders on the platform. "My father groomed Theron for rule. I was supposed to be a princess! I was supposed to be beautiful and have beautiful things! I was never supposed to be anything more, and you *stole* it from me!" She swept her arm about the room, accusing them all with the gesture. She spun, laid both hands on the desk, and stared into Maranath's stormy blue eyes. "You put this crown on my head, and you *never* warned me how heavy it would be!" She stepped back, blinking against tears. *Not now!* But they were coming, and she swept them aside in fury and humiliation.

"You have no right to blame it all on me! You left me to sink! You never told me what to do, or why, or what it would cost! At least have the balls to admit it! None of you want the job. Who else besides me is stupid enough to take it?"

A stunned silence fell upon the elders. Prandil began to clap softly, and it seemed sincere. Maranath shook his head in admiration. "Touché, my dear," he conceded with a nod. He glanced about, noting that most seemed to agree. "If there are no objections, then, I return this courtroom to the Empress."

"I object," Ariano said, her voice almost a growl. "Her remorse is feigned, and she has no intention of wearing our yoke for long. We should kill her now, and deal with the consequences as they arise."

Kariana stamped her foot and spun toward the sorceress. "If I had *my* boot on *your* neck, would you feel any different?"

"No," Ariano conceded. "But mark my words, child. Defy this council again, and I will use your skin for a canvas and your blood for paint. Then, my dear, you'll once again exist only to be beautiful, and we can all be happy, hmm?"

Kariana felt a chill at this. Ariano meant every word, and she was more than capable of delivering on the promise. *She's the most dangerous person in the room.* Kariana swallowed a lump in her throat and nodded to the old sorceress. "It will never come to that."

Maranath rose from the desk and bowed, then ascended the platform and took his seat. Kariana looked up at them as she circled the desk to take back the judge's chair, and found herself gifted with a sudden insight. *They sit above me because they* are *above me. What a fool I have been.*

She knew she must look quite a fright, bloody and battered. Somehow, it still seemed a bit funny, though. She had managed to pull through, and she had even come out better than she had hoped. Aiul's fate had been torn from her hands, and for that she was grateful. "As you might imagine, I should like to end this meeting as soon as possible. Is there anything else we must address?"

To Kariana's dismay, Maralena rose, looking haggard but resolute. "There is one remaining matter. But I propose a recess so everyone can calm themselves before we continue. It is weighty, and we will want our wits about us. There has been far too much emotional behavior already."

Kariana nodded, relieved. She could kill for a chance to wash the blood off her face. She hammered her gavel against her desk. "So be it. Fifteen-minute recess."

Kariana wasted no time reaching a washbasin. She might have gone to her private chambers, but they were far away, and she settled for the court's public facilities. She splashed water in her face until it no longer ran pink, then examined her work in the mirror. Her lip felt enormous, but it didn't seem to show very much. A little makeup to cover scratches and bruises and things should be fine.

She saw Maralena approaching in the mirror and spun to face her, cursing herself for being foolish enough not to go somewhere more private. Maralena was not someone to whom she ever wanted to leave her back exposed again.

The Elder's face trembled and bubbled like water boiling in a pot. For a fleeting moment, Kariana though the stroke she had been predicting for the last hour had indeed come, but when had she ever been so lucky? When Maralena finally managed to speak, her voice was breathy and trembling with outrage. "You are *insane*!"

Kariana rolled her eyes, and answered in her best bubbly-girl voice, "If you just think of yourself as already dead, then you won't get that shaky sound in your voice." She blinked innocently at the hateful harridan for a moment, then let the pose drop. "The Southlander had the right of that," she growled.

Maralena's clenched and unclenched her fists. "This is no game! You've seen what they can do! You *must* stand with us!"

Oh, look at her trying to restrain herself! She wants to choke me so badly! But it would spoil her arguments. Kariana burst into laughter. "Stand with you to do what? We *failed*, in case you didn't notice the explosions and screams." She patted a towel to her swollen lip and winced, then spat blood on the white marble floor. "Of course, *I* was in a better position to appreciate the full extent of the carnage. Was that your plan, to get me killed?"

"You ruined my plan quite thoroughly," the elder replied, "and you earned the beating they gave you." She paused, daring Kariana to deny it. "Now listen to me. We can salvage things somewhat. If we cannot put Aiul to death, then we shall have his punishment given to his wife."

Kariana found herself simultaneously thrilled and repulsed at the notion. It was difficult not to relish the thought of Lara's death, but not so pleasant a thing to imagine being the cause of it. *I could get used to it, though. I think.* But doing Maralena's dirty work? That was a mouthful of piss. "Why?"

Maralena's face was calm now, with only the occasional twitch. "We cannot kill Narelki's son, but we can still drive a wedge between them. I can force her to side with us. When he learns she voted to have his wife put to death, perhaps he will kill her himself. Or perhaps he'll take his own life."

Kariana's eyes narrowed, and she laughed. "She didn't even flinch when I came at her with the dagger. How are you going to force her to do *anything*?"

"The same way I will deal with the Meites. By using her own values against her. Not everything needs to be resolved with a sledgehammer."

Kariana flashed the old woman a girlish smile. "It's much nicer with a sledgehammer, though. Fragile things make such lovely sounds when you crush them, don't you think?"

Maralena gaped at her. "You're as mad as the Meites!"

"Oh, spare me the superior act. If you weren't dead set on causing your own brand of destruction, you'd just expose Narelki for what she's already done. You're looking to draw some blood here, too, and you want it dripping with irony." She dabbed at her lip with the now red-spotted towel. "I'm surprised you didn't stand to defend her earlier. I almost spoiled your artful little vengeance piece, didn't I?"

Maralena raised an eyebrow. "Yes, I relish the irony, but that's hardly the only reason to do things this way. Frankly, it will cause you more pain, as well. I do not forget your part in Marissa's death. I am merely willing to overlook it to punish the party more responsible."

"And I have to make him hate me just as much, for siding with you!"

Maralena nodded. "It wouldn't make sense for you to do otherwise. He tried to kill you." She smiled, gloating in her victory. "But there is some small chance for you. When he finds out that it was his mother all along, he might even be able to forgive you."

Kariana smirked back at the Matriarch. "There's one problem I see with your plan."

Maralena tapped her foot impatiently. "What, pray tell, would that be?"

Kariana spat blood on the old woman's shoe, eliciting a screech of outrage from her. "I won't do it."

Maralena reached down as if to wipe the mess her shoe with her bare hand, but jerked her hand back before she actually made contact. "You'll do it, you little whore, or I'll expose you for murdering Marissa!"

"And expose yourself for treason!"

Maralena chuckled darkly. "Oh, no, not really. Certain evidence will turn up that will implicate you in Theron's death. We planted it soon after the fact, for just such a possibility. I'll claim we were watching you because we knew this all along. I'll walk away without a scratch, and you'll be disgraced. Perhaps they'll give you a cell next to Aiul so you can make cow eyes at him and suck his cock through the bars!"

Kariana barely restrained herself from attacking the old woman. She could take her, she knew that, but not now! There was one old woman in particular who she most definitely could *not* take, one who was looking for a pretense to make good on her threats. Killing Maralena now would be signing her own death warrant. She reached deep within herself and found enough will to stay her hand, but a low, bestial growl tore itself from her lips. "Bitch! This isn't over between us!"

Maralena snorted. "Oh, I suppose you think that's some great threat, but the truth is that it's never over, not until we're all dead. That's now Nihlos works. You'll get used to it."

Kariana said nothing as she tried to steady herself against the dizzying rage that she dared not express. *Oh, I don't think we both need to die for it to be over. Just you being dead should work fine.*

Once the council resumed, Maralena rose to speak. "Now that we are all calmer, we need to discuss something rather ugly. The political ramifications of these decisions cannot be ignored. Someone must pay as a traitor for the assault on Tasinalta, not because she is loved, but because the leader of Nihlos cannot be perceived as weak, or chaos will ensue."

Prandil laughed out loud. "Oh, my, you're so terribly dramatic, Maralena!"

Maralena gave Prandil a condescending look. "You may know sorcery, but you spend your life in an ivory tower. You have the luxury of dealing with people by swinging a sledgehammer at their heads. You know *nothing* about human nature. The people will demand someone suffer for this."

Prandil touched a finger to his chin and grinned like an imp. "It was my understanding that most of them would rejoice in her passing."

Maralena shrugged. "Probably true, but irrelevant. A crime against the Empress is a crime against them. She is a symbol, else why maintain this charade? They will say, 'If Tasinalta cannot protect herself, how can she protect Nihlos?' They *know* Southlanders have entered the city. How long do you think it will take them to go from panic to rebellion?"

Narelki nodded her agreement. "It is as she says. This is almost a direct quote from the Book of Amrath."

The other elders were in general agreement. Polus, as usual, chose to ask the difficult question. "A lovely sentiment, but whom exactly do you propose to execute?"

Maralena took a deep breath and let it out again, slowly, dramatically, a look of deep disquiet on her face. "You won't like my answer, but it's the only one I have. There are a number of parameters to be met. Someone close to him, someone who may well have conspired with him, so that the public will believe justice is being done." She paced back and forth on the platform, looking at each of them, as if she were actually thinking on the matter. "Someone whose loss he will feel keenly because it is part of his punishment. Someone unhoused, and thus not subject to Tasinal's Mercy." She took another deep breath, then let the words tumble out of her. "I propose Lara, Aiul's wife."

Time seemed to freeze for a moment as the Elders sat in dumbfounded silence. At last, Maranath broke the quiet. "You are mad."

Maralena eyed him with a cool gaze. "I am practical, Meite. That's supposed to be one of your virtues."

Maranath rose to his feet. "She carries House Amrath's name!"

"Irrelevant. She is not of noble blood."

Maranath shouted, "Nobility be damned! A name given cannot be taken back!" He looked to Narelki for support but found little there to aid him. He stared at her a moment, then called, "Narelki."

The Matriarch of House Amrath was ashen, as if she were suddenly very ill. "It is a gray area."

Maralena sighed. "No, it is not a gray area at all. There are several precedents. One of them even involves *you*, Narelki. You had a husband put to death, as I recall."

Narelki's icy manner shattered; eyes burning with rage, she answered. "A *former* husband, who tried to force his way back into my bed and my life! He did not bear the name Amrath."

"I beg to differ," Maralena said coolly. "As Maranath noted, there is no provision whatsoever for stripping a house name from anyone. Even Aiul runs no risk of that. Perhaps it was your convention that he no longer use yours, but it was not a matter of law. There is precedent for what I propose."

Narelki rose to her feet, her face twisting in fury. "Executing a rapist is hardly the same as executing an innocent!"

Maralena failed to suppress a giggle, then covered her mouth with her hand, looking embarrassed. "No one is innocent."

Ariano sighed and joined the debate. "Even if we accept this line of argument, she bears his child. There can be no question that the child carries noble blood."

Kariana grunted. "Oh, I assure you, there can be plenty of questions. A noble father, a common mother, things are *never* settled."

Maralena nodded. "And in any event, the child is unborn, hence unnamed."

Prandil, too, had heard enough. "So you would have all of us participate in your fantasy that because the child is unborn, it is somehow not real? You and our empress share a remarkable ability to retreat into self-delusion at will!"

Maralena was unmoved. "Again, I note that there is *ample* precedent. Unborn children are not protected by the law. Many a noble woman has aborted an unwanted pregnancy with herbs or surgery, and they were not treated as murderers. Aiul *himself* has performed such surgeries. How can anyone argue otherwise?"

Polus nodded, seemingly despite his inclinations. "You know the law well, Maralena."

Maranath bristled at this. "She twists precedent to serve her ends! Those are early pregnancies. Aiul's child is nearly born!"

Maralena shrugged. "It matters not. This is a point of law, not vague morality. And we waste our breath in pointless arguing. We're not going to change one another's minds, are we?"

Maranath raised a hand for calm as murmurs erupted. "Aye, enough of this mental masturbation. Is there even a second?"

Kariana sighed. "As much as I don't like it, I am forced to agree." *There. Quite literally true.* "I second."

Maralena called out, "Then let us vote. Empress?"

Before Kariana could speak, Maranath raised his cane overhead, then slammed it against the floor. "Opposed!" Ariano and Prandil followed suit immediately. Lucreta and Davron also raised their hands.

Kariana officially noted the vote. "Five opposed."

Maklin, still scribbling furiously in his notebook, cleared his throat and called out, "Just a moment, I will vote against you. I vote that we put you to death. I just need…one…more…*there*." His hand shot up, and he grinned innocently at her.

Kariana couldn't actually muster any ill will toward the old fellow, Meite or not. "Noted. Go on with your work."

"Thank you, Empress."

Maranath stared at Narelki. "Narelki! Will you not stand for your own blood?"

Narelki's haunted eyes brimmed with tears as she looked about the courtroom, but she did not rise.

Kariana waited for several moments, then announced in a deadpan, "Six opposed, and one side vote to have me put to death. In favor?"

Prandil snickered. "Of having you put to death?" He raised a hand.

Kariana rolled her eyes. "Oh, I think that matter needs a second and a vote of its own. We have procedures for a reason."

Prandil's grin had turned positively lascivious. *Odd. I should think he would hate me now.*

Kariana raised her own hand. "Well?" Maralena raised her hand. Polus and Olemus also raised theirs in support, followed by Narelki.

Ariano shouted "Faithless bitch!" and started toward Narelki, but Maranath put a hand on her shoulder to restrain her. "Pathetic weakling! We should have killed you the moment we saw your taint!"

Narelki refused to meet Ariano's gaze. "Amrath cursed hypocrisy above all else," she said, her voice barely above a whisper.

"It is not hypocrisy to change your mind!"

Narelki smiled sadly. "I have not changed my mind. I would change nothing I have done."

"A lie for these fools benefit," Ariano declared. "We know the truth. Have a care, Narelki, there are things you don't know that will speed the poison in your soul!"

Maranath turned to Narelki. "A minor inconsistency moves you to abandon your own blood? You are worse than faithless. You are a slave. But we knew that already, didn't we?"

Prandil cleared his throat. "Maranath, that's enough, I think."

Maranath responded with a grunt and turned away. "The level of cowardice in this chamber astounds me. We should never have allowed any but Mei's loyal to stand as Elders!" he fumed.

Sadrina sat in silence, eyes brimming with mischief.

"Choose carefully, Sadrina," Ariano said, her eyes boring into the lone holdout.

Sadrina smirked, obviously pleased with herself. "Why should I? Have I something to fear from you?" She giggled. "You and your kind are nothing but bullies, flexing your muscles whenever you choose, sneering at the rest of us as if we were children."

Narelki spun toward her. "Shut your mouth, fool!"

Sadrina was not inclined to be obedient. "I have been silent this whole affair! Now, I hold the power. I will speak my mind!" She rose her feet, her fiery red hair seeming to bristle.

Ariano clenched her fists in frustration. "You stumble blindly into things you cannot possibly appreciate! There are dark forces that *hunger* for men of will, men who have lost everything! It is madness to create such monsters! Why else do you imagine a tyrant like Tasinal would stay his hand?"

Sadrina sneered. "Please! I have listened to you fools spout about invisible gods and demonic forces since I was born. There is no denying you have power, but I see no special enlightenment in you."

"How can one as blind as you expect to see anything?"

"Go on, witch! Tell the rest of your fairytale, so we can all laugh at you."

Polus stamped a boot on the floor. "You humiliate us all, Sadrina, with your petty jealousy."

"You are a fool, Sadrina" Ariano declared. "The Dead God has *always* lurked, waiting for the right moment. The Fallen prophesied his return long ago! Amrath wrote of it in his book!"

"Amrath is dead, as are all the other founders!" Sadrina shouted. "And they were superstitious fools! There are no gods."

Prandil said, in a soft, menacing voice, "It would be the height of irony to see Tasinal return and rip your traitor's heart from your breast."

"Ignore their threats," Kariana said. "With your vote, I will be empowered to break a tie. You will be on the victorious side."

Sadrina jammed her hand into the air, glaring at the Meites. "I care nothing for the outcome, here!" she told them. "I simply stand against you and your bullying!"

"Then die for your pride!" Ariano shrieked, her voice once again multi-harmonic. Maranath and Prandil, however, sensing her intent, moved to restrain her, hauling on her arms to stop her.

"Bitch!" Ariano shrieked. A missile of glassy, pointed sound shot from her mouth and penetrated the wall inches from Sadrina's head, leaving a smoking crater the size of a man's fist. Sadrina screamed in terror as Maranath and Prandil struggled to restrain Ariano.

"Control yourself!" Maranath shouted.

After a few moments, Ariano calmed enough to allow Maranath and Prandil to guide her to her seat, where she sat in grim silence, staring into space.

Maralena waited until everyone seemed ready to move on, then cleared her throat and spoke. Seeming secure in her victory now, she put on a magnanimous pose. "I understand it is an emotional issue, for some, but it is settled now unless the Meites intend to destroy a thousand years of tradition and defy the council."

Prandil cracked his knuckles and cast a withering glare at her. "If that were our intent, we would have simply done away with you out of hand."

Do I dare? Oh, who am I kidding? Of course, I dare. Kariana cleared her throat and rose. "There is one tiny matter of procedure. The vote is a tie. I do still need to cast the tie-breaking decision." She blinked innocently at the other councilmembers. "Just to be official."

Prandil looked quizzically at her. "Ah, yes," he crooned. "That procedure thing. Just to be official, hmm?"

Kariana offered him a wicked grin. *He knows. I don't know how, but he's figured it out.* She'd made a bargain to vote with Maralena. She'd said nothing about breaking any ties. *You shouldn't have pushed me, bitch. I would have been on your side if you hadn't.* "I have reconsidered my position. I vote to break the tie in favor of the opposed."

The courtroom erupted with shouts of surprise, some of victory, others of defeat. *Such lovely chaos.* Kariana felt herself slipping into near delirium. She felt as if she could pass out. Maralena was right. The irony was quite delicious.

Maralena and Sadrina were looking at her, fury and terror in their eyes. Kariana leered back at them, drinking up their fear. She sat back in her chair, feeling pleased with herself.

She noticed the old woman, Ariano, looking at her. They locked gaze for a moment, and the old woman flashed her a faint smile, a nod of recognition. There was something terribly familiar in those green eyes of hers.

And something terribly, frighteningly young.

CHAPTER 10

FALLOUT

SANDILIANUS woke with a start. Someone had opened the cell door. Was it morning so soon? He was surprised to see not the stern, square face of his hateful guard, Caelwen, but the wrinkled features and burning green eyes of the sorceress Ariano. Prandil and Maranath stood behind her.

Sandilianus leaped to his feet and stood at attention. They were enemies, true, but they had honored him. He would return their respect.

Maranath waved him off. "Relax, Southlander. This is no courtroom. Sit."

Sandilianus assumed a parade rest stance, spreading his legs and clasping his hands behind his back.

Maranath grunted at this, then shuffled past him to take a seat on the tiny cot that filled most of the cell. "Fine, I'll sit, then. We are too old to be so formal. We have some questions."

I am surrounded now. He pressed his back against the wall, facing them all as well as he could, and said, "I am Sandilianus Abu al Khayr, Centurion in Prince Philip's legions, serving under Tribune Brutus Samir, and loyal servant to Ilaweh. I can say no more."

Maranath was picking at something on his robe and didn't bother to look up when he spoke. "Oh, don't think for a moment that we lack ways of changing that. It's just that we were hoping not to have to resort to them."

"I do not fear torture."

"Well, I certainly fear watching it. So let's spare me the grief, shall we?"

Sandilianus shook his head in consternation. These were very strange people. "A soldier does not give information to the enemy!"

Prandil's eyes grew bright, and a broad grin spread on his lips. "Then our problem is solved!" He raised both hands, showing he had no weapon. "We're not here as enemies, Southlander. At least *hear* our questions before you refuse to answer, hmm? Where are your manners?"

Sandilianus looked back and forth at them, weighing their expressions, but if they had ulterior motives, they hid them well. "What kind of questions?"

Ariano offered him no smile at all. "Religious questions. You are not barred from speaking about your religion with 'enemies,' are you?"

Sandilianus considered a moment, trying to gauge their sincerity. There were plenty of ways an enemy might try to trick information from him. "You are not believers. You are kafir."

Prandil's humor vanished as quickly as it had come, his gaze as intense as Ariano's now. "Oh, that is where you are wrong, Southlander. We are very much believers."

Maranath laid back on the bed and shifted about, testing it for comfort that his grimace said he did not find. "There are few of us left in Nihlos. This city is weak, as your eyes have seen, and she grows weaker with each passing day. We rot from within."

Ariano stepped toward Sandilianus, her green eyes almost hypnotic as she looked up at him. She gazed at him a moment before asking, "Why came you here, Southlander? In the court-room, you said you followed a holy man seeking an ancient evil. Had it to do with a prophecy? A prophecy of *Elgar*?"

Sandilianus tried to hide his shock, but he could feel his eyes widening. The three sorcerers nodded at one another, satisfied, and Sandilianus cursed himself for a fool. They had pried infor-mation from him, even though he had not spoken! *These sorcerers have a powerful presence. I must take care they do not charm me.*

Ariano pressed closer. "What do you know of it?" Sandilianus forced his face into a stone mask, refusing to give away anything else, but she was having none of it. She poked a bony finger at his chest. "Fool! You know full well that we are not interested in military information. This is larger than all of us, and you have pieces of the puzzle we lack!"

Sandilianus licked his lips, uncertain of what was acceptable to say. "Why do you need to know this? You sound like Yazid."

Prandil nodded. "With good reason. We've read a summary of Tasinalta's interrogation, though we've no idea how much is true. Yazid stepped forward as your commander, but he claimed no military title. A non-combatant, then?"

They were getting to him. Did it even matter if they did? What damaging information could he even reveal? Xanthia could crush this city at will. Any information he could possibly reveal would simply make them more aware of that, and was it not good for an enemy to fear? "There are no Xanthians who do not fight."

Ariano's eyes grew wide at this. She gasped and stepped back. "No civilians? Even children?"

"I do not remember a time that I did not carry a sword," he answered with a shrug.

Prandil shot Ariano a glare, then turned back to Sandilianus. "This Yazid, he called himself Prelate. What is a prelate to you?"

Sandilianus found himself at a loss for words. A prelate was, well, a prelate, but what exactly did the word mean when it came right down to it? "Prelates fight for Ilaweh directly. They do not recognize earthly authority."

Maranath sat up on the bed, a broad grin of triumph on his face. "I told you it was religious."

Ariano's eyes brimmed with curiosity. "Free wandering holy men," she mused. "Have you organized structures, churches and temples, or is it all informal?"

Prandil snapped his fingers briskly. "Can we please save the anthropology studies for later? If you really need to know all of this, then go with him when we release him. We need to hear what he knows of the prophecy!"

Release? Sandilianus eyed Prandil, trying to decide if the comment was a genuine slip or a clever ruse. Their arguing certainly seemed very natural, as if it were their normal method of relating to one another. "What do you mean by that? I am to die in the morning."

Ariano swung a fist to punch Prandil in the shoulder, but he dodged the blow and grinned at her. She seemed in no mood for humor, though, and for a moment Sandilianus thought she might resort to something more violent, but Maranath intervened, rapping his cane on the floor with a loud crack. The entire cell shuddered, and dust filtered down from the ceiling. He scowled at them a moment, then offered Sandilianus a grin. "I see we once again have your attention."

"You have a talent for that, sir, there is no doubt."

Maranath said. "I had intended to present it with a bit more lead up, but yes, that is our intent. We need people to *believe* you were killed, but as for the actual killing, it doesn't much matter."

Ariano shot Prandil a final glare, then turned back to Sandilianus. "You are here about an ancient darkness, yes? We need not be enemies, Southlander. We are, in fact, quite natural *allies* for your cause."

Sandilianus nodded. "Yazid had done much research. I am just a soldier, so I don't pretend to know the whole of it, but I know what he told us." Sandilianus hesitated, still uncertain as to whether telling the Meites his mission would be a betrayal. The Meites said nothing, giving him time to decide. "There is a prophecy," he said at last. "Made by Carsogenicus."

Prandil waved a hand in a circling motion, gesturing for him to continue. "Odio Sinistera, the Left Hand of Hate. We know him. Go on."

"Xanthius and Amrath had him burned at the stake for his evil. It is said that as the flesh melted from his bones, he laughed and prophesied until he was nothing but ash. One of the prophecies was that Elgar would, a thousand years hence, walk the earth, and his scion would rise from the blood of Tasinal, in the city of nothing."

"Built on nothing," Prandil murmured, his eyes clouded and distant.

Maranath nodded. "Tasinalta."

Ariano's eyes glittered with purpose. "We must slay her at once."

"We dare not!" Prandil exclaimed. "Not without knowing the details!"

"Indeed," Maranath said. "It could be that her death at our hands is a necessary component of some ritual. The Fallen would have found such a thing the height of wit."

"Then what do we do?" Ariano asked.

Maranath rose to his feet. "We watch her. And we wait. We thank you for your tale, Southlander." He rose from the cot and turned to the others. "Shall we release him?"

Ariano seemed far away in her mind as she answered. "How can we not? If we fail here, his people would be the last bastion."

Maranath nodded. "Do you understand what we are saying, Southlander?"

"Aye," Sandilianus said. "The enemy of my enemy is my friend. And who is not Elgar's enemy?"

"Just so. Now, as for *your* fate, we'll need another corpse to show in your place. I presume you've no problem if we substitute one of your fellows? No one here will be able to tell the difference."

Sandilianus smiled. "It honors the dead to allow them to save a life."

"Well said. Now, be patient and wait here. Old men walk slowly, but we'll have you on your way in an hour or so."

Maralena Prosin sat at her desk in her study. It was an austere place, almost monastic, her one concession to a world where everything else must be dressed up with artifice. Here, in her private place, the world was true, a place without lies, deception, or vanity.

She poured a stiff drink and leaned back in her chair, considering. The liquor burned in a pleasant way, as opposed to the acidic sting of her humiliation in court.

At some other time, Maralena would have shrugged it off as simply business. She would have set to work looking to repair the damage, to gain leverage, to find new handholds.

She would have held no grudges. Grudges were for fools. They were barriers to seizing opportunities. Vengeance was not something she had ever had the inclination, much less the luxury, of indulging.

But this was different, somehow. Perhaps it was because she had so favored poor Marissa. Yet she had weathered similar losses in the past and maintained her composure. One did not play at power. Blood was occasionally spilled, often enough one's own.

No, it was something else entirely, something so trivial that looking directly at it was decidedly unpleasant. It was no monumental thing at all that made Maralena cast practicality aside. It was nothing more than the tone of Tasinalta's voice, the sight of her petulant smirk, a childish, petty thing to which Maralena had, until now, fancied herself far above.

But it burned like acid, and it would have to be addressed.

Maralena took up a quill, dipped it in ink, and began to write.

Lara:

You do not know me, and I offer you no name, but I am a good man, and I see much. Know that your husband is not truly imprisoned. He is where he is by his own choice, the better to spend all of his time with Tasinalta. It is a cruel game they play with you, and I will no longer stand by and watch. It is my duty to intervene.

She admired her handiwork for a moment. It was difficult to be certain if the words matched the pattern of a man who rarely spoke his mind, and yet if she could not tell, no one else could, either.

She had no idea how it would play out. She was merely lobbing a bomb into a crowd. Whatever the result, it should be quite explosive. For the moment, that was just fine.

She set the letter aside, dipped her pen, and began another.

Kariana had some trouble giving Caelwen the slip, but for all his vaunted duty, he was still human. She simply waited until nature called, and then fled. No doubt, he was furious and frantic, and he would certainly locate her before long. How long, she didn't know, which made time of the essence.

Negotiating House Noril had been surprisingly easy. She had

expected a chilly reception or an outright refusal, but the slaves had ushered her in without comment. Davron himself had nodded as she passed, as if they were actually on good terms. *He must have visited his goat.* She was lucky that Maranath had remanded the prisoners to House Noril rather than House Luvox, or this would have been a much more difficult proposition.

House Noril's 'holding facilities' turned out to be little more than a section of the manse with doors that could be secured. A single guard stood outside a heavy door. Kariana eyed him as she approached. He seemed strong enough but fairly bored. *Well, it's not as if Aiul is such a threat, but the Southlander might escape at any moment.* She shuddered at the thought, took a deep breath, and approached the guard. "I'm here to see the traitor."

The guard's bored expression did not change as he handed her a logbook. "All visitors must sign in."

Kariana could not help but notice the signatures just above her own. The Meites had been here within the hour. Why? She filed the point of information away for later. She would find out soon enough. She scribbled something unintelligible. No need to duplicate their mistake, after all.

The guard accepted the log, then took keys from his belt and unlocked the door. For a brief moment, Kariana feared he intended to come with her, but he swung the door open and went back to his station. "Scream if you need help," he said with a laugh.

Kariana sneered at him and said, "I'll do that." She began to count in her head just how many times she had made a fool of herself of late. *I don't think numbers go that high.* Of course, the previous times she had at least *imagined* she had the right of it. This? This was idiocy. This was some kind of trick. How could it not be? It was simply too much to hope for.

She reached into her pocket and clutched the letter it contained as if it were a talisman, giddy with the possibilities, but all too wary of a trap. She didn't need to read it again to feel its power. After at least twenty readings, she knew it by heart.

It is not that I could not love you, but that I have my pride. You cannot shame me so in public and expect me to submit to you. If I must bend a knee, let me do it without cruel eyes upon me.

It seemed impossible that the letter could be real. Nothing she really wanted ever worked out for her, certainly not since being forced onto the throne. Yet, here she stood, without Caelwen's 'cruel eyes,' or anyone else's for that matter, chasing a miracle she barely believed. She had been humiliated enough for several lifetimes and was in real danger of it happening again within minutes. How could she blame anyone for wanting to avoid it? It was horrible.

She stepped warily toward the door. *What if the Southlander has escaped somehow, and is waiting behind that door for me?* She stepped back, terrified. "Are you *certain* the Southlander can't get out?"

The guard gave her a quizzical look. "I am certain you are in no danger from him."

"How can you be when you don't even check?"

The guard laughed aloud. "Because he is already dead."

Kariana blinked in surprise. "Good. I thought it was tomorrow."

The guard nodded sagely. "That's the way of executions, Empress. Surprise often means less trouble."

It was good news, but she found herself still wary of entering. Perhaps the truth of it was that her fear of the Southlander was simply a convenient excuse to avoid the real issue. She took a deep breath and let it out slowly, ignoring the guard's quiet amusement, and stepped in.

Kariana found it difficult to think of the area as a prison. It was really just a brick hallway with four doors, two on each side, that could be secured from without, a bit utilitarian, but then, so was the rest of House Noril. Polished brass lamps illuminated several paintings lining the walls, the centerpiece a portrait of Noril himself. The four cell doors were solid enough and had slots at eye and waist level.

She tried to peer through one of the top slots, only to find, to her chagrin, that she was too short to see through the top slot. She hesitated, trying to decide if she could bear the indignity of being on her knees again this day. Was she really going to go kneeling and peeping through each tray slot, searching for Aiul like a lovesick schoolgirl?

He spared her that, at least, calling out from the far end of the hallway, his voice tired, defeated. "Why are you here?"

Kariana stammered a moment, fingering the note in her pocket again, trying to draw some strength from it. She stepped quickly to the door of his cell and knelt at the lower slot, only to find herself staring at his crotch. Maralena's taunts flickered like gadflies in her mind, and she struggled against tears. Her voice cracked as she choked out, "I got your letter. I came like you asked."

"I sent no letter."

Kariana blinked at hot tears, glad now that it was not his eyes on the other side. A trick, then, and a cruel one. *I knew that all along, though. I just had to be certain.* "Is that true? Someone else sent it, or did you do it to toy with me?"

Aiul sighed and settled to the floor on the other side of the sturdy door. He looked out at her, his green eyes not angry or cold, but simply sad. "No. It wasn't me. Why would I ask you to come here, Kariana? We are at war, now."

Kariana couldn't contain her grief. A sob burst from her, and she lay her head against the door for support. "Must it be so?" she choked. "Why can't we just forget about everything? Tasinal,

Amrath, Aswan, all of them, they fought one another like beasts at times, and they got past things. Why can't *we*?"

Aiul slammed a fist against the door. It was solid enough that she didn't even feel the blow, but the sound was enough to make her spring back. When she looked through the slot again, he had bowed his head and covered his eyes with his hand. "Too much has passed."

"It wasn't *me*, Aiul! I swear it! It *wasn't*!"

Aiul lowered his hand and stared at her, considering. "You swore before Mei you would kill us both."

"But it was just *words*! You said it yourself, I was out of my head! I didn't mean it!"

"And someone just happened to attack Lara just after that." He glared at her through the slot, but he seemed less certain, for all his display.

Yes! Someone *willing to frame me with her crime because she so disapproves of her son marrying a commoner!*

But the truth would undo any progress she had made with him. He would never believe her. He would accuse her of being a monster to try to turn him against his own mother. Better to seem stupid. At least it was what was expected of her so it would ring true. "Yes."

Aiul's glare softened. "I don't believe you. I want to, I really do, for what we had long ago. But I *can't*. Do you understand?"

Kariana laid her head against the door again and wept softly. "I won't accept it!"

"What was it that cocky bastard Prandil told Maralena?" Aiul asked. "'You can retreat into self-delusion at will'?" He laughed softly.

Kariana giggled through her tears. "It's all I have. I'd be dead if I just accepted things."

"Yes, Kariana, I think you would."

Kariana sniffled. "I know." She looked at his beautiful eyes through the slot again, not trying to hide her emotion anymore. "Will you at least try to believe me?"

Aiul's eyes narrowed. "You are empress, Kariana. You have much power, as you are just beginning to see. If it is as you say, you can use that power to find the real culprit. Have your man Caelwen bring him to me with his proof. We both know that statue would rather be buried alive than frame an innocent man. Do that, and I'll bend a knee to you before all Nihlos."

"That's not what I wanted. That was the elders. I just want you to believe me. And one other thing."

Aiul said nothing, merely waited for her to continue.

Kariana took a deep breath. "I want you to tell me the truth."

"What truth?"

"That you loved me then, and you still do. Don't you dare mock Caelwen for his 'duty and honor' when you stand on the same ceremony."

Aiul turned away quickly, but not before she caught the trapped look in his eyes. "I don't know what you're talking about."

"Yes, you do. I've taken enough men to my bed to know the difference between one doing his duty and one who wants to be there. It came back to you, just like it came back to me."

Aiul slammed his fist against the door again, but this time she didn't flinch. He turned away, refusing to meet her gaze, his jaw clenched. "I'm *married*!"

"I'm not asking you to leave her. I'm not asking you to be with me. I just want to hear you say it."

Aiul remained silent for long moments. When, at last, he spoke, his voice was husky with emotion. "Prove your truth to me. Then we'll talk of mine."

Lara stood at the door to the prison, trembling with rage. How stupid could they be? They were in a prison! It was designed for voices to carry! Or perhaps they had grown so bold they no longer cared if the guard heard. If it hadn't been for her 'anonymous' friend, there would be nothing to fear, would there?

It was true. All true. What a fool she had been!

The guard laid a hand on her shoulder. "I think you should come back some other time, madam. This can't end well."

Lara ground her teeth in fury, and nodded. "I guess you're right." She eyed the heavy brass candlestick that hung by the door. "Could you help me with my bag? I'm feeling a little dizzy. It's the pregnancy."

The guard nodded, offering her a sympathetic smile, and bent to pick up her bag. Lara reached up, snatched the candlestick from the wall and crashed it against his head, sending him to the ground in a heap. The candle, still lit, flew across the room, bounced off the wall, and spun furiously on the stone floor before settling.

She bent to retrieve his keys. There was a lot of blood. Was he breathing? She decided she didn't much care. One murder, two, or three? What did it matter? She unlocked the door and stepped into the hallway, clutching the candlestick like a lifeline. She imagined how it would feel as it crashed into Tasinalta's skull, the sound it would make, like an overripe melon being dropped on the floor.

She smiled darkly as she closed the door behind her. No guards would be interrupting this dance.

She wanted Tasinalta all to herself.

Kariana knew something was wrong as soon as she heard the door open. She didn't know what, precisely, but it was bad. No one should be here. Suddenly, she regretted ditching Caelwen. Someone had forged the letter from Aiul. Perhaps it *was* a trap.

Aiul's eyes cut toward the door. "Who is it?"

Oh, no! No! No!

He could see the look on her face, she was certain of it. His eyes grew wide. *"Who is it?"*

Lara, dressed in a simple nightgown, her belly large with child, held the candlestick high, like a headsman's ax. She wore a cruel, sidelong smile, and her eyes glittered with madness, malice, and murder. "Your man gave you up, whore! Did you think I wouldn't find out?"

Kariana blinked in confusion. "Find out what?"

Aiul pounded vainly against the door. "Lara! It's not what you think!"

A cruel laugh burst from Lara, short, almost a bark. "You don't even know what I think."

It would have been nice to talk, to work things out but Lara was apparently in no mood. Without warning, she rushed Kariana, swinging the candlestick. Kariana threw up her hands to shield her head, a little too late to fully block the blow, but enough to blunt it. Pain ripped her, poured on the crown of her skull and rolled down her face like molten lead, hot, heavy, liquid. She noted with detachment that, as much as it hurt, it was all very confusing. *Attacking first definitely has enormous advantages.*

Aiul was screaming something, but it was muffled. Kariana couldn't be certain what, and did it matter? This had, in fact, all been a trap, hadn't it? The two of them cooked it up together. Get her here, then have the pregnant woman finish the job and claim she was mad with raging hormones or something. Probably, Narelki would even defend her against the charges. Such irony.

Lara seemed to be moving in slow motion, spittle flying from her lips as she screamed incoherently, no words, just sounds of blind fury. Her face was so contorted with rage that she looked demonic. *Or maybe that's just the blow to my head.* The candle-stick was gone. Kariana felt hands tightening around her throat, and motion, and heard a clunking sound. *Oh, that would be your head impacting against the floor, fool.*

She wondered how it was going to feel to die. It would have been nice to fight back, but her body wasn't cooperating. Even if it had, she was outmatched. Lara was no old woman or soft little spy from House Prosin. She was half again Kariana's size, and hard, a commoner who likely had to fight often as a child. *She's probably killed dozens.*

It was instinct rather than thought that sent her hand snaking into her blouse once again for Sadrik's dagger. Black spots danced before her eyes as the last of her breath burned out in her veins. Her hands seemed to act of their own accord, clumsy, the dagger blade pointing in the wrong direction as she brought it to Lara's throat. Lara leered down at her, triumphant, spittle still dripping from her mouth, now a ravenous maw.

Fine. I can adapt. With the last of her strength, Kariana hammered the butt of the dagger into the bridge of Lara's nose, once, twice, three times. *I must remember to thank Sadrik again for this. It's the most useful gift I've ever received.*

Her vision had faded to full black by now, but the hands around her throat fell away. Kariana sucked in air in great gasps, blind. She had no idea where Lara was, no idea if her vision would even return.

Kariana shivered in fear, waiting for the next blow.

It all happened so quickly that Aiul could barely make sense of it. Lara was out of her head, raving. She hit Kariana with a candle-stick and then started choking her. Kariana hit Lara with something. They were both reeling now, both bleeding. It didn't look too bad, though.

Aiul kicked at the door with all his might, but it was useless. "Stop it, both of you!"

Lara groaned in pain and struggled to her feet. She wiped the blood from her lips with the back of her hand and growled like a dog.

Kariana was clearly having difficulty seeing, and she was gasping and heaving, trying to catch her breath. She turned toward the sound of Lara's voice and slashed the air with a small knife. Where had that come from?

Aiul pounded his fist against the door again. "Don't do this! It's *madness*!"

They circled one another slowly, Kariana trying to buy time while her vision and breath returned. Lara seemed to sense this and charged headlong into a vicious slash. The knife cut through her thigh, drawing a stream of blood, but Lara didn't seem to notice. She tackled Kariana with her full weight and bore the tiny woman to the floor beneath her, one hand reaching for the knife, the other scrambling across Kariana's face, fingers clawing at eyes like a crab pinching its prey.

Kariana bit at Lara's hand and somehow managed to wriggle out from beneath her. It was both hands for both women now as they fought over the weapon, screaming, rolling about the floor, hissing, spitting. Sometimes, Lara had control of the knife, at other times, Kariana. Blood flew each time the weapon changed hands. The floor grew slick with it, and the air reeked of copper and sweat.

Aiul screamed at them to stop, his voice growing ragged, but it was useless. He had no part in this play. He was simply a captive audience. His words, like theirs, lost all sense of meaning, became nothing but sounds expressing fear, rage, and denial, a song of conflict, struggle, and loss.

They all sang, all danced to the savage tune. Aiul hammered himself against the door over and over, his shoulders, his feet, his fists, his head. There was blood here now, too, inside, as he grew more frantic. He felt his own bones crack under the impact. Flame filled his throat, his heart, his mind, but he had no power to change anything.

So much pain, and yet he was numb when the moment came. Their struggles, their flailing and rolling on the floor, was the cast of a die. It tumbled. They tumbled. Over and over. Six. Two. Five. One.

Kariana. Lara. Kariana. Lara. Lara.

Kariana was on top when the die came to rest. Aiul could no longer move or scream. He simply watched as she raised the wicked blade high and plunged it into Lara's chest.

He could have understood this. He truly could have. Kariana was in stark, raving terror, mortal fear. Lara had tried to murder her. It was only natural that she defend herself. He could have forgiven the first stab. Even the second. They were terrible wounds, and to his eye, likely mortal, but there was a chance. If nothing else, perhaps he could save their child.

But he could not forgive the third or the fourth. Or the twentieth. Lara was long dead, and his child as well, and still Kariana stabbed at them.

Numb. He knew the pain was there. He could find it, if he focused, agony of body and of soul, yet he was distracted. There was a noise in his mind, in his ears, an odd sound that he couldn't place. It grew louder and more insistent, drawing his attention away from Kariana's madness.

For all the world, it sounded like crows.

Caelwen ground his teeth as the slave from House Noril fumbled with the prison door key. Kariana was still screaming, struggling with someone. He could wait no longer. He snatched the key from the slave and shoved him aside. "Give me that, idiot!"

The slave staggered backward and tripped over the corpse of the prison guard. He raised a sticky, crimson hand from the floor and wailed in horror.

"Shut up with that mewling!" Caelwen shouted as he turned the key in the lock and swung the door open. "Go and tell my men I've found her and to come at once!"

The slave was only too happy to beat a hasty retreat. Caelwen looked about for a doorstop, found none, and settled for dragging the dead guard against the heavy door. He had no intention of being locked in, and this fellow could hardly complain. Caelwen drew his sword and charged into the hallway.

He didn't get far before he realized that, whatever had passed here, it was over. Tasinalta was the victor, but she was severely wounded. There was blood everywhere, and Tasinalta was still stabbing at her victim's mangled corpse. He felt his gut twist in horror as he recognized Lara.

He slid his blade back into its scabbard as he approached. Tasinalta looked up at him with mad eyes, barely recognizing him, but she slowed and then stopped her arm. Her hair and face were crusted with drying blood. Pink foam bubbled from her lips and ran down her chin.

Caelwen reached out a hand. "Empress, let me help you."

Tasinalta's eyes narrowed "Assassins!" she shrieked. "Assassins everywhere!"

She sprung toward him, stabbing at him with the dagger, but his mail turned her blows well enough. He grabbed her flailing arms and pinned them to her sides. "Enough! You are safe now!"

She seemed not to hear him. She was struggling so violently, she was certain to injure herself. He had little choice. He brought his fist up in a swift strike to her jaw, and she immediately collapsed. Choice or no, he had to admit, it was hardly unpleasant.

"Mei," he cursed. "What have you done now?"

"Come to me, boy."

Ahmed heard the voice, but he did not feel like responding. He continued to dig in the sand with his toy shovel, insolent and rebellious. The sun beat down, it's heat intense on the top of his head, but it pleased him to ignore it.

"Come to me now*!"*

Ahmed threw the shovel down and folded his arms across his chest. "No. I am busy."

Pain exploded in his ear as a fist struck the side of his head.

"I did not ask you, boy. I commanded you."

Angry, Ahmed clutched a hand to the side of his head and looked up and up. Yazid stood over him, glowering, ten feet tall, twenty, maybe even a hundred. How could a boy know? About them burned the desert, wind blowing fiercely, sand stinging his skin. The sands extended to the horizon, unbroken by buildings, trees, or water.

Yazid reached down, a glowing blade that burned like flame in his outstretched hand. *"Take it."*

Ahmed refused. "I am too small. I cannot use a man's sword!"

"You will take it, or you will wear the imprint of my fist on the other side of your head, too!"

Sullen and full of resentment, Ahmed raised his hand for the blade, knowing it simply wouldn't fit his hand, and yet, as his fingers wrapped around the hilt, it *did* somehow. His mood soared as he held the blade aloft, marveling at the play of the light it cast. Shadows rippled over the sand, wriggling like worms.

"It falls to you now. Ilaweh will guide you."

Ahmed looked back to see Yazid was gone. He cast about frantically, feeling lost. The light from the blade was fading, and the darkness drew in around him, barely held back. "Father! What falls to me? *What*?"

The voice called again, far away now, as the wind whipped the sand into a scouring blast that Ahmed felt would strip the skin from him. "*Everything.*"

The flames on the blade guttered, then died completely. The winds rose to a shriek, and the darkness rushed in on Ahmed like waters rushing into a sinking ship.

He awoke with a start and nearly fell from his hammock. *Stupid thing! I hate it! Better to sleep on the floor.*

It was nearly dark in the small room he shared with Yazid, but a small beam of light slipped past the privacy curtain. The light flickered, shadowed by moving people. Voices tight with alarm rang out and were answered.

Ahmed snatched the curtain aside.

Brutus stood outside, looking haggard and thin. Blood covered his armor, his hands, was dried on his face.

Ahmed tried to hold back a sob as the knowledge filled his mind, but he wasn't entirely successful. "Yazid?" he choked, already knowing.

Brutus shook his head slowly and laid a great hand on Ahmed's shoulder. His grip was iron, but brought no pain, only comforting strength. "I swear to you, boy, we will avenge him. When the prince hears of this, he will give me a mighty army. We will return to these barbarians and crush them beneath our boots!"

Ahmed clutched at Brutus's hand, blinking against tears and nodding. It was wrong, this notion of killing them all. Some other time, he would have been able to find mercy for the weak. But not now.

Now, he wanted only their blood.

EPILOGUE

NOT FIRE

SADRIK struck a sinister pose in the full-length mirror, considering the visual effect. He was pleased with the robe, a red-and-black silk affair. *Power colors, surely.* He brushed at a stray hair on his brow, careful to maintain his stern expression. Yes, it was just the right look, a mix of contempt and detachment. It came naturally to him, but given that he was performing, he wanted to be certain.

It had been an eventful season, one full of heart-stopping crises. His idiot cousin seemed determined to get herself killed, and then who would they tap to rule? He had barely managed to escape that fate the last time a cousin had kicked off. He had no intention of being placed in that situation again, not if he could help it.

It had taken some outright groveling to convince Ariano to spare Kariana. Fortunately, she had shown some mettle, even if she was a fool. The elder Meites had bought his pleadings that she could be trained into something more, and had relented. Sadrik was considerably less convinced of his position than he had let on, but what other choice did he have? Kariana had to survive, and he would have to help her out of self-interest.

He chuckled to himself, remembering their earlier conversation.

"You mentioned friends who fix problems," she had said. He had smiled and agreed to serve as her go-between. No need for her to know the truth. She couldn't be trusted with it.

Satisfied that he did indeed cut quite a sinister figure, his need and belief in the mirror faded, and the mirror followed, dulling, becoming wooden, imperfections rising out of the flat surface until it was once again a heavy door. Sadrik smiled and slammed his palm against the wood. It burst from its hinges and imploded inward in a rain of shards.

Sadrik paused at the threshold, admiring the room beyond. The taste, the cost, the sheer arrogance on display was remarkable. The entire outer wall was a single piece of curved glass, the curtains drawn back to reveal all of Nihlos dreaming under orange clouds, silent, majestic, impossible to ignore. Numerous white throw rugs were placed as walkways over the marble tiled floor. A score or more candles reflected from mirrors and the glass wall, filling the room with a warm glow. Lilac-scented smoke wafted gently from censors along the counters. In the center, sunken into the floor, was a huge bath more along the lines of a swimming pool. Steam rose from its surface, only to be whisked away by some unseen wind, leaving the vista of Nihlos unobscured.

Maralena Prosin, naked in her bath, gasped in shock and scrambled to cover herself.

Sadrik took his time with his entrance. Swagger was important, after all. It was warm in here. *Scorching. Something is on fire.* Wisps of flame rose from the throw rugs where his boots touched, leaving a trail of charred footprints. Smoke curled from the debris of the door as he passed, and the pristine white towels hanging from rods above the bath began to smolder. "Good evening, Maralena. Are you surprised to see me?"

Maralena recovered quickly from her shock. She lowered her

arms, giving him a full view of her age-worn body. "I hadn't thought it would be so soon."

Sadrik raised an eyebrow and made a tisk-tisk sound. "Should I have made an appointment?"

Maralena hauled herself to her feet and stood naked, dripping and defiant. "Have your kind ever concerned yourselves with the desires of we lesser beings?"

Sadrik waved a hand, and a towel rose from its rack and floated across the room to her. "No need to rob you of your dignity."

Maralena stepped carefully from the bath, took the towel and wrapped it around herself. "I thank you for that. So tell me, is this negotiable? I have a lot to offer."

"I'm afraid not."

Maralena grimaced but nodded. "Not fire, please. Have some mercy."

Sadrik swept his arm at her in fury, and the curtains burst into flame. "*Mercy*?" he shouted. "You don't even know the meaning of the word!"

Maralena turned her head, avoiding his gaze as she squeezed water from her hair. "You people toss it about often enough. I don't have the luxury."

Sadrik steepled his fingers under his nose for a moment, giving her what he hoped was a merciless scowl while he considered. "What will you offer me, then? In exchange?"

"Truth."

"Ah, now that *is* something of value." He waited, letting her stew a second longer. "Give me the truth, and I'll not use fire." He peered into one of the many mirrors and stroked at his beard as he waited for whatever lie she chose to tell him. "But have a care. I know more than you think."

Maralena stared at the steam rising from the bath, seemingly resigned to her fate, and said dully, "It was Narelki who started it all. Will you be visiting her as well? She's the one who sent the men to kill Lara."

Sadrik shook his head, unamused. "You know full well Narelki is a special case. You're not helping yourself here, meddling in things that don't concern you."

"I've concerns aplenty. I just have no power to address them."

Sadrik stared at her, filled with loathing. *Pathetic mewling bitch!* "That is what makes you a lesser creature."

Maralena stiffened as if she had it in her mind to strike at Sadrik, then seemed to think the better of it. *That, too. If you had the stomach to fight me, this would go easier on you, coward.*

"It was her fault Marissa died," she snarled. "I struck back at her child." She cast Sadrik a proud, hate-filled glare. "There was a time when you people would have called revenge fair play."

Sadrik laughed loudly at this. "Oh, you misunderstand why I am here. It was fair enough." He shook his head, pasting on a look of mock-sadness. "No, it's all of the rest that brought you to this place. It was very sloppy, that business with the letters. I would have expected better of you."

Maralena took a deep breath, then let it out with a slight shudder. "Yes. I did too."

"Is there anything else? Any last words, perhaps, you would have me deliver?"

"I regret nothing."

She still counts it as a victory. Perhaps it was worth it to her. "Very well. Prepare yourself." Sadrik raised his arms dramatically and waved them about in slow, meaningless gestures. *Audiences are always more impressed by big actions.*

Maralena's eyes widened, but she maintained her composure. "Not fire."

Sadrik flashed her the wicked smile again and shivered. *Cold. I've never been so cold!*

The dozen or so smoldering spots in the room snuffed out like pinched wicks. The candle flames wavered in their sconces as bone-numbing chill poured into the room like water filling a sinking boat. The temperature dropped fifty degrees in seconds as Maralena gaped, uncomprehending, and the clear vista window grew opaque with frost.

Sadrik waved a hand at her, a casual gesture, and Maralena staggered and fell back into the bath. Another fifty degrees fell away in an instant and another. Maralena's body dipped beneath the surface, and the water grew thick, less translucent. Her eyes sprung wide in horror as she realized Sadrik's intent, but it was too late.

Sadrik's teeth began to chatter, and his breath jetted from his nostrils in visible clouds as he stepped onto the sheet of ice that now covered the bath. *Ridiculous! I am immune to the cold!* It was a sudden realization, one he had really always known but had never actually considered until now. Of *course,* the cold could not touch him. How could it be otherwise? That wouldn't make any sense at all.

Warmth swept through him, and his teeth calmed. Sadrik looked down at Maralena with a smile as she pushed at the wall of ice to no avail. He watched with detached amusement as she struggled against the inevitable, her lips moving silently, bubbles streaming from her nose, her eyes wide with terror. *Begging for mercy, likely.* Sadrik cupped a hand to his ear for a moment, then shrugged and smiled back. *What's that? Sorry! Can't hear what you're saying, you rotten old cunt!*

He pointed his finger at the ice and gestured. Trenches formed on the surface as if they were chiseled there. He did it slowly, not wanting to make a mistake. Writing 'Tasinalta sends her regards' backward took some concentration, and it would hardly do to get some of the letters wrong. That would make him look quite foolish, which could have severe consequences.

At last, her breath burst from her lips in a great bubble, and her body convulsed in death throes. Sadrik gave it a few more minutes, just to be certain, then stepped down to the floor again. He took a deep breath, realizing that it was, in fact, a lovely temperature here. The great window slowly began to clear, and the sheet of ice in the bath began to melt, slowly at first, then accelerating. Within a few moments, Maralena's corpse bobbed to the surface, her eyes still bulging.

Sadrik spat into the water. "Not fire," he said with a nod.

FROM THE PUBLISHER

Thank you for reading *Dead God's Due*, book one in The Sins of the Fathers.

We hope you enjoyed it as much as we enjoyed bringing it to you. We just wanted to take a moment to encourage you to review the book on Amazon and Goodreads. Every review helps further the author's reach and, ultimately, helps them continue writing fantastic books for us all to enjoy.

If you liked *Dead God's Due*, check out the rest of our catalogue at www.aethonbooks.com. To sign up to receive a FREE collection from some of our best authors (including one from Matthew P. Gilbert) as well updates regarding all new releases, visit www.aethonbooks.com/sign-up

SPECIAL THANKS TO:

ADAWIA E. ASAD
JENNY AVERY
BARDE PRESS
CALUM BEAULIEU
BEN
BECKY BEWERSDORF
BHAM
TANNER BLOTTER
ALFRED JOSEPH BOHNE IV
CHAD BOWDEN
ERREL BRAUDE
DAMIEN BROUSSARD
CATHERINE BULLINER
JUSTIN BURGESS
MATT BURNS
BERNIE CINKOSKE
MARTIN COOK
ALISTAIR DILWORTH
JAN DRAKE
BRET DULEY
RAY DUNN
ROB EDWARDS
RICHARD EYRES
MARK FERNANDEZ
CHARLES T FINCHER
SYLVIA FOIL
GAZELLE OF CAERBANNOG
DAVID GEARY
MICHEAL GREEN
BRIAN GRIFFIN

EDDIE HALLAHAN
JOSH HAYES
PAT HAYES
BILL HENDERSON
JEFF HOFFMAN
GODFREY HUEN
JOAN QUERALTÓ IBÁÑEZ
JONATHAN JOHNSON
MARCEL DE JONG
KABRINA
PETRI KANERVA
ROBERT KARALASH
VIKTOR KASPERSSON
TESLAN KIERINHAWK
ALEXANDER KIMBALL
JIM KOSMICKI
FRANKLIN KUZENSKI
MEENAZ LODHI
DAVID MACFARLANE
JAMIE MCFARLANE
HENRY MARIN
CRAIG MARTELLE
THOMAS MARTIN
ALAN D. MCDONALD
JAMES MCGLINCHEY
MICHAEL MCMURRAY
CHRISTIAN MEYER
SEBASTIAN MÜLLER
MARK NEWMAN
JULIAN NORTH

KYLE OATHOUT
LILY OMIDI
TROY OSGOOD
GEOFF PARKER
NICHOLAS (BUZ) PENNEY
JASON PENNOCK
THOMAS PETSCHAUER
JENNIFER PRIESTER
RHEL
JODY ROBERTS
JOHN BEAR ROSS
DONNA SANDERS
FABIAN SARAVIA
TERRY SCHOTT
SCOTT
ALLEN SIMMONS
KEVIN MICHAEL STEPHENS
MICHAEL J. SULLIVAN
PAUL SUMMERHAYES
JOHN TREADWELL
CHRISTOPHER J. VALIN
PHILIP VAN ITALLIE
JAAP VAN POELGEEST
FRANCK VAQUIER
VORTEX
DAVID WALTERS JR
MIKE A. WEBER
PAMELA WICKERT
JON WOODALL
BRUCE YOUNG